GOD SAVE THE SPY

A COLD WAR NOVEL

JOHN ELLSWORTH

Copyright © 2020 by John Ellsworth

All rights reserved.

No part of this book may be reproduced in any form or by any electronic or mechanical means, including information storage and retrieval systems, without written permission from the author, except for the use of brief quotations in a book review.

ISBN: 9798688089462

Disclaimer

This is a work of fiction. Names, characters, places, and incidents either are the by-product of the author's imagination or are used fictitiously. Any resemblance to actual persons, living or dead, events, or locales is entirely coincidental.

For Noel

You always did let your brother go on

LONDON

PROLOGUE

London, 1961

It happened the day after a slushy March snow.

A jogger approached the Soviet Embassy, her breath puffs of white as she ran along Kensington Road Gardens at the junction with Bayswater Road. She was even with the embassy gates when she stopped, coming to rest, her woolen gloves on her knees. She turned her face to the side and studied the snowy strip between sidewalk and asphalt.

The runner took a step closer, leaving the sidewalk. Another step, bending low to see. She gasped and jerked back. In the melting snow lay two bodies, side by side, empty eye sockets leering back. There was blood at the heads and hands, which explained what had caught her eye. She cried out, frightened, at a passing bicyclist. He paid no attention. Her instinct was to run, run far away. Instead, she jogged over to the embassy gatehouse and waved at the guard on duty. The guard walked over to the mounds, then ran back and picked up his phone and called the *rezident*, KGB General Anatoly Anchev.

Anchev called KGB Colonel Nikolai Semenov. "Dead bodies are said to be in the snow outside the embassy."

"What?"

Nikolai Semenov turned to a second-story window overlooking the scene below. Weak early morning light shone through the plate glass.

He saw the mounds in the snow. "Okay, I see it now." It affected him oddly, the sight below. To think it was dead bodies. It was like something out of a dream. Then he touched the window glass to steady himself. Too terrible to even think—might that be her down there?

Anchev cried, "You need to get out there!" Then the phone went dead.

Nikolai struggled into his coat and returned to the window. His hands shook so badly he couldn't zip. For he was a spy betraying the Soviet Union, feeding Soviet secrets to the British three years now. A spy whose wife hadn't come home from work that morning. Had he been found out? Was the KGB toying with him, sending him outside to discover his wife lying dead in the snow?

He watched from above as London police officers arrived at the curb and gestured with gloved hands, talking across the snowy bodies. One ran back to the car and lifted the microphone. A police van pulled in. A camera appeared, flashes of light all around.

Then Anchev called again. Nikolai picked up and listened while watching the police toe the bodies. Anchev said it was on Soviet Union property. The investigation rightfully should belong to the

KGB. He said Nikolai needed to rush down and claim the inquiry for the KGB. Nikolai wanted to ask, "What about the London police?" but thought otherwise. One didn't argue with the *rezident*.

He placed the phone back in the cradle, hurried out into the hallway, and jogged to the end where he double-timed it down the stairs to the lobby door. His heart was pounding. With each step, it became more and more apparent what he was about to find, and it made him want to cry out in horror at what the KGB had done that Anchev was leading him to see.

He hit the ground running, hardly noticing the early morning London air that tasted of burnt coal and traffic exhaust.

"Hey!" he shouted down the drive. "Don't touch anything!"

The London police officers ignored him. He called again. This time they turned to see the thirty-one-year-old run up to the murder scene, coat flapping, sweeping the hair from his eyes.

"This crime scene belongs to the KGB. Embassy property out to the street." He caught his breath and flashed his ID. "I will decide who comes and goes here." He said this while averting his eyes from the mound of snow, fearful he might be looking down into his wife's face. But then he could stand it no longer, and he turned.

Two females, no faces.

Blood was everywhere. It looked like the slaughter had happened right there.

His breathing shallowed. The world tipped. He pressed his hand against a tree overlooking the scene, steadying himself. When he could let go, he approached, closer this time.

He could see well enough through the mix of ice and snow to make out a white blouse on the closer body. Yulia had the same blouse, but he latched onto a small hope that it was someone else's blouse, someone other than his Yulia.

His gaze traveled down to the hands folded across the woman's abdomen, where he studied the wedding ring she wore. Was it the ring he had saved up to buy and presented to her over dinner in Moscow? The tiny stone caused tears to form in his eyes. He looked away, studying the hair all matted and bloody, unrecognizable. But the teeth—her lips were cut away—perfect save for one eyetooth that stood forward. All Yulia.

He blinked away his tears, fighting the impulse to drop to his knees and dig with his hands and lift her away from the cold. But he knew Anchev was watching from the embassy, and Nikolai didn't want to give him the pleasure of destroying a KGB officer turned spy. Instead, he came fully upright, a confident posture, his face that of a stolid KGB Colonel.

There was a more important reason to show no reaction. It was better for him to assume a mantle of innocence, of one who didn't expect harm to come to a loved one. For he was the father of a one-year-old daughter, and if it was Yulia in the snow, and if the KGB had learned he was a double agent, Sasha would become an orphan. The Soviet Union would own her.

He stepped away from the bodies and crossed his arms. He spoke to the London police as if directing them. This was for Anchev's benefit as he studied Nikolai from his gaudy second-floor office filled with awards from the Party and photographs of him with Stalin—hidden away when visitors came from Moscow—him with Khrushchev, him with his wife mounted on her prize horse at their dacha outside Moscow. Nikolai hated him for his loyalty, yet admired him as well, though he would never admit it.

Nikolai said to the sergeant with the stripes on his coat, "You are definitely needed here. But it is still a Soviet investigation."

The nearby police officers shrugged. "Fine," said the sergeant, and he turned to leave, tugging his partner with him. "Come on."

"Wait," said Nikolai. His position in the KGB had nothing whatever to do with the investigation of homicides. He had no idea what came next, and Anchev hadn't appeared yet to direct him. "I didn't say to leave. We shall do this together."

The police stopped and came back. "We do this every day," said the sergeant. "This is our job. If you will go back to the sidewalk and take these other people with you, we will proceed."

He turned. All around, a crowd had collected, the jogger among them. One officer took her aside. Nikolai could hear him taking down her name and phone number. The sergeant became riled. "Get rid of the crowd!"

Nikolai shouted at them to move back onto the sidewalk but didn't approach them. Instead, he bent down and sat on his haunches to view the closest body.

He looked down at the ring again. Did it have his words inside? *Yulia forever, Nikolai.*

Anchev be damned, he could not restrain his hand as he reached out and brushed at the cover of snow. It was icy, but he saw enough. Her fingertips were missing.

"Bring dogs," he ordered the police. "We've fingertips to find."

Anatoly Anchev finally strode out the gate. As he drew near, he stroked his chin and hummed the Soviet National Anthem. It wasn't lost on Nikolai—Anchev was toying with him. "What little gift has someone left on the Soviet doorstep?" Anchev wondered aloud. "Who do we have, Colonel?"

Nikolai shook his head. "Nobody. We have nobody."

"Nonsense. These women are someone's daughters, maybe sisters, maybe even wives." He gave Nikolai a broad smile.

Nikolai felt Anchev's hand squeeze his heart and not let go while he smiled at the young Colonel's pain. Inside the Soviet Embassy, just back of where they stood, she worked nights in the communications center. When she hadn't come home this morning, he had thought she needed to work late—it happened. But the dead bodies at his feet... They did this to her because they knew about him. Now, what about Sasha, their one-year-old daughter? Was she safe? Was she even still alive? KGB had no limits.

"I have a call to make. I'll be right back," he told Anchev.

"Don't leave me here with these dead women," Anchev said with a smirk. "Although I was married to a dead woman once. Did I ever tell you that?" He turned, but Nikolai was entering the gates.

Nikolai took the stairs two at a time. "Oh, my God, oh, my God, oh, my God, oh, my God!"

He made the call to the babysitter from his desk, one of twenty-five in the KGB officers' room. Mrs. Johnson's voice was worried as she told him there was no Yulia. "What has happened? How long will I stay with Sasha today?"

He panted, swallowing air. "Is Sasha well? She's with you?"

"Of course, she's with me. Why on earth would you even ask?"

"Please wait there. I'll be coming soon, I promise."

He hung up and hurried back outside. He needed to get home and take Sasha away. But first, he had to know if that frozen corpse was his Yulia.

He stood beside Anchev and watched the crime scene techs. One of them broke an arm free of the snow and tested its rigor by pulling it upright, where it remained, accusing the sky. "Limbs frozen and full rigor, Inspector Winnike."

"It's the internal organs I'm concerned about," said the new arrival, the Inspector, a man wearing a trench coat and smoking a pipe.

Anchev taunted, "What can you tell me so far, Inspector? Do we have the killer identified by your forensics?"

The Englishman turned to the KGB commandant. "This blood bath tells us the faces were whittled down to the bone while the women were alive. Someone wanted these ladies to suffer. It reeks of KGB! Does that help get you started?"

Nikolai shuddered—suffered indeed. Yulia had endured torturous pain for his sins, about which she had never even been aware. The daughter of a KGB colonel, she would have turned him in had she known about him. He had to step back to the sidewalk to collect himself. No one noticed the blood had drained from his face.

But still, he remained unable to leave.

After another half-hour, the police dogs arrived and sniffed the bodies. They then sniffed the snow cover along the street and then loped inside the embassy fence. Anchev started to say something when he saw the dogs on Soviet soil, but Nikolai saw his jaw relax. Nothing was said.

Nikolai regained his calm and went back inside. He sat at his desk, giving the dogs time to do their work. He again dialed his house number. He waited for three rings. Then Mrs. Johnson's familiar voice said hello.

"Mrs. Johnson, can I speak with Yulia, please?"

"Yulia is not here, Nikolai. I'm so frightened!" She was keeping her voice down for Sasha.

"I don't know where to start," he said as if in a haze. "I don't know."

"Tell me what's wrong, Nikolai."

"She didn't call you and say she was coming home?"

"No calls."

"Stay with Sasha. Do not answer the door."

Nikolai played it through his mind, her last twelve hours. She left home for work at six last night. Arriving at the embassy, she placed headphones over her ears and eavesdropped on British MI5 agents until midnight. When she stopped, she fitted the headphones back on the hook above her name, ate lunch, then typed reports until four when she should have come home and quietly slipped into bed.

Nikolai rang up Yulia's supervisor and asked about last night. He told Nikolai that Yulia hadn't returned after her lunch break at midnight. "Is she ill?"

He dropped the phone in its cradle. This couldn't be happening. Who else to call? There was no one.

He returned to the crime scene, the blood bath.

More police had arrived, and a few more KGB had come to see. A dense fog had crept in, so the police had set up portable lights. Now they fired up a generator with a hose attached to the exhaust.

The Inspector said to Anchev and Nikolai, "They're not frozen internally."

"And how can you know that? Are you a soothsayer?" taunted Anchev.

"Thermometer, sir. They do have those in the Soviet Union?"

"Go on. What else can you tell us?"

"They've been here maybe since dawn. But we need to move them fast because ice crystals can damage cells and make it impossible to detect certain causes of death. We're melting them out."

Nikolai looked at the mutilations. What other cause of death could there be?

The Inspector added, "The hot air won't even deprecate latent prints."

Nikolai asked, "Is there any ID on the bodies? Any papers?"

"You think they're able to turn out their pockets, Colonel?" replied Anchev sarcastically. "Your face is quite pale. Go back inside and let the English do what they do best, examine their war dead."

Nikolai urgently wanted to break through the knot of men and examine between the near one's breasts for the mole. But even that would be inconclusive. Besides, it wasn't her, he said to himself, forcing his mind to think differently. If they really knew about him, it would be him lying there in the snow, not Yulia. That bit of logic gave him hope.

He jogged back inside and again called home. No answer at all this time. He panicked, pounding his desk. *Hold on*, he demanded of himself. Mrs. Johnson might have taken Sasha next door to her flat. That had happened before and was actually a good thing. He pulled open his desk drawer and found a tin of mixed nuts, which he ate one at a time, planning his next moves. After returning the nuts to their drawer, he wiped his hands on a napkin then redialed his number. This time Mrs. Johnson answered and said Sasha was with her. Sounding much calmer now, she told him not to worry.

"Please take her next door to your flat."

"Is it trouble at work, then?"

At 1 p.m., he went back outside to the scene. Anchev had disappeared. The generator exhaust had finished the ice, and the medical examiner was working backboards under the bodies.

Dog tracks were everywhere across the snow, proof the British investigation was examining every inch of Soviet soil.

He stepped to the street side of the scene when a glint caught his eye. Then he saw it. Seven sausages lay upon tinfoil. A sniffer dog brought an eighth and opened his mouth, dropping it amongst the others.

Nikolai's eyes were riveted on the find. A crime scene technician saw the look on his face. "Distal phalanges—that's fingertips to the KGB."

Nikolai couldn't look away, wondering which of them might have brushed his face.

Anchev strolled back outside to enjoy Nikolai's destruction. He came and stood beside the young Colonel. "The dogs will find the missing parts. My only hope is they"—laughing heartily—"don't eat the fingers!"

"Wouldn't that be sad," Nikolai said, a hot rage rising in his chest. It was the final straw. He knew the KGB was playing a game with him. They had killed his Yulia and mutilated her body and left behind her fingertips so she would be identified—after he had gone through hell waiting to know. He shut his eyes and counted, distracting himself from the fury that would have him draw his Makarov 9x18 and shoot Anchev dead on the spot.

But Anchev must have sensed something.

"I shall go have a drink to the dead. We don't want anyone else dead, now do we, Colonel?" Again, the smile.

"I need to tell you something, General."

Anchev looked up at Nikolai. "You sound serious, and here I am making jokes. What is it, Colonel?"

"Yulia wasn't home when I left this morning."

"Didn't she work last night?"

"I thought so. Now, I don't know."

"I will dispatch a section. A KGB officer's wife gone missing is a severe matter. One the KGB doesn't take lightly." Nikolai knew he was only doing what the Embassy protocol required.

"I'll stay at the office."

"No, you go home and look for her there. I'm going to bet you she's home by now. Her story might not be a pretty one, so be prepared, Nikolai. Women can be fragile. But very wicked, as well."

Nikolai returned to his office and collapsed onto his desk chair. He sat for several moments, then realized he was crying. It wasn't supposed to happen like this. He was supposed to defect to Britain with his wife and daughter and start all over again where they were free. He pulled his handkerchief and dried his tears. Maybe it was best if he drove home and waited there.

A hissing radiator and the scent of ancient pipes sent his skin crawling. He sat with his eyes closed, thinking only of his last moments with her. Had they even kissed farewell when she left last night? What would she have him tell Sasha?

Just then, Maxim Moltoi came bursting into the office without knocking—pure KGB. But he was Nikolai's brother-in-law and good friend, married to Yulia's sister. He was pale, his eyes wide.

"Anchev called me to join the search. Have you found her?"

Maxim was a fireplug but a pugnacious fireplug, always aggressive, sometimes very annoying, always "on" whenever the couples visited, regaling all with his jokes and his interminably long stories. *Irrepressible.* Nikolai had some time ago decided to call him that. But now he was all seriousness. Nikolai didn't know that he'd ever seen Maxim like this.

"Have you called home?"

"Mrs. Johnson answered."

"Sasha's well?"

He was one step ahead. "She's safe."

Maxim's eyebrows shot up. "Do you know something you're not telling?"

He hesitated. It was no time to involve anyone else in his slow death march. "I just want my wife found. I just want her home."

"Of course, you do. What do you need me to do?"

"Go home. Wait until I call with the news."

"That's it? Shouldn't we go looking?"

"Look? Look where?"

Maxim shrugged. Then he slowly turned and purposefully walked to the window. He peered down at the scene. "Did you view the bodies?"

"I did. I was the first officer sent."

"Well?"

"Someone is playing a terrible joke on the KGB, leaving two dead, carved-up women on our doorstep. Someone will swing for it."

"But it's not Yulia?"

Nikolai choked down a cry. "The faces and lips are cut away. They're looking for fingertips in the snow. Dogs are sniffing. Then we'll know for sure."

"Yulia's prints are on file?"

"You know that. She works here."

"Of course. I'm going to take you home, little brother. We can look there. We can be with Sasha. If they call about the fingerprints, you'll need someone with you."

"Unnecessary."

"Maybe, maybe not. But it doesn't cost anything. No, I want to be with you."

"What about Carolina? It's her sister."

"I'll wait until we know."

"All right, then. Let me lock up my files, and we'll go."

"I'll go do the same. Give me ten minutes, and I'll be back to get you."

"Leave my car in the lot?"

"It will be here in the morning when I bring you back. Not to worry."

He wasn't worried about the car. He was concerned about coming undone in front of Maxim when they called about the prints. Because he already knew.

That was Yulia lying out there.

As sure as night follows day, it was her.

1

Three years earlier, Nikolai underwent an interview to determine his fitness for the KGB foreign posting to Great Britain. It was conducted by General Sergei Barishsky, the head of Directorate K, the KGB branch in charge of internal counterintelligence. It was held in the KGB's Lubyanka Building, headquarters of the KGB in Moscow.

Nikolai, twenty-eight years old, arrived at the interview room fifteen minutes early. He was a mid-sized, military tough, Eastern-looking man with a square jaw, broad forehead, and pale gray eyes. He kept his face slick in a time when KGB shaved closely and wore Russian Leather aftershave, though he wore none to the interview.

Nikolai wore a black suit with a white shirt and black tie and carried his overcoat, peaked hat, and gloves over his arm. Sunglasses and a wallet were inside his suit coat.

In a shoulder holster, he concealed a Makarov semiautomatic he'd never drawn on the job.

Nervous and his stomach out-of-sorts with anxiety, he took a seat in the waiting room and shut his eyes. Possible questions came to mind, as well as the answers he had framed over the previous weeks.

General Barishsky entered at nine o'clock on the dot and beckoned Nikolai to follow him down a dim hallway. He pushed open the door to a small conference room and led Nikolai inside. General Barishsky sat down with a great exhalation and spread a manila file before him on the table. "So," he said sorrowfully, "we are going to lose you to overseas. Good for you, Nikolai Semenov."

"Thank you."

The general threw open the file, unfolded reading glasses, and widened his eyes to adjust.

"All right, then. You were born Nikolai Feydorovich Semenov in Moscow in 1930?"

"Yes."

"Your father was an NKVD and KGB colonel; two uncles were KGB illegals?" NKVD was the predecessor of the KGB. Illegals were Russian spies abroad who covertly entered a country by boating ashore at night or parachuting in or entry by phony ID. It was very heady work, real spy stuff, and highly esteemed. The point being Nikolai had grown up in a family of Russian secret service officers. Men who grew up in that environment were known to be extremely loyal to the Party and would dedicate themselves to the KGB for life.

"Yes."

"And you wanted to be like him?"

Nikolai nodded. "Yes. He had a habit of saying, 'The Party is always right,' any time there was a discussion of philosophy, religion, politics, or local news."

"Did you agree? Was the Party always right?"

"Definitely so."

"In 1937, your family moved into the same block building in Moscow as other KGB agents, designated exclusively for them."

"The building was eleven stories high."

"And I'm sure it provided a suitable lifestyle?"

Nikolai wanted to say, "But there was a price to be paid for extra luxuries like refrigerators. The KGB spied on everyone. There was no privacy." But he held his tongue, remembering where he was, fighting for his career overseas.

But it wasn't just the KGB officers who were scrutinized. The KGB, or the Committee for State Security, was established to penetrate every aspect of Soviet life. Still, with rare exceptions, every young man's dream was to be selected for its ranks. None more so than Nikolai Semenov, who was excelling in school and sports and was voted by his classmates as most likely to be allowed to join the KGB.

The interview next examined Nikolai's Communist Party knowledge and beliefs. Three hours later, Barishsky looked up and smiled the smile of the Russian bear. "Lunchtime!"

After lunch was served in the meeting room—turkey sandwiches with the crust sliced off, and iced tea—Barishsky continued with his inquisition. "In 1938, you enrolled in the Gorky

Suvorov Military School. Is that when you began to love the State?"

"The school was the best of the best," said Nikolai without answering about his love for the State. "The Gorky Suvorov School was home to the best teachers and experienced military officers in the Red Army. I loved it because we performed in all the military parades on Red Square. I loved the uniforms, the spit and polish, the conformity that military life demanded. KGB officers spoke to us every week, and I always hated for it to end. Since I was quite young, I have worshipped the Soviet KGB."

Barishsky plunged ahead. "You graduated from military school. That would have been 1947?"

"Correct. I was seventeen."

"You then enrolled at the Russia School of International Relations in Moscow. It was known to be the path to the NKVD, so you resolved to excel there?"

"Again, only to become a Soviet intelligence officer. I didn't go out drinking with friends; I had no girlfriend, I had no money, I had only my books and my goal."

Barishsky stayed on course. "You studied Swedish and English and had one course in German?"

"If you can call it a course. We sat in a circle with our teacher and learned German, such as finding the bathroom or saying we were hungry. I remembered everything about English and nothing about Swedish when I graduated. I had become conversant in German. But in English, I was as good as any native speaker." Only London makes sense, see? With his English skills already in place, it would be a strategic posting.

"Next came Soviet-Sino relations, which you devoured. Following that, you began a two-year study of Russian relations with Europe and America. You learned about the American government, the British government. How did they compare to the Soviet government?"

Nikolai spread his hands. "There was no comparison." It could be taken either way.

"You studied the weaknesses of the American government. You learned Capitalism and all of its failings. You learned American geography, military service, weapons, and military bases. You learned how to infiltrate British and American intelligence agencies, CIA and MI5. Am I leaving something out?"

Nikolai shook his head. "Only to add, we learned how to assassinate presidents and prime ministers, how to target them, weapons of choice, the physical layout and traffic patterns around the White House and Ten Downing Street."

"You would give up your life for a president or prime minister?"

"On a moment's notice," said Nikolai.

"You were moved back to Moscow in 1953. You were moved to a location known as The Hotel, where you stayed for months carrying out *gorodskiye zanyatiya*—city exercises. Did you enjoy being a Soviet spy in training?"

"I found the daily exercises out on city streets stimulating and exhausting."

Stimulating like when they learned how to take a contact to dinner, discuss the menu, and suggest dishes to be ordered. The people they met and tried to recruit were all retired MGB (KGB predecessor) agents, men, and some women who found the junior lieutenants amusing as they bumbled and fumbled and started over again and again. They were turned loose in Moscow and told to look for operational sites—posting signals, meeting people, making brush-contacts, counter-surveillance, thrilling games of cat-and-mouse. Always working in pairs, one student acted as the surveillance target while his partner followed the surveillance to control it if the need arose. Professional teams from the MGB carried out the surveillance, and they would often drive in teams of three—one driver and two lookouts. Exercises lasted three hours, during which Nikolai would have some task to perform—meet an agent, post something in a dead-letter box, make a brush-contact. But the most critical requirement was to carry out *proverka*—dry-cleaning, a series of maneuvers to determine if you were followed or not, and, if so, to lose the surveillance. *Proverka* was pass or fail. The KGB lived by it.

"You reported for work in August 1954?

"Yes, I arrived early." From the Metro, he walked to the MGB headquarters—now known as the KGB—known by all spies as the Center. He arrived at his appointment only to find his orders hadn't yet arrived. So, he was free to experience Moscow nightlife for the first time.

"Then, you married? Daughter of KGB?"

"I met a young woman at an after-hours club through a fellow KGB agent, Maxim Moltoi. He brought his wife with him, Carolina, who had brought her younger sister. Her name was Yulia. She was nineteen, half Kazakhstani, half Russian, intelligent, bright-eyed, and laughed easily. She was training to be an English teacher."

"Yes, her picture is here in your file. Flawless."

Nikolai continued with a smile. "We started dating. Soon we exchanged commitments."

"Go on."

"Nothing much. I told her that I loved her, our engagement followed, then we married without hesitation on either side."

"You were desperately in love with your new wife. She was likewise totally in love with you."

"Yes."

"What does she think about KGB?"

Nikolai spread his hands. "Well, her father was KGB. He's retired, and all he talks about is serving the Party. She understands my job."

"No problem with you being gone weeks at a time?"

"No."

"She doesn't tell you to be careful and not get yourself killed today?"

"She understands my job."

Barishsky called for more coffee and reviewed the last several pages of Nikolai's file. From where Nikolai sat, he could see they were close to the end.

"In 1956, you were deployed to Budapest during the Hungarian Revolution."

"I was. I led a platoon of men."

"And the fighting was heavy. "

"It was. I lost several men."

"And killed many more."

"Many more. More than I care to remember."

Barishsky cocked his head to the side. "Oh? Does killing enemies of the State disturb you?"

"With all due respect, if the General has killed, he already knows my answer."

"Please respond."

"I have killed for the motherland. It will happen again when necessary."

"How do you feel about that?"

"It's part of the commitment the KGB officer makes."

Barishsky wouldn't leave it alone. "Are you still able to be the soldier you were in Budapest?"

"Could I kill again?"

Barishsky shrugged. "Yes?"

"I will do my job. I am sworn to do my job. Yes, I will do what is required."

The general flipped to the back of Nikolai's file. He appeared thoughtful for several minutes. "After the Hungarian Revolution warfare, you were then assigned to KGB School 1010, where you have been teaching small arms and close combat."

"Yes, General."

"How has that been?"

"I have done my very best. I wanted my students to have the best possible chance of success."

General Barishsky checked his watch. Then he made notations on the outside of Nikolai's file. He finally tossed the file aside and put his arms flat on the table.

"Was there anything else?" he asked.

"No, sir."

"I believe we'll stop here for the day."

Nikolai was immediately frustrated. With all the impatience of youth, he wanted an answer now. Was he fit for a foreign posting? Had he passed the interview for foreign?

"Did I pass? Will I get my foreign posting later?"

"You passed. I am recommending a posting to London after the first of the year."

His heart soared as he left the Lubyanka Building. It was time to run and tell Yulia. All the training, the difficult coursework, the deployment to a war he'd hated—it was all coming together with a deployment to the West!

He had never been happier.

2

Nikolai and Yulia arrived in London from Moscow. It was 1959, a cold, overcast day in January with a mix of rain and sleet coming down.

The young couple jogged across the tarmac, holding newspapers overhead, into Heathrow Airport. He watched faces while she looked around at the colors and sunny smiles and heard the laughter. It all stunned Yulia. Nikolai had been out of Soviet Russia before. He knew how it was elsewhere.

He had been dreading the plane touching down for the last hour. Coming into the airport, sweeping the faces with his eyes, he reminded himself that the world was a free-fire zone from now on. Whether he was ready to confront the Soviet Union's enemies or not, they were certainly ready to face him. To kill him, if possible. But the dread he felt wasn't about dying, wasn't about killing. Now that he had escaped the Soviet Union by securing a KGB posting to London, and now that his feet were firmly planted on British concrete and tile, he knew that he wanted to stay. He knew he wasn't going to want to leave. His dread was that he might be made to.

He watched Yulia moving ahead of him. She was slender, blond, and feline in her movements. Her skirt was wool, and her blouse was silk. Her prized leather coat lay draped across her shoulders. He watched as her wide eyes devoured the airport and the people. It was her first time out of the Soviet Union.

Nikolai didn't see the shops or the glitz and glamour of a cosmopolitan Western airport. He saw only faces and matched those to the pictures he'd been told to memorize, the faces of assassins haunting London. Then his sweep stopped. He recognized the man at the bar. Franz Rákosi, Budapest. He immediately needed Yulia elsewhere.

"Look!" he exclaimed, pointing at a gift shop. "A Big Ben mug for your father, Jana Valerov!"

She turned in the direction of the shop. "I need to go in there! Will you wait?"

He looked again at the man's face. The man was acting like he hadn't seen Nikolai. Nikolai knew better; there were no coincidences.

"I'll catch up in the gift shop," Nikolai said. "I'll be back for you."

Nikolai, all eyes, stepped into the airport bar. It opened onto the concourse where skylights lit the walkway. But it was darker inside, so there was a split second when his eyes had to adjust. The man did nothing. Opportunity lost for him.

Up to the bar. "Vodka martini."

Said the man beside him, "I'm only passing through. It's nothing to do with you."

"Will you never be over the war?"

"Done and forgotten, I promise. Just two guys bumping into each other at the airport. It can happen."

"Flight manifest? Is that how you found me?"

"Passing through. Budapest was a thousand years ago."

"Budapest was two years ago."

"If you say so. I'm here to meet my wife's family."

"Who would that be?"

"Anna Maria Rákosi. London born and bred."

Nikolai's drink came. "You sound convinced. You can have five minutes."

The man looked around. Nikolai knew, at that moment, the man wasn't alone. The next steps unwound quickly in his head.

"I'm off to the restroom. Finish your drink and be gone by the time I return. Tell the bartender I'm coming back. Tell him to leave my drink."

"I'll have them leave your drink." The man finally raised his gaze from his glass and looked Nikolai in the eye. "Thank you."

Nikolai turned away and stepped into the concourse. It was crowded with passengers lugging suitcases, pushing carts loaded down with bags, the old staggering along under the weight of their baggage, the young darting through the crowd like pinballs. He joined the foot traffic and made his way down to the blue restroom sign. He went inside and counted urinals. Four occupied. Two stalls occupied. "I'm airport security," he announced in his command voice. "They have reported a bomb in the airport. Please leave immediately and seek the nearest exit!"

Staccato sounds of toilet paper rolls spinning, pants zipping, commodes flushing. The restroom instantly cleared out.

He swallowed hard and went to the far wall, minimizing his exposure. There was no cover, but there was a door to the supply room. He raised a foot and kicked the doorknob, breaking the lock. He pulled open the door and stood to the side in the doorway. Then he waited. *Come on, come on, come on.*

They entered the restroom together, Franz Rákosi, the Hungarian from the bar, and a shorter Asian. Rákosi approached first, coiling his body and raising his hands in an aggressive Wushu posture. Nikolai waited, his breath coming in short bursts. In a blink, the man gathered himself and made his attack. Nikolai countered with a sweeping kick, catching the man on the outer knee. "Aiii!" Rákosi cried and stumbled just enough that Nikolai caught the back of his neck with a blurring chop. The bone snapped, and the man fell to the floor. He didn't move again.

Nikolai studied the Asian. He looked unsure for a moment, just enough that Nikolai stood upright and said, "I'm going to allow you to turn around and leave. It's a good choice for you."

The Chinese man smiled, moved as if to turn and leave, but suddenly drew a silver pistol from his waist and aimed it directly at Nikolai. He squeezed off a shot, just as Nikolai threw himself behind the door of the supply closet. He brought around his silenced Makarov 9x18 mm, aiming for the man's torso. He caught a quick glimpse and fired one round.

"Yiiiii!" the man cried as Nikolai came fully exposed from behind the door, aiming his Makarov at the man, who had crumpled to the floor, holding up one hand defensively. The man threw his gun to the floor, and it skittered across the tile toward Nikolai. "No!" he cried." You don't have to do this."

Nikolai kicked the gun aside. He forced his breathing to slow, took control of the fearsome possibility that more of them could come pounding through the door at any moment.

"Who are you?"

"Chin."

"Who sent you?"

"Franz said you were Russian."

"I asked, who sent you?"

"No one. Franz paid me."

Nikolai approached the man studying his bloody hands, one on top the other, applying pressure to the chest wound where the bullet had found its mark. His look was of disbelief that he'd been shot.

"I should let you live," Nikolai said more to himself than the man called Chin.

"That's right. That's the way."

"But if I let you live, I will see you again." The KGB combat teacher talking through him.

"No! I promise!"

Just then, two college-age young men came into the restroom. They stopped, and their eyes went wide when they comprehended.

"Holy shit," said the thick, blond young man. "You going to shoot him?"

Nikolai turned to the young man. "I don't know. Should I?"

"Shit, man, I don't think so. But I don't know."

"Tell you what. Do you have a coin?"

"I've got a quarter."

"Good, you're American. This man is your enemy. We're going to do a coin toss. Chin, you call it. No call, you die."

"Shit, man," said the blond young man. "I don't think I want any part of this!"

Nikolai swung the muzzle of the gun, pointing it directly at his head. "Do it now."

He dug a quarter out of his pocket and flipped it into the air. The young man expertly caught it and slapped it down on his arm.

"Heads!" cried Chin.

The young man lifted his hand and then looked at the Asian, his face white, and his mouth agape. "Tails. I'm sorry, man."

"You're not sorry," Nikolai said. "You don't know him well enough to be sorry."

The other young man turned as if to leave. "I don't want to see this."

"Wait," Nikolai commanded. "Describe me."

The young man's back turned to Nikolai. "I didn't see you that well."

Nikolai swung the gun toward the blond young man. "Now you."

"It all happened so fast I didn't get a good look."

"Good. Now get back to college, both of you. Remember what you didn't see."

They ran for the door, fighting each other to exit first.

Nikolai turned back to the Asian. "You have a gun. You were going to shoot me."

"I have two daughters!"

Nikolai's eyes narrowed. "It isn't that easy now."

"Their mother is gone!"

Nikolai walked up to the man and put the muzzle of the gun on his forehead. "Who sent you?"

"Budapest."

"Why?"

"Ten-thousand dollars for you."

"Who's buying?"

"Budapest."

Nikolai squeezed the trigger. The 9x18 drilled a polite hole, and the man toppled over. Nikolai stepped over him, replacing the gun under his coat. He saw that his hands were steady. He felt his heart beating normally. He crept to the door and looked out. Chin's belly gun had merely popped, a tiny sound. The silencer on his powerful Makarov had done its job, and everyone looked oblivious as they hurried for their planes, baggage, restrooms, exits. Nikolai was relieved. He disappeared among them.

He made his way through the crush. He stepped right, left, paused before he continued, and took care not to collide, not to call attention. At the gift shop, he sidestepped his way inside. She was standing at the cash register, holding two small boxes. He approached and touched her shoulder.

"I had to have them. See?" She opened one box and pulled out a coffee mug. On its side, it said *London*. She turned it around—Big Ben.

"I couldn't resist," she said, excited to be in her new city.

"Jana Valerov will treasure it." Her father was retired KGB, had been stationed in London for twenty years. Now retired in Moscow. Nikolai's father had been KGB, too. Two to live up to.

"Did you hear those noises? The clerk said they're doing construction."

"I didn't hear anything. Ready for breakfast?"

She paid and followed him out of the store. A phalanx of police and armed airport guards surrounded the restroom entrance. They were turning people away. He spied the two college boys heading in the direction of the loading planes. They wouldn't look at him.

As they were walking down the concourse, Yulia grasped his arm. "Wait, let me stop and look." They stepped aside so others could get by. Yulia let her gaze roam along the wall where there was a mural depicting a summer hayfield brushed with golden sunlight, a silver airliner flying in toward reaching arms. Yulia turned and smiled at Nikolai. She held out her free hand. "Now, I'm ready. Come." He took her hand, and they rejoined the moving crowd.

Nikolai looked off beyond the two-story windows to a gray industrial haze smothering flat-roofed buildings from the runway to the horizon. Would this be his home? Even gray and old, it was better. The crush of people bumping up against him drew his attention back inside, and he set about studying the citizens he was to penetrate.

Amidst the tramping feet and jostling bodies, attached to Yulia at the hand, he allowed the crowd to direct his walk as he swung along with the flow, determined to join them.

3

On the ground level of the airport, they found a restaurant advertising *Authentic English Breakfast.* They ordered bacon, fried eggs, sausage, mushrooms, baked beans, toast, grilled tomatoes, and coffee. They hadn't had a meal since entering Swedish airspace and were hungry. This was their very first feast, their welcome to the land of plenty.

He said to Yulia, "General Masirov warned me not to like London too much." General Masirov was Nikolai's commander in Moscow, the head of the First Chief Directorate (Foreign Operations).

"He was afraid you wouldn't want to return to Moscow?"

"I think. If I had to choose a city to demonstrate Western democracy's best, he said I could hardly do better than London."

"General Masirov said that?" she asked, testing a bite of toast slathered with authentic marmalade. She smiled and said about the toast, "This is wonderful."

Her porcelain skin, unmarred since she came from a land without sun, shone even in the artificial light. She ate right-handed, keeping her left hand in her lap, just as she'd been taught at the young ladies' school. After every bite, a demure dab at the lips with the linen napkin. Bite-dab, bite-dab, bite-dab. But there was another side to the lady. Like her husband, she was a marathon runner, a competition she savored. Sweat and 10k road grime weren't usually a young ladies' style, but fit Yulia like a glove. "He said you could hardly do better than London? It sounds like he was encouraging you about your choice. That was thoughtful."

He looked at her like she'd just stepped off the moon. KGB *thoughtful*? He suppressed a smile. "He did say that. We were in his office yesterday morning. But when he said it, he'd already been drinking."

"That explains it then."

The young KGB officer ate otherwise than his wife. He was all elbows and hands and exuberant bites, determined chewing.

They finished their meals and signaled for the bill.

Just as they were paying, Ninel Turinov arrived. They had graduated KGB School 1010 a year apart. They greeted each other as brothers.

"Am I late?"

Nikolai smiled. "Your timing is perfect."

"Don't tell Anchev. I'll owe you."

Ninel was tall and wiry, uncoordinated, and knew it as he carefully pulled out a chair and sat.

"Welcome to London." He smiled and then turned to Yulia. "I am Ninel, and you are going to love it here. My wife is waiting to meet you. We have a baby." Then he turned back to Nikolai, and his voice dropped to a whisper. "And the Brits, impossibly naïve! It's an intelligence feast every day!" His bright eyes sparkled, and he laughed at their good fortune.

They walked outside. A car from the Soviet Embassy was waiting with a driver. It drove them into the West End of the city, a desperate urban sprawl, old houses lining street after street, garbage in the gutters, and traffic on all four sides, some moving, most not.

"It's exciting," Yulia said on the ride over. "Our first look at London!"

Nikolai was watching out his window. "It's so dirty here. Streets running willy-nilly, doubling back, crossing each other. It's bewildering and chaotic. Perfect for KGB takeover."

Laughter followed.

They pulled in through the electric gates at the Russian Embassy, a large, older building of white sandstone. Nikolai saw it was three stories, maybe four if there was a basement. It had been well-preserved, and the Soviet flag hung above the main portico. At No. 13 Kensington Palace Gardens, it was only a short distance to Bayswater Road, the main thoroughfare along Hyde Park, making it easier to get around town.

Turinov showed both husband and wife into the ambassador's office to meet the man under whose posting Nikolai would work. Nikolai took the chair indicated by the ambassador. Turinov remained standing while Yulia sat down beside Nikolai and planted her feet solidly on the floor in young ladies' school style.

The ambassador bustled around his desk to shake hands. "I've heard good things about you."

"Well," Nikolai said, "let's hope I can live up to them. How do I begin here?"

The ambassador wasted no time. "That will be up to KGB London, but I would look for entry into a gentleman's club if I were you. We haven't cracked that nut yet, but that's where the bluebloods go after five."

"Gentlemen's clubs? I will make a note."

General Anatoly Anchev, the *rezident* of the KGB station, paged them. Turinov showed them to his office, done in amber wood with wall hangings of Moscow winter scenes. Anchev, the *rezident*, welcomed the newcomers and offered coffee. As the mouth-breathing sixty-year-old poured, Nikolai studied him and saw a friendly enough character who copied Elvis Presley's sideburns—Elvis, whom the Party hated. But Nikolai knew there would be another side to Anatoly Anchev, too, a KGB side, when those eyes would flash with lightning and strike dead Russia's enemies.

Anchev spoke to Nikolai in English, asking about his training in the language, the plane flight, etc. Then he announced that Nikolai would immediately enroll in two special KGB English language classes for localization. He would learn what Britons called everyday items, what different geographical accents sounded like, and how to tell social levels apart, place names and pronunciations—all the things that would make the Britons comfortable with him.

"I would like that very much," Nikolai responded.

"Good, consider it done. You will begin tomorrow, your first full day on the job." Anchev then paused before he continued. "Turinov, would you please show Mrs. Semenov around the grounds while I speak with Nikolai momentarily?"

"Of course."

After they were gone, Anchev's smile faded. "One of my officers witnessed the melee at the airport."

"It happens."

"Who were they?"

"Franz Rákosi, Hungary. First name unknown—Chin, Beijing."

"Why?"

Nikolai shrugged. "Rákosi lost a platoon in Budapest in the Hungarian Revolution. I'm on their list."

"Lost them to you?"

"My soldiers, yes. We captured him. He was lucky he got out alive."

"Was he tortured?"

"Yes."

"I see. So, he was looking for you?"

"I didn't torture him personally."

"That wouldn't make any difference. You captured him."

"Yes."

"What about Chin? What do we know about him?"

"China. Said I was on the flight manifest, ten-thousand U.S."

Anchev shook his head. "Welcome to London, Major Semenov. It can happen here as anywhere."

"To their regret."

"Go home now. KGB flats are beautiful in London. Your wife will be very happy here."

"She is already happy." He was as well. But the man sitting across from him was the last man he could ever let know.

"Take these keys. Black Morris Oxford in front."

Nikolai nodded. "*Spasibo*."

"Now, please find Ninel. Moscow will be calling to complain."

"Rákosi was waiting when we arrived."

"Can't be helped. Ninel's job was to be there before you arrived."

"Solid KGB, Ninel."

"Consider it handled." He brushed him away.

Nikolai went outside to the grounds and found his wife and Ninel. "Your turn," Nikolai told him. "I tried, for what it's worth."

Ninel took off at a trot.

"I know," he said to Nikolai without looking back.

4

In the first days, he drove London streets, walked London downtown, learned entries and exits, and dead ends. He monitored dead drops and received microfilm canisters in brush-bys. Defense industries and military emplacements came next, photographing those he intended to penetrate. He felt very professional and now understood all the intense training and preparation the KGB required. It was good they had taught him to deceive, to coerce, to blackmail. He was going to need these skills to produce intelligence if he wanted to stay in London.

He threw himself into learning colloquial English, spending four afternoons a week in the station's classroom setting and three nights a week at Berlitz Language School at his own expense for help with his dialect. Yulia enhanced the rest of his study with her degree in teaching English. Within weeks, he spoke English like a native and received his certificate. He took it home framed and hung it in the kitchen.

On the night of the certificate, Nikolai went hunting. KGB expected him to apply his new language skills and start recruiting.

He would go where the British were vulnerable, where the lubricant of alcohol loosened tongues. He had studied the local papers and decided the most popular watering hole was the Flamingo Club in Soho. He wore his best Savile Row suit of clothes, provided by Moscow, and a gold Rolex watch. It must appear that he was a very successful businessman.

Into the Flamingo Club he went at ten p.m., walking in mid-tune on the band's cover of Chuck Berry's "Maybellene" that wafted through thick cigarette smoke and the smell of a grill weeks past the recommended time for a good palmetto brush. The noise level was three decibels above cocktail hour. Young professionals and businesspeople crowded the dance floor and bar while duck-tailed waiters balanced drink trays and collected money. When Nikolai approached the bar, two young women giggled and talked behind their hands about a woman they swore was Mary Quant, who they overheard discussing something new called the miniskirt.

Nikolai selected a man for his fitted suit and perfect haircut. His dentistry was Western, and his gold Rolex crept out from under his pressed sleeve from time to time, as Nikolai observed.

He moved in, slid between the man and another with his back turned, and ordered an English ale. When his pint came, he paid and threw down a hefty tip that made the bartender smile. He stood with his back to the bar, awaiting a pause in the conversation on his left.

Meanwhile, the target kept right on talking to the young blond woman. At long last, she excused herself for the restroom, and the man turned back to the bar, gulped down his drink, and ordered another.

"She's lovely," said Nikolai.

The man's head turned toward him. "The woman? I think maybe she charges." He laughed. Nikolai faked it.

"Is this a good place for the ladies?" Nikolai asked. He had left his wedding ring at home with Yulia's understanding he was working.

"Probably the best in London. There are other cheaper places to drink, but the women aren't as nice as the Flamingo Club. It's a difference in social status."

Nikolai stuck out his hand. "Nick."

The man shook his hand. "Daniel. What do you do, Nick?"

"I'm in business."

Daniel grinned. "Now, what in the hell does that mean? That's a bit vague. Business in what way?"

Nikolai chuckled for effect. "Imports and exports with the States."

"Oh, well…that sounds interesting." His voice said not really. Then he asked, "Have you ever been to America?"

"Not yet, but I've always wanted to." Which was true. The closest truth he'd spoken all night. "What do you do, Daniel?"

"I'm vice president of European Travel out of New York. London is a favorite with our clientele."

"So, you're here to make sure your customers enjoy London?"

"Something like that. The lady in the restroom is from San Francisco. She came here on her two-week vacation to have a fling. She's part-owner in a dining ware company in the San Francisco Bay Area. They make melamine stuff, the kind of plates everyone uses when there's no company. We'll be having a midnight dinner at Jaruls Kök."

"Is that all you do, European Travel?"

Daniel had another drink, and like the last, gulped two swallows. Nikolai judged he was feeling no pain.

Daniel opened his hands. "I also do some work for the Stars and Stripes now and then. Just general snooping. Nothing that would get my name in the paper."

"Stars and stripes?"

"America. I carry its water from time to time."

"Sorry, I don't know what that means."

Daniel shrugged. "Well, there are people here who pay to know some of the things I find out from my customers."

Nikolai sensed the man was fishing. Typically, it would take two or three lunches. But he went along. He knew the man might be CIA, but that didn't stop him. Recruitment by the CIA would be reported to KGB Moscow and approved. Nikolai's major score was that he would penetrate the CIA for information valuable to the Soviet Union while giving up only disinformation.

"People who pay for things? What things?"

"Like when a new business moves into the area, such as IBM. Certain people want to know how many employees, what they're making, who they're selling to—especially if they're selling to the Soviets. Sorry, I've had too much to drink. Forget I said that."

"Hold on, that's kind of what I do. You're paid according to what these people say it's worth?"

"Yep."

"Same with me. I wonder—do you think it would make sense for two guys like us to trade information? Maybe make more money off of what the other guy knows?"

"Are you a spy?"

Nikolai's eyes narrowed, and he made direct eye contact. "The truth? I'm a businessman who likes pleasant things. My wife likes pleasant things. All it takes is money. I'll sell a little information here and there if it helps fatten our bank account."

"Soviet information?"

Nikolai raised an eyebrow. "American information?"

The woman returned. She held up her glass and called to the bartender, "Ding, ding, another?"

When Daniel didn't turn back to her right away, Nikolai knew he had said some right things.

"How much would you pay? Let's just say I'm asking for future reference," Daniel said.

"One-hundred American dollars for each meeting that gives me some good information."

"That's amazing. Where do you get your money?"

"See, I have my sources. I'd rather not disclose, or you'll go straight to them. I mean, it's only a possibility."

Daniel nodded his head. "No, no, no, I get it. I'm sorry I said that. Look, there's a new American hydraulic outfit moving into London to address waterway erosion. I'm helping find housing for about fifty workers. Would something like that interest your people?"

Nikolai smiled. He didn't want to reel him in too quickly. "I think so. I could find out. Shall we meet again?"

Daniel said, "I'm here every night. You talk to your people, I'll put some information together in a packet, and we'll meet next Monday night. Is that good for you?"

Nikolai was very wary. It was too easy. It sounded more like the CIA as it went along. "Monday would be perfect. I'll bring one-hundred-dollars in twenties."

"Won't hurt my feelings. All right, Nick"—Daniel held out his hand—"I'm going to need to get back to my lady before she ditches me. But we'll meet next Monday. Be prepared, like the Boy Scouts say."

They shook hands, and Nikolai patted Daniel's shoulder. "She wants another drink. Your chance to shine. What's your name again?"

"Daniel Danbury."

"Nikolai Semenov. We'll talk soon."

He finished his drink and moved off. It was early, only 10:30.

Time to move on to the next club.

His efforts paid off. By the end of the month, he managed three contacts, two of them with insider information about British defense industries. Moscow was pleased and sent its encouragement.

Nikolai grew into his posting and had fleeting thoughts of staying forever, but what would Yulia feel about that? Like his father, her father was KGB, too. She was KGB through and through. Would she have the same feelings about staying in Britain the rest of her life? Or would she turn him in if she knew his intentions?

One night in bed while they were reading, Nikolai tossed something out to get her reaction. "Lively music, cheerful people, openness. More and more, I look at the Soviet Union now as cold with little sunshine. General Masirov was right. I do enjoy it here."

"What about KGB? What about the Party? You love KGB."

"Yes, KGB is my home."

"But Britain is the exact opposite. How do you do it?"

"I do both."

"What if MI5 tries to recruit you?" She was whispering with the covers pulled over their heads when she said this. KGB bugged all flats.

"Shush. I'll recruit them instead."

She was sleepy and dreamy. "Good."

"Maybe we'll never return to Russia."

"Don't be ridiculous," she said.

He said no more about it that night. Maybe she would grow into it, the more she came to realize they were living where the stores never ran out of food, where you could read anything you wanted, where you could publicly criticize the government.

He would wait for her to catch up. He would have to wait, for he adored his wife. But would he return to Russia if she insisted? Was his love boundless?

He rolled over and shut his eyes. Some answers would be slower to come than others. For now, remaining forever was a topic he wouldn't broach again, not with Yulia.

She was more KGB than him.

5

News arrived from Nikolai's aunt in Leningrad. She had written two weeks before, sending the letter to *KGB Moscow* to find Nikolai. He opened and began reading, wondering why his mother's sister, whom he hadn't spoken to in a decade, was writing.

He found out why as he read and learned of his mother's arrest and 100 rubles fine for attending church. She had tagged along with a friend, a woman dying from cancer. While his mother hadn't changed her mind about such foolishness as religion, she had attended a service as support. Aunt Tania found the news article in the Leningrad paper since the government papers had reprinted to warn the populace that they should avoid church.

But then the letter continued. Mother had gone to Leningrad, to Aunt Tania's home, as the Party had ended Nikolai's father's KGB pension because of the arrest. Now she was penniless, without income, and relying on her sister for food and shelter. Finally, the letter swore Nikolai to secrecy but asked, in the humblest manner, whether he might send a little something now and then.

It shocked Nikolai. It was so unlike his mother. And he was confident the entire foolishness of church and religion amounted to naught in her life. But for the Party to step in and take away his father's pension? The pension that he had earned as a loyal Russian intelligence officer after working all his life? His first reaction was shock—and shame—but then he grew angry. Why hadn't the Party given her credit since Nikolai was serving in the KGB? Did his loyal service, like that of his father, mean nothing after all?

He fell into a pit of anger and lashed out inside his head at the Party members surrounding him every day, the diplomats and their Communism, and the KGB officers who blindly followed the Party and its leaders and government. His mother's predicament turned his head, especially after contacting his bank in Russia, and learning money couldn't be transferred to his mother. Her name was on a list of undesirables, and she couldn't receive charity.

He became furious, shouting and stomping around the flat at night, Yulia running after him, reminding him of the electronic ears everywhere.

He told her in a whisper he wanted his mother out of the Soviet Union. And that he wanted *them* out of the Soviet Union if that's how loyalty got rewarded. It shocked her when he said these things, though she made like she understood. She cradled her husband's head at night and shushed him and didn't argue as a good KGB wife should do.

Then, one night after tender lovemaking with Yulia, while he was lying and staring at the ceiling and she had drifted off, he realized he liked Britain more than he'd ever liked Russia. He had good feelings about the people he knew and the town he lived in and struggled with spying against them.

He got up, went into the kitchen, poured a small glass of vodka, and drank it off. More anger surfaced, and he made a decision. He would bring his mother to England. He would provide for her, and she would never have to return to Russia.

He set his glass down on the kitchen counter and looked out at Yulia's small strawberry garden she'd potted on their flat balcony.

He was going to be recruited.

6

Franklin Bolling was an MI5 officer who had met Nikolai at a Danish Embassy cocktail party. They had spoken briefly when, much to Nikolai's surprise and great liking, Bolling began speaking to him in flawless Russian. Their conversation had continued another half hour and ended with a plan to meet for coffee. Nikolai found himself quite liking his new contact. Bolling was blond and intelligent, spoke English with an upper-class accent—as Nikolai had learned to recognize—and had been a top student at Oxford in Russian history and language.

Bolling toiled away in a windowless office at MI5 with just enough room for a modest desk and chair. Tacked to his west wall was a map of Greater London with red thumbtacks pinned on some of the MI5 key meeting places around the city, places like Mornington Crescent Tube Station, Tin and Stone Bridge, St James's Park, In and Out Club, Piccadilly, 54 Broadway, Boodle's, 28 St James's Street, White's, 37-38 St James's Street— all locations monitored by MI5 photographers.

Before they met for coffee, Bolling went to work, examining every document and file inside MI5 that contained any reference to Nikolai Semenov. Most of what he found was recent since the KGB agent's London posting was recent. He learned that Nikolai had been very active in recruiting maybe a dozen contacts from whom he purchased information regularly.

Gordy Radenko's name came up in Nikolai's file. He cross-checked Radenko's file. Sure enough, Nikolai's name popped up in the Gordy Radenko file. Radenko was a junior officer from the Polish intelligence service. He had been a Polish Olympic hopeful who had trained for a short time in Moscow. Later, he had taken a holiday in London soon after a Soviet military incursion into his homeland and vanished while away, surfacing in Soho, where he formally defected. He wanted to settle in Canada.

Bolling contacted Radenko and met him for coffee. "You want to defect and live in Canada?" he asked the young spy.

Radenko spread his unusually large hands—large because he had been a weightlifter on Poland's Olympic team. "I do want to live in Canada. Someplace where my only neighbors are geese and bears. I no longer want much to do with people."

"That's honest."

The young spy shrugged. "Four years in the service of my country and four in the military before that—it is enough. I'm ready for peace and solitude. I'm thinking of British Columbia."

"I wanted to meet and ask about people you know who maybe I should know. For example, the names of other Polish agents? Have you been asked this yet?"

"Yes, I gave my handler a complete list a month ago."

"Excellent. I'm sure I have that in your file. We also know you have an intimate grasp of the structures and methods of Polish intelligence, and you have been debriefed on those matters at some length. That much of your file I have read myself. Now, I'm wondering, who do you know from Russia who MI5 might like to know about?"

Radenko, wanting only to go to Canada, stared into his coffee as if thinking about how much information he'd have to provide to secure his relocation to Canada. "Let me think."

"Take your time."

Bolling ordered a refill on both coffees. When it was poured, he stirred cream slowly into the hot liquid. At long last, Radenko looked up and snapped his fingers. He began reeling off names, some of whom he knew a few things about, some more, some less. The names were primarily Polish. But five of them were Russians, and one of these stood out.

"I know this Russian named Nikolai Semenov. He is a distance runner I have trained with in Moscow. We did weight training." Bolling was pleased. He had found his man.

"Tell me more about this Nikolai Semenov."

"If you need to meet a KGB officer disillusioned with the Soviet Union, you need to meet him. I think he's ready to recruit. Also, a tip. He loves James Joyce."

"The writer?"

"Go figure."

Bolling flagged Nikolai as a "person of interest" and gave him the code name ULYSSES for his interest in James Joyce.

Bolling next contacted MI6 in Moscow. What did foreign intelligence have on KGB officer Nikolai Semenov? They got back to him two days later with a complete dossier, tracing Nikolai from first grade into KGB School 1010, his Berlin posting, and even referenced the problems Nikolai's mother was having since her arrest. This part of Nikolai's file was of great interest to Bolling, for it represented an entry point. The mother's problems could be used by MI6.

7

It was a Saturday morning when Nikolai and Yulia rented bicycles to enjoy their city. They studied their map at a café just around the corner from the rental shop. The ride began at Westminster Pier, right in front of Big Ben. For energy, they both had a scone with cream and raspberry jam. Nikolai chose coffee while Yulia got a pot of tea.

After they were finished, Nikolai suggested, "We can follow the Thames."

"With many marvelous sights and shops," Yulia said. "And look at this downtown street and its cafes! I love the freedom here."

"To come and go as you please without eyes watching," Nikolai said. As he spoke, he looked behind them to prove his point that they weren't being followed. He didn't believe they were.

They stopped two hours down the road to enjoy a fine view of the Palace of Westminster. At the gate, Nikolai struck up a conversation with a couple standing on his left.

"Do you work?" he asked them in his friendliest tone.

"Not right now," said the man. "We just had a baby, and I'm on parental leave."

"Parental leave? What is that?" asked Nikolai.

"You're not from here, okay. But your English is superb. Parental leave is when your employer gives you ninety paid days off work to take care of your new baby."

Yulia's eyes widened. "They pay you to stay home?" she asked in her excellent English.

"Yes," said the new mother. "Not everyone gets it. It depends on who you work for. So, watch out."

"Where are you from?" the young father asked.

"Moscow," Nikolai said.

"Oh, well, good talking. We have more shopping to do for our new one. Goodbye now."

The couple turned and left. Only then did Nikolai see that on the other side of them was a baby carriage, a pram they began pushing down the sidewalk.

"Well," Yulia said, "that was a conversation-ender."

"You noticed. Wow."

They resumed riding their bikes while dodging pedestrians, other cyclists, and ice-cream trolleys. It was a beautiful, warm day, and London was buzzing with people out and about. They pedaled from Wandsworth Bridge to the Thames Path for the next two hours, where signs then instructed them to dismount while taking in the views. After a long push of their bicycles, they finally passed Fulham Palace and ended at Kew Bridge. The mid-afternoon sun shone red and orange and gold through the cocktails and beers on the outdoor tables.

"I'm hungry!" Yulia called Nikolai from behind. "Can we stop?"

They found they could get a small picnic at a converted greenhouse café. They took their basket out on the green alongside the river and spread their blanket.

After their picnic, they laid back and draped their arms over their eyes against the low sun. Late afternoon was coming on. Yulia said her butt hurt and her arms were aching, and she wouldn't mind starting back. But she knew he had someone to meet before they went home.

At four o'clock, Nikolai told her it was time.

"Someone for work again?" she inquired. She never wanted details, like all good KGB wives. Only enough to make her plans around her husband.

"Someone I met at a British Embassy party. Could you find some shops for an hour? That's all I need."

Nikolai and Yulia went their separate ways at Seppo's, a coffee and sandwich café. He watched her pedal away, then went inside and ordered coffee. It was only four, so seating was plentiful. He found an empty table farthest from the sidewalk where watchers couldn't eavesdrop. Then he waited. He looked down at his shaking hands. It was an unscheduled meeting with a man who might very well be from British intelligence. If KGB caught him at an unscheduled meeting, it could be fatal. He stuffed his hands in his pockets to hide the fear while his eyes studied every face, every look, anyone who glanced his way. He told himself he could always get up and leave. The reality was the man could be KGB himself, and the meeting could be a setup to test his loyalty. He had to fight down the impulse to bolt and run.

Five minutes went by. Nikolai checked his Rolex. Then another five. He was getting ready to get up and leave when he saw his contact, the man he had met in a gentleman's club, not an embassy party. Sometimes it was necessary to lie to Yulia. But it was for her own safety, so Nikolai never felt guilt over the fibs that passed his lips.

His contact was riding a bicycle that wobbled up the sidewalk. When he almost ran a young couple into the street, Nikolai couldn't suppress a smile. He leaned the bike along the cafe's low fence and entered through the gate. He walked past Nikolai without acknowledgment and went inside to return several minutes later with a cup of tea. He sat down across from Nikolai and pushed his glasses onto his forehead.

"I'm Franklin Bolling. Thanks for coming."

Nikolai shot a look around. He nodded.

"Gordy Radenko says I should meet you."

"Gordy defected from Poland, last I heard. I knew him from Moscow when I was weight training for my long-distance running. A loyal Pole."

"He represented Poland in the Olympics."

"So, what do you want with me? You approached me, don't forget."

Bolling stretched and looked both ways over his shoulders. "Radenko told me you were disillusioned."

"I don't know what that means," Nikolai replied. He didn't know this person and wasn't about to answer.

"I work for MI5. We have heard things about you, Mr. Semenov."

"Oh? What things?"

"We have heard you are upset with the Soviet Union. We heard they took away your mother's pension. How am I doing so far?"

It stunned Nikolai. He knew MI5 had investigated him before they gave him an embassy visa to come to London. But the information about his mother? That was found out *after* they granted his visa. Why had they kept investigating him?

He inhaled sharply but then regained his inner footing. The chess move came to him, and he leaned across the table. If he was being recorded, he wanted it loud and clear what he was about to say. "I love my job, and I love the motherland. I don't know why you're saying these things. Maybe it's you who is disillusioned with Britain."

Bolling took a large swallow of his tea and then looked up and gave a slight smile. "Maybe I've misunderstood Gordy. If I have, I apologize. But if you're saying these things because you're afraid or think I'm recording you for the KGB, I am not. Look." Bolling stood and lifted his shirt. There was no wire.

"I don't know what you mean," Nikolai said. "I need to leave now."

"Don't rush off. We have much to talk about."

"Forget it, please. It's been a mistake."

He left the table and went searching for Yulia. She was located three stores down the street, modeling a white blouse in front of the shop mirror. "Oh," she said and kissed his cheek, "I thought it would be an hour. Are we ready?"

They biked back to the bicycle rental and turned in their Phillips bikes. Nikolai received his deposit, and the couple caught a taxi back to their flat.

Yulia went into the bedroom and laid down while Nikolai made two teas and took them to her bedside. She was already asleep, so he retreated to the main room and sat on the couch.

He finished both, then joined Yulia on the bed. At first, he couldn't sleep, thinking about his talk with Franklin Bolling. It had been an exciting few moments, but he realized something. There would have to be trust, something the KGB warned against. This would not be easy.

Five minutes later, he was asleep, exhausted from the long ride.

8

Bolling wasn't satisfied with his chat with Nikolai. He knew they could do much better. Plus, he had only just begun. It was very rare that MI5 had a chance at recruiting a Soviet KGB officer.

He approached the director of K4, MI5's Soviet residencies branch, Jason Donovan. Donovan was blond and wiry, resembling Tab Hunter of American TV and movie fame. He had the total respect of his team, and they jumped when he asked.

Donovan listened to Bolling, having him repeat what Gordy Radenko had said about disillusionment. He listened to the mother's problems. Then he made a decision. He would approach Nikolai Semenov himself and feel him out. A disillusioned KGB officer was a huge win.

Donovan was an old-school British agent, always cheerful around the office, charming to Embassy and MI5 staffers. His father had attended Sandhurst and was heavily decorated for his efforts leading soldiers in World War II in Africa and Belgium. His exploits were more than any son could hope to equal, so Jason had gone his own way, attending Oxford to study romance languages. In his senior year, he was tapped on the shoulder and asked whether he'd ever considered serving his country. Donovan played the role of the diplomat perfectly, his cover for his spying. He swiftly became a familiar figure on the London diplomatic party circuit.

Bolling agreed to have Donovan approach Nikolai. Bolling brought out the file and showed Donovan a picture.

"Oh, yes, I've seen him all over town at embassy parties—good looking kid. And probably mean as hell, these KGB fellows. Well, let me have a run at him."

It was time to meet Nikolai Semenov.

9

Nikolai was away from the embassy to prepare to meet friends for Friday night drinks. It was a chance to meet British embassy contacts, and he was studying literature at the London Public Library. He was familiarizing himself with English novelists in case books were discussed.

It was early, nine a.m., when a man he knew from the embassy parties only as Jason came and took a seat across from him at the library table. Nikolai looked up and started to smile, but there was something profound in the man's eyes that caused Nikolai's face to go KGB blank.

Jason looked all around and then whispered, "We need to talk. Can we go somewhere private?"

"The library demands total quiet," Nikolai said.

"Bring your book with you," Donovan replied. "Maybe you'll teach me something."

"There are rooms upstairs."

Donovan had inspected the entire library before making contact. Quiet and small rooms, yes, but too many bare windows. The talk would be elsewhere. "No, let's meet for lunch in three days, noon, at Pillio's."

It was a place Nikolai had never heard of, so he knew it was off the beaten path, away from the usual embassy lunch restaurants. He agreed, saying he would be there.

Back at the embassy, Nikolai played it brilliantly, for he knew he'd been watched. He went straight to the *rezident*. "What do I do?" he asked Anchev. "This fellow from the British Embassy has invited me to lunch. Should I accept?"

"Is he MI5?"

"He has to be."

"Be aggressive! Do anything to recruit an MI5 officer!"

* * *

Three days later, Donovan walked behind the Soviet Embassy, crossed the busy Kensington Palace Gardens, headed two blocks north, one block west, then waited just inside Pillio's overhang where he couldn't be seen from the sidewalk. After ten minutes, no one appeared, so he entered the restaurant and took a seat at the rear, facing the window, where he could watch who entered and who left. It could still be a setup, KGB taking out a vulnerable MI5 officer.

Nikolai arrived precisely on time, darting his gaze around the small restaurant, and took a seat without speaking. Donovan knew they were being watched. He felt it all around them, too. It was a narrow line Donovan and Nikolai walked, and they were on their best game. They ordered and were served.

Donovan was very soft-spoken as they ate. Then he made the first plunge into a request for secret information. "Why," he wondered, "does the KGB send so many intelligence agents abroad? There must be a hundred of them in London alone."

"Good question," Nikolai said between bites of sirloin tips. "What do you think is the answer?"

Donovan knew now. Slow the hell down.

"Have you been to any London art galleries yet? Are you taken by European art?"

"We went to a gallery showing Impressionists. Like nothing I've ever imagined. What's your favorite?"

"Impressionism is lovely. Do you read?" asked Donovan. "Who do you read?"

"I'm reading Joyce. You?"

"I'm reading Homer in Greek. It's a weakness of mine."

"The *Odyssey*?"

"You've read it?"

"Only in Russian. I'm afraid I'm not much of a student of Greece."

"Not yet, maybe, but there's time. Especially in the West, where so much of the world's great literature has been penned."

"Western literature, I agree. It isn't Dostoevsky, but only Russian writers are capable of a *Karamazov*, am I right?"

They talked on and played at the edges of why they had agreed to meet. Donovan quickly learned how slowly Nikolai wished to play it, in contravention with other KGB agents he'd tried to work with who had, in the end, proved too eager, too ready only to receive and never give. That wouldn't happen again, Donovan had resolved, which made him feel good, actually, about Nikolai's pace.

In the end, Donovan moved his chess piece one square closer, asking, "Do you have to report our discussion to KGB Moscow?"

"Yes, but it will be very neutral. It will contain no mention that you asked about KGB strategy and strength."

"Thank you for that. I'm paying the bill. So, should we meet again?"

"I'd like that very much. I'll brush up on my Homer, and you pick up Tolstoy."

Nikolai had tipped his hand. He had opened the door to more.

Nikolai stood and worked his fingers with his napkin. "Oh," he said without looking up. "Twenty-five."

"Twenty-five? What, pounds? Rubles?"

Nikolai smiled and tossed down the napkin. "Twenty-five KGB agents at the Soviet Embassy London. Not one hundred after all." He did an about-face and left the restaurant.

10

Donovan and Bolling prepared a recruitment request for the MI5 director and sent it to his office. Then they waited. The next day, the response came: *Proceed ULYSSES. Handle with extreme care. Randall Cummings to lead. cc: Randall Cummings.*

Two weeks later, Donovan and Nikolai met at Metovolk, a plain little restaurant with a bland menu. But the food was not the point since Donovan, this time, wanted to talk. "You're KGB," he said out of the blue.

"Of course."

"Then tell me, who is the PR line deputy in your station?"

Nikolai was shocked. Did they know nothing at MI5? Suddenly he broke into a smile and said, "*I* am! You've made me think you know everyone, but you don't even know who I am!"

"Really." Donovan appeared thoughtful. Then, "Let me tell you something personal. I've learned more about your mother."

"What about her?"

The British spy nodded his head sympathetically. "We can't blame you for being upset with the Soviet regime. They've hurt her badly, and unless I miss my guess, you're quite angry with them."

"I'm not willing to say how I feel one way or the other."

"Understandable. Nobody's asked you to. But sometimes, a country like Great Britain can be a haven for political refugees. It might be good for an officer like you someday. And your family."

"What do you know of my family?"

"Here is my good faith. Your mother has now received five-hundred rubles."

"That's impossible!"

"No, it's impossible for you. It's not impossible for friends of mine."

"We should meet again," Nikolai said.

"Then, I'd like you to meet someone else you should know, a senior officer in MI5."

One week later, Nikolai dry-cleaned his KGB watchers by running in and out of stores, trains, buses, and finally disappearing down an alley. With no more KGB following, he was free to meet. He took a taxi to the meeting with Donovan.

It was the same restaurant. Except this time, the MI5 agent was waiting outside when Nikolai arrived.

"Come," said Donovan, "let's walk."

Nikolai shivered and looked around like a frightened rabbit. Had he lost them?

"If the KGB were to spot me here with an MI5 officer, on an unannounced meeting, I would be thrown into the dungeon at Lubyanka. Or worse."

"Then let's walk faster."

Nikolai walked with Donovan, even knowing everything was at risk and knowing he was entering enemy territory. Another thought, an even uglier one: What if Donovan was actually a KGB double-agent? What if Nikolai was walking into a KGB trap? He shivered as they walked down the next street. He was quickly losing his confidence and thinking seriously about breaking off and turning back. Instead, he reverted to a habit the KGB had broken him of—biting his nails. He accidentally tore one and began cursing in Russian. Donovan looked at him. "I do speak Russian swear words. Sorry for your pain."

They turned into a small, one-level apartment complex in the third block. Inside, Nikolai was introduced to a bull of a man named Charles. Small talk and vodka followed. Gradually, Nikolai shared information about the KGB and its operations.

The walls were down, and the meetup deemed a success. It was time for Cummings to build his team. Cummings spoke with Bolling and Donovan, who provided background and intelligence access of the potential asset—what secrets he could come into contact with and what secrets were outside the scope of his job.

Randall Cummings then wasted no time in selecting the ULYSSES team members. He penciled out a list:

- Jason Donovan: director of K4, MI5's Soviet residencies branch.

- Charles Lightner: political division, one of Nikolai's handlers

- Emma Magnuson: geography expert, the overt movement of spies from country to country, city to city, and town to town.

- Franklin Bolling: Soviet analyst, one of Nikolai's handlers

- Randall Cummings: ULYSSES team leader. Deputy chief of MI5 counter-intelligence London.

- Martin Crawford: MI5 overseas liaison and one of Nikolai's backup handlers.

ULYSSES was in play.

Plans were then laid, and their first meeting was in mid-August. Franklin Bolling's first topic of business was access to the safe house MI5 had acquired between Kensington High Street and Holland Park.

"Here is the key to the safe house. You can come here at any time. You can go to ground here if necessary. Bring your family—or don't, whatever is best for you. We will meet here once a week. Then we can talk."

"Who will I be meeting with?"

"One, Emma Magnuson. She's the officer who will devise your escape plan if you ever get kidnapped back to Russia. Other MI5 officers will also appear here with certain requests for information. Depending on their department and what they need most."

Nikolai smiled. "The plan of escape. That's very important. You don't want them to torture British secrets out of me."

Bolling shook his head. "Not at all! I'm your handler, and I care about you. Nothing bad will be allowed to happen to you, not on my watch. The escape plan will bring you back to Britain, where you will live a wonderful life. We want that for you."

In leaving the Soviet Embassy for these weekly meetings, Nikolai checked out by telling Anchev he was "going to meet a contact." Contacts were sacrosanct under Anchev's rule; he preferred not to know their identities, which played directly into how Nikolai wanted it anyway. Microfilm no longer was used; it was all documents now. But the Brits had cameras galore at the safe house, ready to snap whatever documents Nikolai brought along.

On the ULYSSES team, Charles was eventually replaced by Martin, a Brit the polar opposite of Charles: always smiling, chuckling at his jokes, quick to make sure Nikolai was comfortable and had everything he needed, ever solicitous about Yulia and whether she had any special needs.

"Her needs are simple, like mine." Nikolai concealed it all from Yulia. She was KGB through and through and trusted he was, too. And she was innocent and couldn't have knowledge the KGB might one day try to extract. She was a dry well, and Nikolai planned to keep it that way.

11

The Soviet Embassy utilized its officers and their spouses as much as possible. When the *rezident* discovered that Yulia was a graduate of Moscow State University with a teaching degree in English, the ambassador approached her about teaching English to children of the embassy staff, all non-native speakers. Yulia jumped at the chance. She soon had a classroom for children on the second floor of the embassy in a room that had once been a "maps and strategy" room, whose previous occupants had moved to a larger space. She purchased pictures of everyday objects the children would come into contact with and titled them with both Russian and English names—buses, trains, automobiles, jackets, restrooms, family members, addresses, and on and on. Then the children were introduced into her classes, which met three days a week after regular school.

One day, Russ Zeleny remained after class, pretending to be slow in gathering up his books and bag.

"Russ," Yulia said to him, "is there anything you need to tell me?"

"No."

"Is everything okay in your life?"

Russ broke into tears when she asked. She went to him, age six, and wrapped her arms around him, patting his back. "What is it, sweetheart?"

"Papa hits my mama!" the boy cried out, bursting into sobs that no amount of patting and hugging would help.

"Did you see this happen?"

"Every night. He drinks and drinks and gets angry. He tells her he hates her and hates me! I don't want my papa to hate me! I told him I'm sorry!"

She continued holding him close and patting his back. "There, there, we'll see what we can do about this, okay?"

"O-o-okay," he said, stuttering now.

She had noticed how sometimes he couldn't finish his sentences in class.

"Does it make it difficult for you to say words?"

"Yes, it scares me! I'm scared, teacher!"

It was the children's mothers' job to pick them up from the embassy after Yulia's class. She decided that day she would speak with Mrs. Zeleny. She pulled in through the embassy gates at 3:45 that afternoon, driving her red MGA coupe. Yulia stood in the driveway, Russell's hand in hers, as the car came to a stop. Yulia approached with Russell and pulled open the passenger door.

"I'm wondering if I might tell you something," Yulia said.

Mrs. Zeleny was wearing sunglasses though the day was cloudy and had been raining. She pulled them down on her nose. "See?" she said as she revealed two black eyes. "Is this what Russell said?"

"It is. He's such a good student, but he's having trouble."

Russell trembled beside Yulia, and she couldn't get herself to hand over the child. "Maybe we could go inside and talk and let Russell play in my classroom? I have the toys he likes."

Mrs. Zeleny parked and came inside. She followed Yulia down the hall to her classroom. Yulia induced Russell to play with the toy cars at one end of the room. Yulia and Mrs. Zeleny talked at the other end while Russell was distracted.

"Russell told me about the hitting."

Mrs. Zeleny burst into tears, then abruptly stopped, pulling herself together using willpower. "I cannot let this be known. They'll send us back to Russia where there's no help at all. Here, I am saving up to divorce him."

"What does he do?"

"He's KGB."

"He's Mitkov Zeleny?"

"Yes."

"We know him. He's been at meetings with my husband. He's a top officer."

"I don't agree with that. I only know he's a hitter. He drinks."

"What are your plans? Have you thought about talking to the *rezident*?"

"No! No *rezident*. That would only put him in a rage. He would kill me!"

"It seems to me he's slowly killing you anyway."

Mrs. Zeleny cast her eyes down to the desktop. "It seems he is."

"You want to divorce him. All right. Do you need money?"

"I need fifty pounds more. Then I have enough."

Yulia pulled open her desk drawer and removed her purse.

"What are you doing?"

"Wait, please."

She pulled out two twenty and one ten-pound note and pushed them across the desk. "Take the money and get away from this bastard. Now, what comes next?"

Mrs. Zeleny brushed away tears that filled her eyes.

"I—I'm a nurse working the midnight shift. I've talked to Immigration. They said I could stay in England because of my trade. I'm going to divorce him and get a flat of my own. Then Russell can grow up safely without violence. His mother will see to that."

"I couldn't be happier. When does this happen? You're not holding back?"

"The divorce papers are waiting for me to sign. I have enough money to rent my own flat now. I will skip work tonight and look in the morning early. Then I'll take only what we can carry and leave him. The rest of my belongings will be returned in the divorce."

"I'm happy for you. Do you mind if I tell my husband about Colonel Zeleny?"

"Why would you do that?"

"KGB will expel him. They will return him to Moscow in shame."

"I wouldn't mind, no. As long as he doesn't hit me for it."

"No, Nikolai will make sure of that, I promise."

And Nikolai did, confronting Colonel Zeleny about his abuse and telling him he was on report, that Nikolai had spoken to the *rezident* and his wife, Rina Zeleny. The next day, Colonel Zeleny was sent home to Moscow, discharged from his career at KGB. KGB not only wouldn't keep a KGB officer guilty of violence in the home, but there was also the possibility his rage would involve local authorities, the last thing KGB would abide. They wasted no time shipping him off.

Russell stuttered no more and cried after class no more.

The Soviet Embassy would allow Mrs. Zeleny to stay in her flat for a full year without rent. But she moved anyway, preferring to begin again with Russell in new surroundings without old memories.

Shortly after this incident, in October of 1959, Yulia announced she was pregnant. They began shopping for baby clothes. They decided to remain in the same flat; the baby would sleep in their room at first. Embassy friends threw a shower. Gifts poured in.

She delivered mid-summer 1960 on one of the hottest days of the year with no complications. The baby was named Sasha, Yulia's mother's name. She was a happy baby and started sleeping through the nights at six weeks—much to everyone's amazement.

"She's so easy," said Yulia.

"She is that," Nikolai agreed. "We are blessed."

12

Sergei Makov's KGB career was collapsing in on him like all spies who leave British fighter aircraft specs on double-decker bus seats or throw up their dinner on the table of the Brazilian deputy ambassador. Or make a pass at the *rezident's* wife at the United Day party just past. Makov had done all this and more, every day more. He drank too much and talked too much, and his batting average at recruiting British spies in London was all but non-existent.

Makov was married to a twit of woman who wanted only to return to Kyiv and take up her place in blue-blood society there, such as it was. Worst of all, it was a sexless marriage, and Makov was at the age when some middle-aged men began keeping score. Zenda, his wife, was someone he had decided to scrap in favor of someone younger and sexually ravenous if such a one existed and had an eye for him besides.

Makov lived more in his head and his imagined future than he ever lived in his present reality. Late to work, he was so hungover he wore sunglasses to hide the bloodshot, was unable to concentrate, and threw up in the men's room. Leaving "for the field" after lunch, Makov failed to produce any intelligence of any value. His *rezident,* Anatoly Anchev, was distant, hated Makov, and wanted to replace him with someone whose numbers made him look better to Moscow where promotions were issued.

That winter, Makov was slipping into a rut: disgruntled, lonely, peevish, and disappointed, but too lazy and boozy to do anything to arrest the slide. Then Dona Maria came into his life, and the lights came on.

Dona Maria Cantrell was the head hostess at the Cantrell Restaurant in Piccadilly, an upscale watering hole and eatery for London's well-heeled, upper-crust citizens out for a night of drink and fun and debauchery. But there was more, for Dona Maria was also the madame of a string of a dozen lovely young women who would spend the night with you for one-hundred pounds. Makov met her on one such outing, and he fell in love with the madame. She also was rolling in money, and when he told her he was a physician—making up a huge lie right on the spot like all good KGB officers were trained to do—who specialized in delicate heart surgery, she took him home with her that first night. She kept him up until dawn with creative mattress athletics that left Makov so terribly exhausted he called in and canceled his "surgeries" for that day. He disappeared for days at a time while he "operated in several hospitals around the city" and was too busy to call.

While Dona Maria was patient with her new physician over those first weeks, she soon grew morose and moody and jealous of his other love—heart surgery. Of course, there was no heart surgery; he was performing as a KGB officer in London. Unaware of any of this, Dona Maria began asking for more time with her lover, persuading him with ever-greater orgiastic beddings, wearing herself out trying to turn his head away from his professional life and focus on her instead. At first, he responded. But reality soon created storm clouds because, as Makov was learning, Dona Maria was also immature, needy, and greedy. "How much do you earn for a surgery?" she asked him. "Should we have a bank account together? It would make me safer if something happened to you."

Exhausted by her sexuality and her money-grubbing, he sat her down one night and leveled with her. She learned her new Soviet lover was already married, teetering on bankruptcy, and a KGB spy.

"How can you stand KGB? They are all thugs! They break my girls' noses and steal their money and refuse to pay!'

Makov sidestepped it, promising he would divorce Zenda as soon as possible and marry Dona Maria. They would move to Moscow and live a perfect Soviet life.

"Moscow? I have no desire to live in that horrible place! I will live here in London. But I won't live with you on a pauper's salary. Now go out, find a real job, and make me proud."

Makov responded by promptly stealing Soviet secrets, KGB personnel lists, and embassy employee charts, then selling his treasure to the British. Almost overnight, his fortunes turned. The lovers opened a joint bank account into which he deposited one-hundred pounds. Soon, there was another two-hundred.

She welcomed him back into her bed, where they made plans for marriage and a life of long nights and candlelight dinners right there in London.

Moscow be damned.

13

Yulia was an excellent teacher; parents had only good things to say. But she wanted to earn money for her family, too, and teaching was volunteer work.

"What would you think if I looked for a job so that we could afford a bigger flat?" she asked Nikolai one day.

"Doing what?"

"I don't know. Working at the embassy? Is there work there?"

"There's a bulletin board with jobs. Perhaps take a look when you are there next."

"You would have to watch the baby at night."

"That's no problem except nights when I work. What then?"

"Mrs. Johnson next door. She mentioned if I ever needed help with the new baby, she'd be glad to earn some extra money."

"That could work. You sure you want to work outside of the home?"

She smiled. "Very much. I love my baby and my home and you. But I need something away from home, too. It would feel nice."

She searched the job board at the embassy and found an opening for an English-speaking listener at the Soviet Embassy in London. She didn't know what a listener did, but she applied anyway. She was immediately offered the job, where she would be paid for her time.

Yulia's assignment was the radio room. All British radio broadcasts were monitored for local information, political climate, military facts and maneuvers, and public discourse—anything KGB Moscow could glean from public dissemination. Across from her sat two other workers, both women, monitoring British television. Yulia soon graduated to tape-recording MI5 agents whose cars had been bugged by the KGB. She then filed reports on what the Brits said while pursuing the Soviets.

Across from Yulia sat Anya Donchev, a blowsy woman with thin hair and a mouth that didn't take lipstick well. With the askew mouth and flat hair, she appeared like a member of the chorus line third row. But Anya was very bright and successful in her listening job. Yulia liked her and always made a point of getting along, for her job was important. She and Nikolai needed the money—his eighteen-hundred rubles each month wasn't enough to enjoy life in a Western country where goods of all colors and sizes were available in the stores. So, Yulia's extra six-hundred gave them a very nice lifestyle and helped with Sasha's growing expenses.

At ten o'clock one night, she listened in on a conversation between two British MI5 agents. It took place in their bugged car. The garage had just told them their car was slick, free of bugs, but it was not.

The one agent went by "Buzz," and the other went by "Saw."

Said Buzz, his voice crackling in the night air heavy with radio sounds, "Did you count Sergei Makov's gift?"

To which Saw replied, "One-hundred pounds—unmarked bills, used, as he wanted."

"Here he comes, getting out of his car now."

Over headphones, Yulia heard footsteps approaching what sounded like gravel and then listened to the car door open.

"Did you bring my money?" asked a man's voice.

"Lieutenant Makov is one-hundred pounds richer with this," said Saw. Yulia heard the sound of a paper bag passed hand-to-hand.

"I want to count."

"Of course," said Buzz.

Yulia was electrified. "Come, listen," she whispered to Anya Donchev, sitting next to her that night, wearing headphones. Anya plugged her headphones into one of Yulia's phone jacks. The women concentrated.

"It's all here," Makov said.

"One-hundred pounds," Saw said. "I counted it myself from the bank."

"So, your people asked about Soviet war plans in England? First, if war breaks out in Europe, England will be swamped with Russian soldiers, aircraft, rockets, tanks, a complete army of occupation. KGB will install radar trucks along your Atlantic coast. Maybe thousands of troops in London," said Makov.

"You know this how?" said Buzz.

"My position as Soviet Army liaison gives me access to all war planning. It would be the job of the Soviet station in London to prepare radar sites ahead of time. Our people have already done that, and we monitor those sites against tall buildings, antennae going up, aircraft operations in the vicinity, anything that could impact our ability to identify incoming aircraft from the Atlantic."

"What about documents tonight? What have you brought for your money?"

Papers rustling inside the automobile.

"These are the Soviet plans, hot off the press. I copied these myself, one-hundred-fifty pages."

"They are genuine?" said Buzz.

"Do you doubt me? Why did you recruit me if you didn't trust me? That was ill-advised."

"No, no, no!" exclaimed Buzz. "Of course, we trust you. I was merely asking if they were the most recent. That's all I was asking."

"Look at the date on the bottom. Here, use my lighter."

The sound of a cigarette lighter wheel spun.

"See? Along the bottom? The note has it in September. That's as recent as it can get."

"So I see. Good enough."

The sound of a Zippo being snapped closed.

"Is there more?" Buzz then asked.

"Paper? I have all of Europe."

"How much for all of it?"

"Europe is very difficult to sneak out. I could be caught and shot. Two-hundred pounds."

"How long would it take?"

"Two weeks. I can only copy at lunch hour. Maybe less than two, but I could guarantee two at the most."

"As recent?"

"The same vintage, I'm sure."

"Two weeks from tonight, here, same place. We will bring two-hundred pounds."

"You do that," Makov said. "And I will bring Soviet war plans for Europe. Everything, I will bring it all."

The meeting broke up.

Yulia looked at Anya. "It's recorded," Yulia said, stunned. This was huge.

"I know what I would do," Anya offered with a smile.

"What is that?"

"I would play the tape for Lieutenant Makov. Sell it to him for one-half."

Yulia recoiled from the whisper as if from a hot stove. "No!"

Anya smiled the smile of a collaborator. "Oh, yes."

"My husband would watch them shoot me and applaud," Yulia mused.

"He might. Or he even might buy a new flat to live in. Prices are good right now."

"One question," Yulia said. "Why would Makov say these things inside a car he knows is bugged by the KGB?"

A knowing smile from Anya, reeling Yulia in with her boldness and insider's view. "He knows if anyone ever listened to these tapes—which no one ever does—he would claim it was disinformation. That he was feeding false information. He would then say he took the money to recruit other contacts. You just happened to hear it going on."

"I listen to all my channels," Yulia hastened to say. "It's my job."

Anya snorted, "You are one of many, a jewel, but a poor one. Do you want to split with me or not? It is a perfect chance. It's been done before around here."

"Has it?"

"Of course. Clerical knows everything Operational knows. Why wouldn't we?"

Yulia was frightened. Anya couldn't know Yulia was the wife of a KGB agent and strictly committed to the system. So she declined. "I cannot do it."

Anya scowled and reached for the reel of tape. It was mounted on a Teac tape machine. She rewound, then pulled the reel free and slipped it inside her purse. "Now, you don't have to worry," Anya said. "It's my problem now."

"What will you do with the tape?"

"Turn it in. KGB must hear this."

Yulia was relieved. "Then I feel better. Thank you."

"I'm going to Lieutenant Dachev right now." She got up and left her post. Ten minutes later, she returned.

"You turned it in?"

"I did. It was disinformation. KGB knew all about Makov if that makes you feel any better."

"Then I will sleep tonight."

Anya never returned to her seat after that night. Yulia asked around, but she was never heard from again.

14

In March 1961, Sergei Makov answered a knock at his door. It was yet early, and Makov still wore his pajamas. A young woman he didn't know was standing there. "I have a tape recording you should hear," she told him.

"Who's that at the door?" Dona Maria called from the kitchen on one of the rare mornings when she cooked breakfast. Makov didn't answer. He was outside the flat, the door closed behind him, trying to understand who this twit was who would dare come by the flat of a Soviet KGB officer and present a tape recording.

"I work at the KGB listening room. The tape is a recording of you accepting a bribe from Buzz and Saw. Don't bother trying to grab it away. There are other copies."

"What is your name?"

"Anya."

"You work at the KGB taping room?"

"Yes."

He whispered, edging nearer, "What do you want from me?"

"One half."

"Of?"

"Of everything you have taken for bribes. Congratulations, Officer Makov, you have a new partner!"

"Wait. I must verify you are who you say."

She told him her full name, then her address, too, when he asked where he could deliver the blackmail.

"Who else knows about this?" he asked.

"Just my friend, Yulia Semenov."

"Nikolai Semenov's wife, Yulia?"

"Yes, she's really an English teacher. But she needs the KGB job. We will split whatever you pay us."

"She knows about this tape? This one right here?"

"Of course. We're partners."

"All right. Be home tonight and answer the door when I knock three times. I'll have your money."

"I work tonight."

"What time do you get off?"

"Five in the morning."

"Yulia Semenov gets off, too?"

"Yes, we work the same shift together."

"So, I can pay you both when you get off?"

"Okay. Be waiting at the back door of the embassy. We'll come down the stairs. Be waiting there. I'll tell Yulia the boss wants us to do an errand in my car. You follow us to Azmah Park and pay us there."

Makov smiled. "You've got this all planned out."

"I just want the money you owe us."

"I owe you?"

"You heard me. Be there tomorrow morning and have the money, or else I'm taking the tape to Lieutenant Dachev."

"I promise. I'll be waiting."

He shook the snow from his clothes and went back inside. Hurrying to the blinds, he parted them with his fingers and watched Anya climb into her car.

He would be there the next morning. She would become an example to silence others who might have heard things.

15

The following morning, the sun dodging in and out of the gray sky, two bodies were found outside the Soviet Embassy in London.

Nikolai relied on his brother-in-law, Maxim Moltoi, to drive him home from the Embassy when Anchev told him to go home. Yulia still hadn't arrived there. Nikolai was panicked, having trouble with his breathing. His face was flushed as he thought of what he would tell Sasha about her mother. She was far too young to understand much. But still, she would ask, "Where is *mamochka*?" What would he answer back?

Maxim drove slowly through the frosty London afternoon. It began raining. The Alvis coupe's windshield wipers beat out a rhythm that sounded to Nikolai like, *That is her, that is her, that is her.* He couldn't help it. That the dead body was her had become visceral.

They arrived at Doring Road. They ran from the car to the stairway overhang. Upstairs they climbed to the second floor.

Nikolai turned on a light when they entered. "Yulia!" he called loud enough to be heard throughout the flat.

"Yulia's not here," Maxim said with an air of suspicion. "We mustn't lose hope."

There was a note. Mrs. Johnson had Sasha next door. They would watch TV until someone came to her.

"We're not killing anyone, Max. We don't know about that yet."

"I've got a feeling she's off with him," Maxim insisted. "I don't think that's her in the snow. God, I hope not."

"Don't we both."

They hung their coats on the door peg.

"Coffee? Something stronger?" Nikolai asked.

"Kubanskaya. I know you keep it."

"Be right back."

"Are you drinking with me?"

"Just one. To clear my head."

"Of course."

Two hours later, they were on their third vodka when the phone rang. Nikolai jumped at the sound, then picked it up from the table beside his chair. "Colonel Semenov."

"Comrade Semenov. Nicole Reynolds calling from the crime lab. We expedite the fingerprint analysis in homicide cases." The London police crime lab. Anchev had given the police his name and home phone.

"Yes, go on, please."

"The fingerprints match the ones provided to us by the Soviet Embassy. It is your wife in the snow. I'm so sorry to tell you, but Anatoly Anchev said do not hesitate to call. I called him first. He said you'd want to hear it from me if you have questions."

"Oh, God!" cried Nikolai. "How can you be sure of this?"

"Our crime lab gives us two-hour support in suspected homicide cases. Your wife took priority."

Nikolai was softly weeping. But he didn't want to end the call, not just yet.

"Which—which body was it?"

"The body in the white blouse. She was closest to the gates, according to my drawing."

"You matched the fingertip to the finger?"

"It was very easy to do. They were cut with pruning shears. Or maybe tin snips. Do you know anyone with pruning shears or tin snips?"

"Thank you for calling," Nikolai said without answering her. "Good evening."

He replaced the phone on the table. He wiped a forearm across his eyes and wept, then swiped the tears from his eyes. He was crying openly in front of another KGB agent and didn't care.

"I heard it all," Maxim said quietly. "I'm sorry, Niky."

Nikolai went into the bathroom and returned with a box of tissues. He thought he was done with the tears, and it was time to blow his nose. Except he didn't get that far as he felt the tears well up in his eyes. He used sheet after sheet of tissue until the box was empty.

Maxim stood. "Let me get a tissue. Bathroom?"

"Please." Nikolai lost it again, rocking back and forth, murmuring Yulia's name over and over.

"Shock," Maxim said, handing him a wad of toilet tissue. Maxim placed his hand on his shoulder. "There, there. We'll find whoever did it."

"We will. Oh, my God. Who would want to harm Yulia?"

"That's the question. Maybe her lover? Maybe she was going to tell his wife if he didn't leave her?"

"Oh." He couldn't stop the tears.

"That is a logical explanation. The bastard must be located. Look, someone at the party. He would have to be KGB to be there."

Nikolai's tears still rolled down his cheeks. He dabbed and turned away. "Sorry, Max. I—"

He shuddered. He could hear Sasha laughing and playing through the thin flat walls. Mrs. Johnson's TV was blaring. How would he ever tell Sasha?

The phone rang again.

"Colonel Semenov? General Anchev. I'm sorry to hear about Yulia. Terribly sorry. I have put you in charge of the investigation."

"Me? Seriously? My own wife?"

"You would rather it was someone else?" Now Nikolai heard the sarcasm. The game continued.

"Yes. I've never heard of the KGB investigating their own family member. I don't think it's a good idea."

"Fine, I'll give the case to someone else."

"Yes, I mean, I'll probably be a mess for a day or two. You want someone on it without delay. What about Maxim? He's sitting here with me. She was his sister-in-law."

"Put him on."

Nikolai handed the phone to Maxim. "Sorry," he whispered.

"General? This is Major Moltoi. I am at your disposal."

"It is your investigation, Major. Make us proud."

"Yes, sir."

"Be prepared to take the lie detector first thing tomorrow."

"Sir?"

"We have to rule you out."

"Yes, sir. I see."

"It's standard practice. We can't have you investigating yourself now, can we?"

"No, sir."

"Same thing with Colonel Semenov. Have him here for the test along with you. He must be ruled out. *Standartnaya rabochaya protsedura*. SRP."

"Understood. I will bring the Colonel with me."

"Excellent. That is all. Good night."

Maxim handed the phone back to Nikolai. "Hello?" Nikolai said into the phone, but it was dead. General Anchev had hung up.

"Lie box?"

"Both of us," Maxim said. "SRP. We must find her lover. Has anyone called her? Any man called here looking for her?"

Nikolai forced a smile. "Taking your new assignment seriously, are we?"

Maxim scowled. "I will find him for you, I promise. When I do, I shall shoot him. There will be no arrest."

"Then you're in trouble. No, we'll let the KGB shoot him. That's good enough for me."

"All right, then. The KGB gets to shoot him. Let's have one more," said Maxim, holding up his empty glass.

"Agree. Then I can get Sasha and tell her. It's going to be terrible!" The tears were building.

"I will leave you to it."

Nikolai went into the kitchen for drinks. While at the sink running water, tears exploded in his eyes. He leaned his head over the sink and washed his eyes beneath the fixture. The water was cold—London water was all but freezing in the winter. But it felt good and helped him focus. He poured the vodka, added two cubes to each, and rejoined his guest.

They drank while Maxim outlined the steps he would take in the investigation. First, he would talk to every agent at the United Day celebration. The KGB had a list—the KGB always had a list. He would get to the bottom of the lover situation. "No one dares lie to an official investigation." It was true. The crime of lying to the KGB was always worse than the crime under investigation for perpetrators and witnesses alike. So that consideration was on Maxim's side.

"One thing troubles me," Nikolai said with a steady voice.

"Burial?"

"There needs to be a memorial service."

"Carolina can arrange that. It would help if you took time to grieve and reflect, but I'm sure there will be time for that later."

Nikolai couldn't stop the tears but had a message to share. A nagging thought demanded confession to his brother-in-law. "Maxim. I must tell you this. The KGB might think I'm spying for the Brits and—"

Maxim's eyes widened, and he jumped on it. "Then you are a threat! KGB killed Yulia. I have no doubt. They are silencing you forever. They have left your daughter, but she would be next."

"That means I got Yulia killed because they distrust me!"

"I have no doubt. Please don't talk to anyone until I check with some contacts. Hear me?"

"I hear you. My lips are sealed."

"Good man. Now have another drink, then read to Sasha. Tell her slowly. She's young and won't understand. She'll cry for her *mamochka* for some days."

Then Maxim was off, and Nikolai was left alone with his growing self-recriminations for getting Yulia killed.

He had another drink, but it was half-full when he tossed it out. He retrieved Sasha from next door and brought her inside. He placed two fingers inside the diaper and found it was wet, so he changed her diaper then read her Dr. Seuss in Russian. He put her to bed early, found the teddy bear, and tucked it in with her.

He went into the living room, watched the news on TV, then slipped into bed. He moved to Yulia's side and buried his face in her pillow. He smelled her and remembered how clean she always smelled. Of all things to remember.

He climbed in bed at midnight and slept two hours, but was up the rest of the night, berating himself for causing Yulia's death. On the one hand, he was raging at whoever had murdered his beautiful wife, but he sobbed and vowed revenge on the other. At last, at five a.m., he fell asleep sitting up in the living room chair until six when Sasha woke him with her crying.

16

That morning, he dressed in his uniform and took Sasha to Carolina for the day. Her eyes were red-rimmed as she gave him a silent hug. Then, "Niky. I'm so sorry."

He called at noon. Sasha wanted her *mamochka*. She wouldn't stop crying. But meanwhile, Nikolai had to deal with the KGB.

He went into the office for his lie detector test. It was administered in the building's basement with only the polygraph operator present, seated behind Nikolai while the questions were asked and answered.

"Did you murder your wife?"

"No."

"Did you pay to have your wife murdered?"

"No."

"Did you want her dead?"

"Never!"

"Yes or no, please. Did you want her dead?"

"No."

"Have you received money you're not entitled to?"

"No."

"Are you spying for a foreign government?"

"No."

"Let me ask that again. Do you work for a foreign government?"

"No."

"Are you giving secrets to a foreign government?"

"No."

"Are you spying for a foreign government?"

"No."

Thirty minutes later, they were finished.

"How did I do?"

"Flying colors. No problems."

"I'm cleared?"

"You're cleared."

"May I see the strip?"

"No, you may not."

Five minutes later, the polygraph examiner was meeting with Anatoly Anchev.

"Colonel Semenov failed the test."

"Which part?" said the *rezident*, looking shocked. "He murdered his wife?"

"No, I ask baseline questions to make sure the apparatus is working properly. I asked if he was spying for a foreign government. He said 'no,' but it was recorded as a lie. Your man may be a spy."

Anchev's eyebrows arched. He thanked the examiner and sent him on his way with the admonition that all results were top secret. "If word gets out about them, I'll be coming after you," Anchev told the man, who was white-faced at that.

"Yes, sir. Lock and key."

Anchev cabled Moscow. "We may have a mole in our station. Permission requested to follow and turn him against the British if it plays out."

One hour later, Moscow Center replied. *Permission granted. Indisputable evidence requested. Double surveillance. Transcribe all bugs and forward to Moscow Center. That is all.*

17

Nikolai knew he had failed the polygraph question about spying. He called an emergency meeting at the safe house.

"Is there a plan to escape from Moscow yet?" Nikolai asked Bolling once they were both there. "In case I am kidnapped back to Moscow?"

"We have several ways to escape from the Soviet Union. It is always necessary to be thinking that way, ULYSSES," Bolling said.

"ULYSSES?"

"Your code name. For our work together."

"James Joyce? His book?"

"One of your favorites."

"What don't you know about me?"

A subtle smile. "We have yet to find that out."

"What of our work together? Should we quit while the investigation about my wife is proceeding?"

Bolling wasn't ready for that. "Let's think this through together. MI5's own KGB officers have said nothing about a spy. There's no mole hunt, and the KGB did not kill Yulia. Someone unknown killed her. She knew something, and someone silenced her. That someone needs to be found. Maybe KGB will find him. Maybe the London police will find him. And that's good. But we cannot let it interfere with our work."

Nikolai was sitting with his arms crossed on the kitchen table, deep in thought. "You're right. KGB didn't kill her. My guilt cannot be trusted."

"Good. Can we talk now?"

"We can."

"Here's what we need. MI5 needs clarification on KGB's London station. We need to know who the actual diplomats are and who the intelligence officers are. We need names and assignments as well. Even better if we had the names of spies being run by KGB London station, especially those who have penetrated MI5."

"We've been over all that, Franklin."

Bolling nodded. "We have, but it's always changing."

"I can help with the first part, the names of intelligence officers and assignments. In the second part, the spies who have penetrated MI5, I have never seen a list. I will investigate. I will do what I can."

"Excellent. And what about KGB Moscow itself? We'd like a chart of the directorates and directors and deputies."

"I have that already," Nikolai said, touching the side of his head. "I have it up here."

"Great and, Nikolai, let's not quit just yet. There is so much you can help us with. We will make a plan for your escape. It will be a good plan, I promise."

"What more can I turn over?"

"What about the documents you're dealing with? We want everything that crosses your desk. A spy camera? We can offer that."

"It would be instant death if I were caught with a spy camera. They would shoot me on the spot, and you would be short one spy. I think I have a better idea, but it's more complicated."

"Tell me then."

"What I want you to have is all documents we receive from Moscow. These come to us by microfilm."

"Microfilm. Of course. Go ahead."

"I intercept the diplomatic pouch the microfilm comes in. The pouch comes to my desk every day. I can bring the microfilm outside of the office over my lunch hour. No one would know because it's in my possession over lunch anyway."

"And we could acquire a microfilm reader, take a brush-by, run and copy it, and get it back to you before the end of the lunch hour. I like that. It will work."

Bolling was elated. He relayed a request to MI5. He needed a portable microfilm copier. Did they have any such thing? They replied he need only stop by Technical Services and check one out.

18

Leaving his flat to run his five kilometers, Nikolai would check the Vauxhall Cresta parked in front of his building. If it faced in, it was a signal to check under the fender. If it faced out, no message. The rest was up to him. On July 10, he saw the Cresta facing in for the first time in weeks. When he returned from his run, he bent down to tie his shoe and felt beneath the fender. A note tied with a rubber band around a stone. He palmed it and ran upstairs to his flat.

He opened the note and read. It was from Wilford Staley, an investigator with MI5. Nikolai had never heard of the man. But the note puzzled him: Staley had been approached by a KGB officer Makov. Makov had been working with MI5 for almost six months. He had complained that he was the victim of blackmail. Nikolai was told to meet Staley for lunch at a particular restaurant in South London on Tuesday next at one o'clock.

Nikolai kept the luncheon date, arriving precisely at one, to find a man wearing an outrageous pink necktie sitting near the rear in a booth. Wordless, Nikolai sat down across from him.

When the man didn't speak, Nikolai asked, "Well?"

Staley spoke softly while looking beyond Nikolai, over his shoulder. "Makov came to me a month ago. Blackmail. He was selling documents to our people—a KGB clerk overheard the transaction when the KGB bugged the British agents' car. The person who overheard was a young woman. She wanted two-hundred pounds in return for remaining silent. She played the tape for him, where he was selling secrets to MI5 agents. She said she had another copy of the tape, not to bother ripping it away. She was smug and she had him. He asked for MI5's help. We said certainly we would intervene.

"But a strange thing happened. The girl disappeared. Poof, gone like smoke."

"What does this mean for me?" asked Nikolai, confused.

"Anya Donchev was the blackmailer's name. Mean anything to you?"

"No, should it?"

Staley leaned closer. "She was found next to your wife in the snow. That was the second victim."

Nikolai grew dizzy. He shut his eyes, a sweat breaking out across his forehead. For several moments he couldn't think, as unreal as the words sounded. "Tell me that again."

"Anya Donchev was working with your wife the night Makov sold his first documents to MI5."

"All right, all right. Let me think."

"Certainly."

Staley sat back in the booth and stirred his coffee.

"This Anya and Yulia worked together? They were listeners. They heard the KGB microphones. They heard the sale of the documents. Then what? Are you saying they both blackmailed Makov?"

"That isn't what I said at all. I said Anya Donchev blackmailed him."

"Wait. How do you know about Anya and Yulia working together?"

"Please, Mr. Semenov. We have people, too. You don't really want to know."

"Let's be clear about what we're saying then. Are we saying Makov murdered my wife? And this Anya?'

"You said that. Not me."

"Why are you telling me these things? Why aren't you protecting Makov?"

For the first time, Staley smiled. "Because your friends at MI5 are bigger than his friends at MI5."

"Did MI5 help?"

He spread his hands. "We did not engage."

"Sorry, I need to think. I know Sergei Makov. Lieutenant Sergei Makov. He's one of us."

"Sure."

"What can I—? What if I—?"

"Kill him? Sorry, we can't have that. He's too valuable. Just like you."

"Then why are you telling me? Surely you don't think I'm going to be able to live with it? Have you lost your minds?"

"No. You can kill him, certainly. Just not now. We need his sources too much. Sergei Makov is off-limits to you, Nikolai."

"How long?"

"Until we tell you. I will tell you when we're done. Then you can do whatever you feel you need to do. Until then, no."

"Why are you telling me now?"

"Because you and Major Moltoi are looking for a man from the last UD party."

"What? You cannot know that!"

"What, you thought only the KGB attended your little party? Come now, Nikolai, give us an inch of credit."

"Stunned."

"We don't want you poking around that party. You might uncover a partygoer we don't want put under a microscope by you or the KGB. Leave it alone. Now you know the truth. Leave the UD party-list alone."

"What else aren't you telling me? There's more. I see it in your eyes."

Staley looked down at the table. Then he lifted his gaze and looked directly at Nikolai. "This next, you didn't hear from me."

"I swear it."

"Makov was acting at the orders of KGB."

"KGB ordered Makov to murder my wife? And Anya?"

"Keep it down. Makov went to the KGB *rezident* and told him he was selling disinformation to the British. He said two listeners were blackmailing him over that. The KGB would not have one of its officers blackmailed, so they green-lighted him. Makov did the rest. All right. I'm finished here."

Staley slid sideways out of the booth and stood.

"You can buy my coffee," he said and walked right up the front and out the door.

Nikolai sat stunned. The KGB had ordered Yulia's murder. He closed his eyes but only saw red as he tried to think who, above Makov, would issue such an order. The *rezident*, Staley had said. Anatoly Anchev. The waitress stopped by. He ordered coffee and lemon meringue pie. Thirty minutes later, he paid for his pie and both coffees. He understood clearly. But was Yulia really in on some blackmail, or had her name just been used by Anya? Whichever, he planned to strike back. Makov and Anchev. This could not be allowed to stand.

He changed buses three times to get back to the office. KGB missed spotting him as he dry-cleaned.

Sergei Makov. He had killed Yulia. Anatoly Anchev had given the green light to kill a KGB officer's wife.

It would come full circle. Until then, the spying would double, triple, everything would go to the British.

Everything.

19

Nikolai's Yulia was dead and gone. Staley had given him proof it was the KGB. His mother had been arrested and stripped of all property by the KGB. He was in a rage, and, in his way, he was hurt. What about the loyalty he had pledged to the KGB and the Party? So far, it was a one-way street. It had taken so much from him, so thoughtlessly, without regard to him as a real person, that he had finally reached the end of his rope. He made a decision. He was going to give the British every last piece of intelligence he could lay his hands on. At the moment he'd made this decision, he realized that his loyalties had shifted. He might not be British, but maybe that would happen one day. Whatever else, he was no longer Soviet. His own country had turned its back on him.

On a warm day in late July 1961, Nikolai appeared as a nondescript man wearing nondescript clothes, ordering coffee from a small café in central London and carrying it outside to a white steel table. He sat down and opened the newspaper. He slowly stirred his coffee with a spoon. The restaurant was full since it was the noon hour, and some people were standing outside along the fence, eating their sandwiches and laughing. Nikolai studied the crowd over his newspaper, looking for KGB surveillance--he knew KGB faces when he saw them, but this time it was all clear.

Soon, another nondescript man, Franklin Bolling, appeared outside, balancing a coffee in a saucer and a sandwich on a plate. He approached the first man's table and nodded at the extra chair. "May I?"

"Help yourself."

Bolling sat down and began eating his sandwich and sipping his tea. "Would you pass me the sugar?"

Nikolai passed the sugar and, as he did, dropped an aluminum container of microfilm into Bolling's hand. The exchange took one second to complete. Bolling wolfed down his sandwich and abruptly left.

Once off the square, Bolling turned up a flight of stairs, flew up to the landing, and let himself into the first flat. There, he fired up a copier about the size of a Bible and pulled the microfilm slowly through the copier face. Then he waited, counting the minutes.

Thirty minutes later, the same two men did a brush-by exchange as they passed in front of the shoe store window. Now, Nikolai had the film returned and was on his way back to the station with it inside his pocket, where Bolling had planted it.

After dozens of brush-bys and drops, Bolling and Nikolai met at the safe house to discuss a month later.

"Is it helping?" asked Nikolai somewhat tongue-in-cheek.

Bolling couldn't help beaming. "Is it ever! You have given us a river of documents every day. We've never had so much information from one source. There is so much information on spies and agents and illegals, and where they operate, we've had to bring in extra agents to handle the deluge. But don't stop! Don't think for a minute it's too much!"

"We have to be extremely careful. Our drops are the most dangerous moment in the whole game. If a KGB officer were to witness, he would shoot me on the spot. So we need to become more creative."

"We'll set up a dead drop. We'll set up one for each day of the week. That way, we can alternate, so we repeat the same handoff two weeks apart. Does that help?"

"Agree. A dead drop might be that much friendlier. But the time is still thirty minutes with you. I must return before my lunch hour is up."

"Understood."

Nikolai knew that with every exchange, he was risking his life. One slip-up—just one—and he was dead. Imagine, he thought, a KGB officer caught outside headquarters with microfilm so top secret it was transported by diplomatic bag. He had to shake his head and pinch himself at times. Was he really doing this? He was. Would he continue? He would, and even more of it. But still, he was terrified. He would return each time to the embassy shaking and sweating head to toe. He kept his hands in his pockets the first hour after so his coworkers didn't notice him shaking.

The contact sites varied: a phone booth, a toilet, a filling station, a drugstore magazine display, a dentist's outer office, a grocery store bathroom. They changed it every day.

As the *rezident's* deputy, Nikolai had access to hundreds of documents containing code names, operations, directives, and a 150-page report outlining all Soviet intelligence efforts in Britain. The volume was enormous, and London was now underwater. The information was still painstakingly distributed, sometimes to MI5 and sometimes the British homeland intelligence agencies if it affected national security. Other than MI5, only the Brits received Britain-specific ULYSSES files.

The gap closed between Bolling and Nikolai Semenov. The Russian knew MI5 was watching him. He knew they were recording him, even against their earlier promises they would not. However, he still identified every KGB officer, every illegal, and every source feeding the KGB's greedy mouth. Bolling convinced Nikolai to accept money in the form of underground deposits into a secret Semenov account in London that would be available to him should he ever decide to defect to Great Britain. The time would come when Nikolai would most likely defect.

But until then, documents would continue to swamp the Brits.

20

In August 1961, Bolling approached Emma Magnuson concerning the escape plan.

"My boss is going to ask me about the percentages. What are we talking about here, as far as chances of the plan of escape working? Forty percent? Sixty percent?"

She grimaced. "Ten percent. Maybe only five."

"Really? That's all?"

She tapped her pen on her pad of paper. "All of Russia is a prison. No one comes, no one goes without special written permission."

"Make it better. Director's orders."

Emma took on the assignment. She had to make it fit Nikolai and Sasha. She was a Cambridge graduate in political science with a second degree in political geography. Her skill was movements across the face of the earth, particularly the overt movement of spies from country to country, city to city, and town to town.

Bolling set up a working meeting. He watched her work to see how it was done.

"First, we begin with the seaports. What if we forged a seaman's documents? What if we get that seaman listed on a crew bound for neutral soil?"

"Makes sense," Bolling said, "as long as the Russian Coast Guard doesn't board it and shoot everyone who looks suspicious."

"Let's see," she said, opening and marking her place in three books. "It appears that Soviet security on the waterfront and ports and even ships themselves is even tighter than airports and automobile crossings."

"Don't forget," Bolling added, "that official Russian documents require watermarks. Impossible to forge. What about a private boat to carry Nikolai and Sasha across the Black Sea to Turkey? Or the Caspian Sea to Persia? Or Finland to Stockholm?"

"Back to your Coast Guard again. They're thick as thieves along the Baltic. I've even heard horror stories about spies who get discovered and tossed overboard."

"So that's out."

"Airports? There's a ferry from Turku to Stockholm. I rather like that."

"By way of Helsinki. Perhaps Moscow to Leningrad, Leningrad to Tallinn, Tallinn to Helsinki."

"Let's see. He takes a train, a bus, a ferry, a car, a ferry, a jet plane. But there's one problem. The Soviet Union officially closed the ferry between Tallinn and Helsinki. One exception is this: the Silja Line out of Helsinki is allowed to dock one ferry a week at Tallinn and load and transport back to Helsinki. It's a commercial exception to allow trade, sales, teachers, and remote workers to travel back and forth on Sunday afternoons."

"So, all this has to happen on a Sunday?"

"Sunday afternoon."

"Afternoon."

She opened another book and read, then looked at Bolling. "How do we get him out of Russia? The security is tighter than a banker's ass."

"According to Geneva, they can't search diplomats or their vehicles. Pop him in the trunk, I suppose."

"Like the KGB are worried about the Geneva Convention. Don't be ridiculous."

"You think?"

"Well, let's put the border down as a variable. I don't think we can guarantee either way at the border."

"But we can stack the odds. What if we cross the border when they're swamped? Maybe they get too busy to search everyone's trunk. We need research on when and why this might happen."

They broke off their talk and went their separate ways. Bolling made some calls and got MI6 Moscow on the ground to check things out. He ran their spies to find Nikolai's path to freedom.

She called Bolling on a secure line two weeks after their meeting.

"The most heavily traveled international border in the Soviet Union is located in Tallinn in Estonia. An enormous amount of commercial traffic passes through that seaport. As well as an enormous amount of private traffic—automobiles, buses, military vehicles."

"Go on."

"I still think if we get him across that channel on a Sunday afternoon when it's hectic, he's a free man."

Bolling had a reservation about that. "Not necessarily. The Finns are terrified of the Soviets. They might turn a fugitive back to Russia if they find out Moscow wants him. No, he'll have to get out of Finland before he's safe."

"I'll add on. I'll be back."

She studied the Tallinn seaport. It was a two-day drive from Moscow, allowing breaks along the way and a night of sleep. Western diplomats frequently visited the port both for its access to the sea and proximity to Helsinki. This included diplomats from Moscow, passing into Finland as diplomats might.

She called Bolling again. "Getting a man from Moscow to Tallinn in an embassy car is impossible. He will have to get there on his own. Perhaps the train, it goes to Leningrad, then to Tallinn."

"They'll be swarming the Tallinn train station. That's a no."

"Then he goes to Leningrad by train and takes a bus to Tallinn. That's one way."

Bolling had his reservation. "What about the KGB? They follow us everywhere."

"Your man is KGB. The world's best dry-cleaners."

"He has to get away on his own. They don't know where he's gone. He heads for the train to Leningrad and sneaks on board."

"Then the bus to Tallinn. Anonymous and fast."

"So he arrives at the ferry, the border. What happens there?"

"No, he meets MI6 officers outside of Tallinn, someplace easy to find. He gets in the trunk of their car."

"And his daughter gets in with him. Problems with the kid being quiet, but there are ways for that, even."

"Drugs."

"I didn't say that, but yes, a mild tranquilizer for Sasha."

"One problem right off the bat," Emma said. "The embassy cars they're driving to Tallinn… KGB mechanics service those. Bugged stem to stern."

"Easy. They don't talk in the car. They play opera on the radio. No KGB officer wants to listen to opera all that time on the drive over."

She laughed. "Maybe not."

"Still, the MI6 officers will be followed by the KGB. How do they shake them so they can pick up Nikolai and Sasha?"

"That's the most difficult part of the equation. I haven't solved that yet."

"Nor I."

Getting human cargo to the Tallinn port in an embassy car was next to impossible because the KGB had officers assigned to watch all vehicles. Any British embassy worker attempting to leave Russia was stopped, his documents examined, his reason for the trip written down, and his trip delayed long enough for the KGB vehicles to fall in behind.

Magnuson spent a solid week teasing out answers. But in the end, she framed a plan because MI6 had promised a plan to Nikolai and the Prime Minister. First, Nikolai would somehow need to let MI6 know he needed out. Second, he needed to get to a rendezvous point his own best way. The rendezvous would be near the Tallinn seaport. He would have to get there without being followed. Third, a diplomatic car driven by an MI6 officer would have to escape KGB followers and reach the rendezvous point alone. Nikolai and Sasha would then have to hide in the diplomatic vehicle. Fourth, the Russian Border Guard, swamped as they were at the border, would have to forego searching. Then, if all these things could happen on the same day, he might escape by ferry to Finland. But only on a late Sunday afternoon.

She was tearing her hair out by the time she was done.

But it was the best she could offer. She revised her percentage-of-success estimate with the Prime Minister downward. Five percent. It was the best she could offer.

Still, it was all they had. Emma Magnuson's plan activated as TINKER.

MI6 Moscow undertook to find a rendezvous point near the Tallinn seaport. The rendezvous had to be easily accessible from the main road and discreet for the pickup to occur unobserved. Moscow MI6 asked how Nikolai would reach the point in the first place? The answer came back from Magnuson: Nikolai would have to get himself there.

The MI6 station chief drove to Tallinn from Moscow and made his notes and took his photographs as he traveled the road. At a church down a side street, he found what he was looking for and pulled over. More pictures, more examination of the area, visualization of his parked car from the roadway. The church could not be a weak point in the plan. There were enough weak points already. He was also taking into account the militia posts every twenty kilometers, as were on all Soviet roads. The GAI posts monitored all traffic, assigning arrival times at each post, and estimated arrival times at the next post. All traffic was monitored, and if the flow was interrupted, KGB cars were dispatched to investigate. So, Nikolai's rendezvous and pickup would have to be accomplished in less than a minute to avoid KGB investigators on four wheels.

TINKER included an exchange of signals between Nikolai and MI6. His signal would set TINKER into action.

She decided Nikolai's signal to the MI6 watchers should happen inside some building or structure when pedestrian traffic thinned. She began with Red Square and immediately saw her target, Saint Basil's Cathedral.

She searched MI6's graphics and design department in London and found the cathedral's interior layout and plans. She made calls from payphones to tourist guides and even Moscow hotels to establish when the cathedral would be open and closed and days of the week. She studied the interior layout. Built around the 156-foot high central nave were nine small, separate chapels aligned to points on the compass, four were raised to designate their position between heaven and earth. The chapels were dedicated to the Protecting Veil of Mary.

The ninth chapel honored Saint Basil. It was somewhat remote from the others, and it was usually dark in that area.

It was this chapel where Magnuson laid her plan. The signal would consist of a votive candle placed at the feet of the statue of the Virgin.

Then she had second doubts. What if cleaning crews spied the votive and removed it in the act of cleaning? But then she studied the floor plan, and a more reliable signal came to her. On the priest's podium at the front of the chapel would be a bible. Nikolai would signal for help by placing a hymnal beneath that bible.

When he was in Moscow, the chapel would be checked twice a day by MI6. If the hymnal was so positioned, the plan would be activated.

Then the second stage of the plan would activate. Nikolai would catch the train to Leningrad after shaking off the crumbs. The dry-cleaning would need to shake them for good, so he was free from surveillance. On arrival in Leningrad, he would take the bus to the rendezvous point. Nikolai and Sasha would hide and wait there. The rendezvous was a church about two kilometers south of the Tallinn ferry.

Meanwhile, two MI6 officers driving a diplomatic car would leave Moscow and go straight through. The MI6 officers would arrive at the rendezvous at exactly 4:30 p.m. and hide Nikolai and Sasha in the trunk. The escape plan was code-named TINKER after Peter Pan's fairy, Tinker Bell, an oblique reference to the ferry that would take Nikolai and Sasha to Finland.

At their next meeting, Nikolai politely listened as Bolling outlined TINKER from start to finish. When he finished, all eyes went to Nikolai. Well? They asked.

"I have never seen a more unworkable plan," he said in a low voice. "It is far too complicated and relies on a series of fortunate events completely outside our control. If one step goes wrong, the whole plan falls apart. I won't ever take it seriously and never expect to activate it, as you put it. I am at sea without a life raft. There is no plan."

The MI6 agents looked at one another.

They had no response.

21

One noon when Nikolai was preparing to leave the Soviet Embassy for a lunch meeting with Bolling, Anatoly Anchev called. "Come to my office now!"

Nikolai had bent beneath his desk to retrieve a pencil and stuffed one inch of papers inside his coat. He sat back up and found other officers were paying little heed to his problem. His heart pounded in his chest. He decided to leave his coat in his cubicle, draped over the back of his chair. Almost jogging, he hurried to Anchev's office. The bully hated waiting. The secretary was expecting Nikolai and sent him right in.

Anchev was scowling when he looked up.

"Look at this," he immediately began. "This is your August summary. Not one recruit, nothing useful from your contacts. How are you spending your time, Semenov? You are making me look terrible here. KGB Moscow is complaining about your lack of production."

Nikolai shook his head. "I have been remiss. My wife's death."

"That is a horrible thing."

Nikolai went on. "Plus, my mother's troubles."

Anchev's eyes narrowed. "What kind of trouble?"

"They arrested her for helping a friend with church," he said, improvising.

"Let it go. That's an order. If you cannot, back to Moscow you go and remain. Your first duty is the Party, not your mother. Have you forgotten that?"

"No, sir."

Anchev shook his head. His scowl deepened. "Protocol. We're finished here. Go find me a traitor!"

Nikolai was keenly observant. He had seen an uptick in the surveillance of him by internal KGB officers. Anymore, they watched everything he did. The bugging, the tails, the inspection of work at the office or in the field. Everything he touched was checked and re-checked by other officers. What did he take to the post office? Payment of a utility bill? They bribed postal workers, getting the clerks to spy for them. They bugged telephones and telephone utility employees to warn of out-of-area phone calls. Nikolai knew it came from Anchev. But he was doubly careful and gave them nothing more to indicate he had crossed over.

Nikolai, his inside coat pocket bulging with top-secret documents, left the confrontation with Anchev and walked casually downstairs to his car. Over the next twenty minutes, he shook the eyes following behind by driving through heavy traffic to a remote parking garage and parking on the fourth level, hurrying to the stairs, and chaining the door shut behind him and locking it with a Bulldog padlock. Then he ran down one floor and jumped inside the sedan left there for him to use by MI5. He had seven sedans in seven different garages dedicated to his use and his use only.

Nikolai met Bolling and pled his case for immediate intelligence meant to placate Anchev. "Of course," said Bolling, "we'll provide you with all the intelligence we can spare. We need to keep KGB London happy with you."

The sharing began: Royal Navy maneuvers in the North Atlantic. Troop gatherings in preparation for the Cuban crisis, looming large on every nation's radar now. Strategic arms' talks with the U.S.

MI6's provision of useful information was unprecedented and meant to dissuade the KGB from recalling Nikolai to Moscow as a failure. Above all else, MI6 needed Nikolai right where he was, working hand-in-glove with them in London. This time around, the information provided was valuable intelligence. It was also available to any citizen with a TV, a map, and *The Sunday Times*. Whatever else it might have been, it began having the desired effect. Anchev became less hostile. KGB Moscow sent its approval in the form of a demand for more of the same. So the Brits complied, slowly parceling out low-level intelligence intended to secure Nikolai's London longevity.

When they ran out of low-level information and began crowding the line between low-level and secret, London turned to James Ellis, a young MI5 officer they added to the ULYSSES cell to do one job: make Nikolai look good in KGB London.

He went to work combing open-source information such as magazines and newspapers for facts and "secrets" Nikolai could parade across their desks. Ellis then turned to politics. He made a great showing of Nikolai's interest in and mastery of American politics as well as British. Who would run against Kennedy in 1964? Who had his ear? Was Robert Kennedy going to break up the UAW? Were Chinese-American relations on the thaw? He even researched where Jackie was getting her hair coiffed and who she was wearing that spring. Ellis, creative beyond hope, then took to making it up. His mind knew no limits. He reported intelligence about American nuclear emplacements in Colorado, about the American air defense system known as NORAD. He reported on ghost British MI5 agents, names, and stations, who "Nikolai thought approachable."

Best about it all, with rare exceptions, was that the KGB had no way of confirming or disproving the intelligence Nikolai produced by the pound. Reports poured in every day. KGB officers assigned to follow and listen in were called off the case—too risky to be found out and expose Nikolai's cover. Too great a chance at him being branded as a Russian spy and losing him to history.

Within the KGB *rezidentura*, Nikolai's reputation as a top agent doubled and redoubled. Even Anchev started talking to him about British soccer. Nikolai made Anchev look good every time he signed off on one of Nikolai's reports. In the end, Anchev reported back to Moscow Center that the lie detector hit was an anomaly, that Nikolai was 100% loyal. Moscow Center replied that Anchev should call off the dogs. No more surveillance than was used for all KGB officers.

Nikolai was promoted on a Monday morning to the chief of political intelligence in the *rezidentura*. He now had access to *all* PR Line files, not just his own, from which he copied the names of all Soviet spies who had penetrated MI5. It was a pitiful list, only three low-level names, giving MI5 a moment to breathe a great sigh of relief.

22

In mid-August, Nikolai arrived at the safe house, worried.

He told the team, "There's a rumor at London station that KGB is leaking. MI5 has ousted Soviet spies known only to other Soviet spies. Someone is talking."

"Love to see any leads," Bolling replied. "Any chance?"

"There's also a rumor I could be going back to Moscow."

"What? Impossible! It would be time to defect. We will take care of you."

Nikolai continued. "Not yet. But all microfilm exchange has to stop."

"Yes, that would be correct. They'll be watching too closely now. We must protect you."

"I think it's time we have a serious, fool-proof plan to get me the hell out of Russia if the roof caves in. Help me now."

"The plan is being constructed even as you and I talk."

Bolling walked into the kitchen and returned with a bottle of vodka. "We need to have a drink and talk this through."

"I can't abide the thought of going back to Russia," Nikolai groaned after a second swallow. "Three-hundred-million souls—and me—know it is a prison there, nothing more. We are living in a *gulag*, and if they're honest, everyone wants out."

"I'm sure. Isn't there always the possibility of revolution by the people? Aren't they capable of throwing off the bondage of Communism and repression? For us at MI5, that is our ultimate goal, to incite such a revolution."

Nikolai smiled. "So you can install your monarchy in Red Square? Or so the Americans can spread their republic to Russia? I think people will never do that. In a word, the reason is this: KGB. We are everywhere, and the people are terrified. That is our goal; to terrify the populace. What a horror show! And now they're sending me back there to spread even more horror! What can I do except go?"

"Just think of the good you've already done for people. With every document you've brought us, one more restraint on the Soviet people has loosened."

"Aiii, if only I could believe that."

23

Despite his efforts, Moscow recalled Nikolai in September 1961. He said goodbye to MI5, his friends from the Soviet Embassy, and packed Sasha and her things. They were flown to Moscow by Aeroflot in five hours. Their household would follow. Nikolai spent two days lining up a babysitter, one for days, and one for nights when KGB business took him away. They settled into their new flat and made it as homey as Nikolai knew how. His mother came to stay for two weeks and then decided she would remain with him while he was in Moscow. Now Sasha had a new friend, and the tiny family grew.

At the First Directorate HQ in KGB Moscow, Nikolai received a call at his cubicle. Masirov wanted to talk. The General came to his cubicle, and wearily took a seat. He loosened his tie and fanned himself with a handful of Nikolai's papers.

"Hot," he muttered. "Maybe it's my weight. Sila says I'm getting fat. What do you think, Colonel Semenov? Is the General filling out?"

"The General is in superb condition. The General's vigor in his duties would allow no less."

"Now that's very politic. Say, Nikolai, everyone knows we're hemorrhaging agents in the UK. Were you ever aware of any malcontents in the service in London? Someone who might have crossed over and exposed any of our officers? All it takes is one bad apple."

Nikolai took a deep breath and held it down, counting to ten while he pretended to think. "There might have been one or two who weren't enjoying their post, but no one seriously out of step."

Masirov gave him a long look. "You should know."

"Let me review my personnel roster."

"If anyone comes to mind, you call me, eh, Semenov?"

"Yes, sir."

The General plodded off, and Nikolai let out a long stream of breath. Had he looked genuinely puzzled? Had he said enough? Wouldn't any officer have known of at least one or two malcontents in the corps?

Nikolai felt the noose of that KGB spy hunt, which had now morphed into its most massive KGB spy hunt. It was tightening around his neck every time a spy was outed by London MI5. Who had fingered him for MI5? It had to be someone in KGB London, someone high up enough to know from inside the MI5 himself.

Nikolai announced he wanted London.

"It isn't right, keeping me in Moscow against my will," Nikolai all but shouted at Masirov one evening over vodka in Masirov's plush office."

"Easy," Masirov said with a glower, "remember who you're talking to, Colonel."

"Yes. I apologize. I'm just so—so—"

"Let me look into it. We will look at London. Give me a few days, please."

Nikolai thanked his superior officer and left.

But his hatred for all things Soviet, especially the KGB, smoldered. He had proof the KGB murdered his wife.

There was no coming back from that.

24

It wasn't until January of 1962 that Nikolai wrangled a London posting out of Lieutenant General Masirov, whose own star was rising within the KGB, partly because of Nikolai's excellent job in Russia. He didn't want to lose his young Colonel, but Nikolai's superior skills at convincing Masirov that he could make Masirov look even better from London won him the job. So, he applied for a new UK visa as a member of the Soviet diplomatic corps, which was granted in twenty-three days, a record in KGB Moscow. It raised eyebrows.

"It's strange they sent your visa so quickly," Masirov said in a voice filled with suspicion when Nikolai went to pick up his visa. "What surprises me the most is they must know who you are, and yet they seem anxious to take you in."

The truth was, London's ULYSSES team was on top of the application and had pushed it right through, which was unusual to the casual observer because Nikolai had hints of Soviet spy written all over him following his days in London. As a matter of policy,

London would reject all visa applicants who sounded like intelligence officers, but not this time, because they wanted Nikolai back on board, feeding them new information. Luckily for the ULYSSES teams, no one at the British Foreign Service was watching them all that closely or, if they were, they understood the need to have Nikolai back in the fold and looked the other way.

Delay set in, however.

Nikolai used a desk in Room 122 of the KGB British department's political section for almost one month. Files filled every inch of wall space: files on what agents were operating in Great Britain, names and personnel records, and current assignments. While waiting for Moscow's permission to leave the country, Nikolai spent his days at the office reviewing those files, memorizing agents. He also studied KGB plans for political operations in the UK, committing to memory the embassy workers and illegals who would be working toward political manipulation and upset. He would be ready with names and strategies as soon as his plane touched down at Heathrow.

Then, a new opportunity opened to him, a cross-posting to the Soviet Military intelligence service, GRU. GRU sought out the KGB's expertise in sealing leaks since Khrushchev was planning a significant move into the West. Rather than have Nikolai spend his time lounging while waiting for Moscow's permission to leave Russia, Nikolai was temporarily loaned to the GRU to act as a liaison. Quite soon, Nikolai had learned the GRU structure, names of the top-ranking officers, and the secondary corps that made the whole service work.

The strategic work was known as Operation Anadyr. Nikolai read the entire plan of military operations. Soviet missile systems, troop strength, vehicles, weapons, strategies, logistics, and timing were all laid out in front of him as part of his job in strengthening its guard. He spent months learning everything. His hours away from home were doubled, as he was now serving two masters. But he never blinked.

One night, listening in secret to the BBC on his shortwave radio, Nikolai learned that London had expelled three of his former colleagues. These were KGB officers working under diplomatic cover. Nikolai saw an opening. He approached Lieutenant General Masirov about the gaps in London that the ejection would cause.

"I would like to spy for the Premier in London."

Two days later, Masirov summoned him to his office and greeted him with the news he needed him in London to rebuild the Soviet team. "Would you enjoy working in my department?"

Semenov stammered. He would like nothing better.

"Then leave it to me."

Masirov invited Nikolai to have lunch with him in the General's office on Tuesday afternoon. Nikolai jumped at it.

An aide brought a menu.

"You have a menu?" Nikolai asked. He'd always known the KGB to be Spartan in its benefits to its officers. Here was a menu?

"I have a menu. My doctor says lean meats, no fats, rarely fruits for the acid."

"Impressive. I usually bring my lunch from home. Some cold cuts or leftovers."

"Nikolai, I want to be clear with you about what you know and don't know. For example, you were taught how to approach a contact, correct?"

"I was taught how to approach a contact, ask them for lunch, suggest a menu item, and pay the bill without looking at it. As the Americans say, I learned to razzle-dazzle."

"Well, that's all good. So, what can we do to enhance your recruitment in London?"

"Keep me away from useless tasks in the station."

"Such as?"

"Stamping documents, RECEIVED!"

Lieutenant General Masirov waved a cautioning finger. "Don't let me down. Always remember the town in Siberia where the toilets don't flush, and the water is carried from the river."

"I remember," Nikolai promised.

FINALLY, THE KGB'S FIFTH DEPARTMENT GAVE NIKOLAI THE ALL-clear to travel to London. On March 28, 1962, he boarded the Aeroflot flight to London. It was difficult saying goodbye to his mother. But in a way, he thought maybe she knew she wouldn't see him again. She was very wise and had seen his behavior at home.

She was right. If his work for Britain succeeded, he would eventually have to defect and never return to Russia.

Nikolai's mind was freighted with details accumulated from months of intense scrutiny of documents in the KGB archives as the plane took off. Then the months with the GRU, tightening the seam around the top-secret missile system and plans. Written notes of what he had uncovered would have been far too dangerous. Instead, in his head, he carried an entire war plan. He brought memorized details of the missile system and Soviet army and Khrushchev's date to deploy them in the West.

Operation Anadyr. Did the West know of it?

25

It was on Nikolai's second assignment in London that General Anatoly Anchev started softening beyond anything Nikolai had experienced in the KGB. Not only was he even more appreciative of Nikolai's excellent results, but he'd proven his loyalty by coming back to the KGB London again and working under Anchev.

He started using Nikolai as a sounding board, but many times it was just small talk over tea. The general liked his Typhoo tea strong with milk and sugar, while Nikolai forewent the sugar but enjoyed it just as strong, seeping the bag until the water turned a dark amber.

"Say, have you heard?" Anchev started casually, "we've just received a pouch from Philby."

Harold Adrian Russell Philby, also referred to as Kim Philby, was a British intelligence officer and a double agent for the Soviet Union. Since World War II, he'd been working with the Soviets with a group of five spies. He was one of KGB London's best sources.

Nikolai asked, "What is he telling us now?"

Anchev's voice grew excited. "Nothing except a map of all British missile silos encircling London. Moscow's delirious with joy."

Nikolai joined in the celebratory words and praise for Philby, all the while knowing he had to contact MI5 in the next hour and let them know what Philby had divulged to the Russians. They would be horrified.

But Anchev wasn't finished. "And speaking of missiles... Would you like to see something exceptional?"

"If you think it's safe."

"I'm the *rezident*. I decide what's safe."

Anchev then proceeded to show Nikolai photocopies of two highly classified documents, giving the full order of battle between Soviet and American forces once the Americans became aware of missiles in Cuba.

"What missiles?"

Anchev hadn't yet gone far enough, but Nikolai had to act like he didn't know. "Operation Anadyr. Khrushchev is preparing to establish Luna missiles in Cuba."

Nikolai's jaw hit the floor. The items he'd memorized back in Moscow at the GRU headquarters came rushing to mind. It had all been true then. World War III was possibly on the horizon.

"*Bozhe!*" Nikolai said softly. "My God! Where did these come from?"

"Moscow. Special courier chained to his wrist on military aircraft. Directly to me. Handed personally to me. There are no restrictions on KGB eyes. You're the first to see them."

"I'm thinking other staff should be excluded," Nikolai said.

"Posh! If you're trusted, they're trusted, too. Our people must be aware. We say every day we're fighting a war. Well, here it is!"

"Yes, it's a war, indeed," said Nikolai, out of words.

Nikolai was on fire to learn the documents' authenticity, but he came across as calm, almost dismissive on the outside. "This is what you wanted to show me?"

Anchev's mouth tightened, and his whole face became a boil of anger. "Isn't it enough, Semenov?"

"Impressive. Very impressive." It was all he could do not to yawn. But on the inside, he saw himself running madly for the safe house. Then he wondered if he could make copies of the war plans. Now, *that* would be the cherry on the cake. But he doubted it. He didn't even know where Anchev would hide the plans. Probably in the basement safe, guarded around the clock.

Standing at Anchev's desk and studying the war plans, Nikolai let his eyes wander across the *rezident's* desk. There were letters—one from someone called Lana—and a plan to dry-clean his way to an important meeting with the GRU, plus a list of all KGB agents in London. Nikolai saw his name there and saw that he was rated a 5 and that 5 topped the ratings. Most of the others were 4s.

He made up his mind at that moment. He swallowed hard. "Should something happen to you, Comrade Anchev, what should I do with these war plans?"

"Do? Take them into custody. Top-secret custody. No eyes."

"Where will they be kept, in case I need to retrieve them?"

Anchev raised his gaze from the war plans, looked Nikolai in the eyes, and stood upright. "Comrade, I think we should talk about something else. Top secret is top secret."

"Certainly. I just want to do my best job for you, comrade."

Anchev weighed the moment in his mind, then his face relaxed. "There are plans in place for that. Alinsky will take over in my absence."

So, he might have been a 5, but there were other considerations. He hadn't seen Alinsky's rank on the paper, but now he kicked himself for his boldness, hoping he hadn't raised suspicions. Which, it went without saying, he had. Suspicions were always in the air. There was no reason why he shouldn't be the subject of one of those now.

Still, he thought of the war plans, and he thought of the miniature British cameras. What an incredible score it would be. Just for five minutes alone.

But he didn't dare bring a British spy camera into the embassy.

Did he?

26

It was time to test document turnover, Nikolai to MI5. Nikolai couldn't wait to begin. At lunchtime, he slipped into his sports coat. He surreptitiously located a fabric shop, and the clerk found a leftover piece of dark fabric, the size of a schoolboy's pad of paper. He painstakingly sewed the material into his jacket's right inner side and tried it out in front of his bathroom mirror. He found he could easily hide *The Sunday Times* inside the pocket without creating a visible bulge.

Nikolai gathered the papers from his desk, station-wide directives from Moscow station. Included were top-secret documents he had checked out. As he stuffed the papers into his inner pocket, a bead of sweat broke out across his forehead. He swiped the sleeve of his coat across the sweat and took ten deep breaths. He told himself he wasn't going to panic.

There was no check-in/check-out protocol in London like at Moscow station, where officers were patted down and searched as they came and went. KGB officers were loyal and raised almost since childhood to never betray the service. So, Nikolai was able to take the elevator down to the lobby and walk right out to the parking lot that first day. At the safe house on Bayswater, Bolling ran the documents through a Xerox machine in ten minutes while Nikolai ate a cold steak sandwich. He then stuffed the documents back into his pocket and left without a word in case KGB bugged the house between meetings. It was swept daily for bugs, but Nikolai preferred the silent approach, nonetheless.

In the weeks and months that followed, Nikolai left KGB London at various times of the day with top-secret KGB documents hidden in his coat. Sometimes the meetings with Franklin Bolling took place only blocks away from KGB London, at a particular office supply store, and its copier used for a small price. Or sometimes at the safe house itself. It didn't matter where; the documents flooded MI5 right away.

A half-dozen senior MI5 officers gathered in River House in London to discuss Nikolai's top-secret files. They didn't know the spy's identity, but they were stunned with the top-secret information.

For the most part, Nikolai's months of debriefing served to prove to MI5 and the Prime Minister, who was now listening in on ULYSSES, that the KGB wasn't a vast flotilla of thousands of agents scattered around London spying. Rather, the KGB was much less than it had once been, especially since the British had expelled so many of its members.

27

Anatoly Anchev was dining out with friends, enjoying laughter and lively conversation followed by coffee.

Anchev requested the bill. It arrived in a plastic binder, which Anchev flipped open. But there was more than the dinner bill inside. The binder also contained a white envelope. Anchev was enough of a spy to know it could not be opened there in front of his guests, so he slipped it into an inside pocket. But the envelope had electrified him: the return address was *K*, an alternate name for MI5.

When he returned home that night, Anchev tore off his jacket and sliced open the envelope. It contained an MI5 document marked TOP SECRET. Anchev began reading. What he found was that he'd been given the MI5 brief for expelling Mila Petrova and the two GRU men, including details on how MI5 had identified all three as Soviet spies. Anchev's pulse quickened as he read on. The sender offered to provide more secrets. He gave Anchev detailed instructions on how to contact him. It was signed *Lana*.

Lana was obviously a code name meant to keep his real name unknown—maybe forever, maybe only until trust was earned. Lana said he wanted to spy for the KGB deep inside British home intelligence, MI5.

Anchev fixed a strong vodka and sat down on his couch with his stockinged feet on the coffee table. The letter from Lana lay beside him on the cushion. He knew his political capital inside the KGB was about to soar.

Now to decide how it would best elevate him up the ladder.

First, however, came the response to Lana.

He locked his door and mixed a second drink and turned off all the lights. He returned to the couch, took a swallow, and shut his eyes.

After several hours of reflection, his spirits had soared over the Lana letter then plummeted just as quickly. It required more consideration. The message might be a KGB dangle intended to lure him and see if he might cooperate with a British spy.

He mixed another drink, vodka and ice.

On the other hand, what if the letter was real?

The specificity of the document's instructions turned his head. Anchev would need to indicate his willingness to meet with Lana by putting a single thumbtack into the side of the Arrivals and Departures sign at the Buckingham Underground station. Anchev knew it well. He felt safe enough so far. Lana would then deliver a canister of film to Anchev's post office box in Wembley under the name of Reginald Riverdale, two names taken from a popular comic book series in America. Anchev couldn't begin to conceive how the spy knew about the phony postal box he kept for illegals to reach him. It could only be MI5. It had to be real.

Upon reading the document yet again, Anchev concluded he had nothing to lose. All the way through, he would be acting as any KGB officer should act given the circumstances. A chance to parlay an approach by an MI5 operative? Who at KGB London could ever blame him for jumping at the opportunity? He first thought of sending Nikolai or one of the other senior officers, but then thought better of it. If there were successes ahead, they wouldn't be shared.

Then Anchev weakened and decided against leaving a thumbtack. There was too much risk to his career—even his life—if it went awry.

Two weeks passed, and a second offering arrived in Anchev's home mailbox after failing to pin the thumbtack. Lana wasn't fooling around, said Lana. This time, there were two photocopied pages. Anchev was stunned. The secrets they contained were verifiable.

He needed a second judgment, someone whose opinion he trusted. Anchev called Nikolai into his office, closed the door, locked it, and asked, "Would you like to see something out of this world?"

"Certainly."

Anchev pushed the two photocopied pages across the desk.

"My God! What are these names?"

"All of our officers in London who are double-agents working for the British. He knows them all!"

Nikolai scanned down the list. It included all known KGB agents working for the British as double agents. He scanned almost to the bottom before coming to his name—ULYSSES. He saw ULYSSES graded as "more or less identifiable." It was enough to get him shot should his real identity ever be teased out. "More or less identifiable." What the hell did that mean? Lana undeniably had accessed top secrets. But ULYSSES remained one step removed. He shuddered inside.

He handed back the document. "Is it accurate? Those are KGB officers spying for the British?"

"Yes," said Anchev. "They've done well."

"Because?"

"Because we already know all of them...but one. They have long been identified and passing disinformation to the Brits. There is only the one we don't know about yet, but we will."

"As an aside, what are you going to do with the known spies?"

"Kill them."

"Of course."

"The one we don't know is ULYSSES. Why that name?"

Nikolai shook his head. "It makes no sense."

"ULYSSES is one of us. We will find him. How would you like that assignment?"

Nikolai all but gasped. "I would like that very much. Where do I begin?" Did he hear correctly? Was Anchev about to assign to him the task of ferreting out himself?

"I will open all the personnel files to you. You will go from there."

"Why would you do that?"

"You are my chief of political intelligence. It should naturally go to you."

Nikolai managed a stony-face for his superior officer. But inside, he was beside himself. The personnel files of all KGB agents opened to the spy himself!

Anchev's eyes narrowed. His eyebrows lifted. "Just one thing. If ULYSSES is you, Nikolai, I will know that. Do you know why? Because you won't find the mole in all of the other officers. You will come up empty-handed, and then I will know it must be you. So, start digging. Bring me a name to match the bullet in my gun."

Nikolai left Anchev's office and returned to his desk. He was stunned. He put a sheet of paper in his typewriter and typed: *Approach to be used to find ULYSSES.*

Then he sat back in shock.

He was looking for himself. Suddenly, he needed to urinate and ran for the restroom. After he was finished and washing his hands in the basin, he raised his eyes to the mirror. "You have got to be kidding me," he muttered, a Briticism that fit.

He decided two things must happen, and the identity of Lana was the first. This was because ULYSSES could be identified at any second by a second letter from Lana, and it would be the end for him. He returned to his typewriter. His hands shook to such an extent he could not type. He slowly calmed down and began thinking. How would he identify Lana before Lana identified him? MI5 was the key. They would have to identify Lana from their side of the street.

But Nikolai would also need to generate search results, lists of names, and strategies for the hunt. These would keep Anchev convinced the search was legitimately underway.

28

At lunchtime, he slipped out and called the emergency number. Emma Magnuson was on the other end after one ring.

"What's going on?" he asked her. Then he explained.

Her reply came instantly. "Nikolai, we need to meet."

Randall Cummings, deputy chief of MI5 counter-intelligence, and Emma Magnuson were waiting at the safe house an hour later when Nikolai arrived.

"Is it you?" Nikolai asked. "Wouldn't you tell me first?"

"No, my God," said Cummings. "It's one step away from you, Nikolai. We would never do that!"

"Then who?"

Cummings raised his hand, pledging, "We will get to the bottom of it. I promise you."

"It would be too obvious if you went into hiding," Emma said. "You must continue to show up every day and make advances in your work like before."

"I agree," said Nikolai. "I don't intend on running. Nor defecting. There is too much work to be done yet. How will MI5 proceed?"

"We will find him. We're already working on it," Cummings said. "We know that what he's turned over is political sources. So he's someone on that side."

"What is your timing?"

"Maybe months. We'll need him to repeat, which is your domain. When he repeats, you must be the first to know."

"I don't know. This time, Anchev was excited to show it to me. There are no guarantees he will do that again."

"No," said Emma. "We know Anchev. Extremely emotional and unpredictable. He showed you this time for his ego. He needed to be viewed to be as successful as you are. That's his M.O. He'll repeat."

"He's going to be difficult, Nikolai. Going in, this spy is very highly placed. We know that. No one but the second level has access to those names. That rules out ninety percent of our people right there."

"What are you doing to find him?" Nikolai asked this question partly to assure himself all stops were being pulled out to find Lana and, equally important, to obtain ideas for mole hunting. As of two hours ago, KGB had assigned him the task of finding himself. He decided he wasn't going to inform MI5 of this development just yet. He needed more time to assess and consider. No one could be trusted completely. Not yet.

"What are we doing to find him?" Cummings was thoughtful. "First, we are looking at access to that list. As always, we have three clerical people in the mix. But a clerical person isn't going to cooperate with the KGB."

"Why not?"

"Because they know we will kill them if we find out."

"I thought England didn't have capital punishment. I thought its courts—"

Cummings interrupted. "Did I mention courts? I thought I said they know we will kill them. They have no doubt."

"All right. And upper levels? They aren't equally frightened?"

"They know how we work. They know how to avoid being caught. There are always ways. You know that." He smiled now, and Nikolai got his meaning.

"So, now you've launched your internal mole hunt, and it might take months. Meanwhile, I'm in grave danger. If ULYSSES becomes known, we won't need TINKER. I'll be dead before you know it. All that will remain of me is a memory. They will never announce what happened to me. It's happened many times before on my watch. We go to turn someone, and we get turned instead, instant death."

"Here's why it's so slow going. If someone inside the Soviet *rezidentura* gets wind of our investigation, they'll know we got tipped off. Now they only need to find out who had access to the case. That might be three people, all within immediate reach of Anchev. KGB would have that person talking in an hour. Or less." It was clear to Nikolai, the way Cummings said this last part, that he respected the KGB's methods, but not in a good way. Nikolai supposed that he did, too, a matter of professional pride. The point was made: the KGB could not know MI5 had launched the hunt.

"Your name wasn't revealed, which tells me the ULYSSES team doesn't include our mole. So, I will use the ULYSSES team as hunters. That way, it remains walled off."

"Smart."

"Exactly," Cummings said. "We have our team, and we have a KGB asset to find. If we keep it to the team, he'll never know we're even after him."

"Nor will the KGB," said Nikolai. "Much better."

"The hunt will be led by Jason Donovan."

Nikolai knew Donovan was highly placed, the director of K4, MI5's Soviet residencies branch.

"He's a ULYSSES member, you will recall."

"Of course, I know Donovan well."

But he still drank too much vodka that night after putting Sasha down.

Steady, he told himself, *make your own lists now.*

29

Anchev was in his office with the door shut and all sound deflectors in place. Seated across from him was Viktor Bucharov, Colonel KGB. Bucharov's assignment was counterintelligence, the KGB arm that spied on its officers, keeping them honest. He was six feet, olive-skinned, blue-eyed, with hair that looked blond in daylight and brown at night. With a finely trained hockey player's physique, he ran, worked out every day, and easily bench pressed 325 pounds. Which was appropriate, because Bucharov liked nothing better than hand-to-hand combat unless it was brain against brain. He had graduated first in his class at KGB School 1010 and had attended the U.S. Military Academy at West Point under a ghost identity. The Americans had missed him every step of the way. He had retired from the American army just before American soldiers went to Southeast Asia.

"Comrade, we have a severe spy problem in London."

Bucharov, rigid in his chair, fastened his eyes only on Anchev, missing nothing. "A serious problem with KGB London. Tell me more, General."

When Anchev showed Bucharov the Lana document, he caught on instantly, saying, "So, I am to track down ULYSSES?"

"Exactly."

"Have you made a station assignment to find ULYSSES?"

"Nikolai Semenov. One of my most trusted agents. I have told him, 'bring me a spy or I will settle for you.'"

"He's very likely the spy, then."

Anchev sat back, looking like he had just been slapped.

"How can you say Colonel Semenov is ULYSSES?"

"Never mind. Get rid of him. It should be my job and my job only."

But Anchev trusted what he alone controlled. The Second Directorate and its mole hunters would have to operate independently.

"I will have Semenov, and I will have you."

Bucharov shrugged. "It's your station, General. I can only make suggestions."

Anchev winced. "Oh, no, Colonel, you can do much more than that."

"Pull Semenov's personnel record. It will make my work that much easier."

"Very well."

They spent the rest of the afternoon absorbing every last detail about Nikolai Semenov.

Questions came up. Where did Nikolai Semenov disappear so often at lunchtime? Who was he talking with? Bucharov knew he would begin by confirming what Nikolai's reports said about this.

For once, contacts would be questioned about conversations and comparisons would be made.

30

Inside a combination vault on the second floor of the Soviet embassy in London were the personnel records. Access was "eyes only," as no records were removed or copied. With one exception: General Anatoly Milanovich Anchev, *rezident*, could remove and copy documents. He was trusted 100% by KGB Moscow.

Nikolai knew that he was looking for himself. Only a perfect plan of deceit was going to save him. He thought he knew how. First came action, convincing Anchev the KGB mole hunt was underway.

At the personnel desk, he presented the written authorization from Anchev. The clerk read it through, then stamped it and slipped it inside a file.

"All personnel records?" she said. "You must be a very special spy."

He didn't respond except with a grunt of disapproval that she should try to discuss it with him, as any good KGB officer would respond. Chagrined, she asked where he'd like to begin.

"Begin with the A's," he told her.

She studied a list inside a folder.

"Arkady Asimov?"

He knew Arkady, one year ahead of him in KGB School 1010. Poor Arkady.

"Yes, that's who I want."

"Very well. Please take the file with you into room B. It is reserved for top-secret files. Come and ask if you have any questions about abbreviations or dates and times. We close at five. All files returned at four-forty-five."

Nikolai picked up the file and headed for room B. He had brought along two pads of paper for notes he would make. He went inside and pulled the chair away from the table. Then he settled heavily into the chair.

Take notes? Did he say take notes? Notes of what, his own spycraft?

He flipped open the file and began reading about Arkady. First up was a full-face photograph where he wore his new KGB uniform on graduation day from KGB School 1010. Next came two pages of family history. Then four pages of educational history showing all courses studied at university. Asimov had served on active duty for three years. There were KGB Station reports and scores on his work, and his results took up a good inch thickness of the file. Before London, he had served in Poland and Germany. So, he was fluent in Polish, German, Russian, and English. Standard there.

Nikolai stole a look around the monitored room. He was sitting on a treasure trove and was all but speechless. Access to all KGB spies serving in London. The room was small, no bigger than a study carrel at any university library. He wondered whether there was an overhead recording what he wrote in his notes. He threw his arms back, turned his face up, and yawned as he took account of the ceiling. Two nozzles from the sprinkler system, two fluorescent tube light fixtures, ceiling tiles with tongue and groove joints symmetrical and all but invisible. No cameras above. There was just no place.

Which meant he could take notes. But could he remove his notes from the personnel office? There was only one way to find out. He spent the next two hours copying all actionable facts out of Asimov's file. The facts include the fine points MI5 might like to act on, such as honeypots for the sex addict, family that could be threatened in exchange for some traitorous act by the agent, pending bankruptcy or financial hardship, susceptibility to blackmail—the kind of points any spy agency would desire. All of it was written out, together with Nikolai's numerous comments and action items. It had to appear from his notes that he was searching out any deceit in Asimov. He concluded his notes with future action items:

1. Eavesdropping measures

2. Report tracking, e.g., compare reports filed by Asimov to information contacts supplied via documents, recordings, photographs.

3. Lunch watch, night watch

4. Neighbors

5. Bank records: large unknown deposits

6. Trips to offshore havens

7. Lie box

8. Statement agent/spouse

9. Friends

10. Premises inventory

Here was the KGB's Rule of Ten surveillance map. It was meant to be used at the outset of all investigations.

Nikolai sat back and examined his notes. There wasn't anything on the list he couldn't accomplish.

He had an idea and returned upstairs to Anchev's office, where he requested a meeting. Anchev told him now was a good time.

"I've been thinking," Nikolai said. "We have twenty-five KGB officers in KGB London."

"Including you."

"Including me, that's right. The Rule of Ten for twenty-five officers means 250 inquiries, some of which will take days. That's going to take too long. I am here to request permission to locate the traitor from the British side. I am requesting permission to penetrate, target our mole's handler, and obtain the identity of the KGB officer code-named ULYSSES."

Anchev sat back, quite surprised. He clasped his hands across his protuberant mid-section and drummed his fingers. "I like it. How do you get close to the British?"

"Allow them to recruit me."

"That might take time."

"I know people."

"I'm sure you do. Let's jump ahead. What techniques will you use to identify our traitor?"

Nikolai spoke confidently. "Infiltrate records."

"You are convincing me, Colonel Semenov. I say, let's do it. There is no risk."

"I will need copies of all personnel files."

Anchev's brow furrowed. "Why is that?"

"So I can quickly access officer details. It won't do to allow the records clerks to know who I am looking at by requesting one file at a time. That's a certain tip-off."

"You're thorough, Semenov. I like that. Copy all files. But remember this, you must guard them with your life as if I checked them out."

"I understand, sir. Will do. Sir, one other matter. KGB Moscow watches KGB officers like me. Please caution Bucharov to keep his distance. It would ruin everything I'm trying to do if the Brits discover him while he's tailing me."

"That's an unusual request."

Nikolai tried hard not to scoff or smile. He had seen Bucharov surveilling him. Ironically, it would have been unacceptable to KGB Moscow had he failed to discover the trail.

"We will make our arrangements. Any more than that, I cannot divulge. Just go about your business, Semenov, and I will go about mine."

"I understand. Thank you, sir."

31

Nikolai met with Bolling and Donovan at the safe house on Friday.

"I've been ordered to find the identity of ULYSSES," he told them.

"What?" said Donovan, surprised. "You've been ordered to find yourself? Anchev must really trust you."

"Yes, Anatoly Anchev has assigned ULYSSES to me. I have been told I find the mole among the twenty-five officers of KGB London, or it will be me who is the mole."

"Interesting," Bolling whispered. "No one saw this coming."

"Good and bad," Donovan said.

"Here's one reason it's good," Nikolai said, handing over a folder with copies of the personnel files of all twenty-five KGB officers of KGB London. "You're not going to believe what I just handed you."

Donovan was already placing it in his bag. "What is it?"

"Twenty-five personnel records. Complete records on all twenty-five KGB officers in London."

"What?" exclaimed Donovan. "That's nothing short of a miracle!"

"Of course, what we do with them is a whole other matter," Bolling said, adding a note of caution. "They cannot be expelled, lest Anchev knows who passed the records. All we can use them for, basically, is recruitment. Likes and dislikes, that kind of thing."

"And the discovery of buried agents."

"Obviously that," Bolling agreed.

Donovan was thoughtful. The head of the ULYSSES team would have the final say in how MI5 would handle Nikolai's predicament.

"He's thinking," Bolling said over a cup of tea. "I know that look."

Nikolai smiled. "Let's hope he thinks the right thing."

"All right," Donovan said slowly, ignoring their comments. "Here's what we're going to do. Every month we'll load Nikolai down with disinformation he has discovered about the mole. Eye color, age, things of that nature, and secrets divulged to us—all of it fictitious. But the identifying characteristics such as eye color and hair color and weight and appearance, all of that we'll lift from our files on MI5 agents in London, and we'll use those, dance around and make it seem like it's this one, then that one, but then, no, this one over here, and on and on. That should get us quite far down the road. Until..."

"Until?" asked Bolling.

Donovan shrugged. "Until Nikolai defects, and there's no longer a reason to keep up the ruse."

"Open-ended," Nikolai said. "Explanations for the delay in finding the mole."

"We can help with that. I'll put Charles Lightner on it. Charles's very creative."

"Charles has been accommodating. We meet around the city and talk. He's provided me with consistent disinformation. I'd be very pleased and feel very safe with Charles," Nikolai said. "My choice, indeed."

Donovan nodded and looked at Franklin Bolling. "Franklin?"

"Nikolai just said it. Charles has all of MI5 to help him. I'm onboard with Charles."

"Make arrangements next week when you see him," Donovan said to Nikolai. "If anything beyond that is needed, just let me know immediately, and I'll make it happen."

Nikolai smiled. "This is very good."

"Right-on. Enjoy your mole hunt."

Nikolai shook his head. "Enjoy my records. I'll see what else I can come up with while I search."

"Excellent."

32

Jason Donovan took control of the first meeting of the ULYSSES mole search. He had the total respect of his team, and they jumped when he asked. First, they pulled all MI5 personnel files. "Let's start with a list of the officers who ousted the Soviet spies."

"The three spies."

"Yes."

"Next," said Donovan, "we need to know who saw the list."

Bolling nodded his agreement. "The only thing is, that list was distributed all over London."

Donovan looked up from the list. "Who received it?"

Bolling drew a deep breath. "Let me see. The list went to the Foreign Office, the Home Office, 10 Downing Street. And the chart listing all intelligence officers, the one Lana delivered to Anchev, was drawn up by K4."

"My God. Who else?"

Bolling said, "Let me think. At least fifty copies went to various departments."

Donovan saw the vast scope of the search. "All right, let's cross-reference the officers Lana identified with the officers who know of ULYSSES. I need this because we're in the dark about how ULYSSES was included on the list Lana gave Anchev."

"Only the ULYSSES team knows there's a ULYSSES. It's one of us?"

The team members looked at each other.

"No, I don't think that at all," Donovan said. "But I think records were accessed from within MI5 by someone, maybe even a clerk."

The ULYSSES team winnowed out names of non-ULYSSES potentials. Two days later, they were down to three suspects, topped by the name of Robert John Ziegler.

Donovan reviewed the shortlist. "Ziegler's a loner who knows too much to get rid of. Who enjoys irony? So, MI5 accommodates his whimsy—he's an odd bird—while at the same time keeping him out of the vault. The long and short of it, Ziegler's been reduced to a high-paid clerk for all his loose screws."

"Look what I've got on him," Bolling said. "At Oxford, he applied for admission to the mathematics department because, he said in his essay, he wanted to improve the hydrogen bomb. During his history course, he dressed in an SS officer's uniform from World War II and told fellow students he was searching down Jews in his dorm. It scared the hell out of people, and complaints were lodged. But he was finally talked down from that and kept in the infirmary for three days, nursing a minor breakdown. He then returned to his studies and eventually graduated from Oxford. How in the hell did we end up with him?"

Lightner, the political expert, had this answer. "His father was a Member of Parliament and saw to it his son was offered a position in MI5. The son was accepted on short notice and assigned to K4, analyzing and combating Soviet espionage in the UK. Haha, funny. He also ran access agents. However, ULYSSES is sectioned off. Ziegler can't know his name, so we've made a complete circle here."

"But the fact ULYSSES exists... Ziegler got that somehow."

"I said he's bizarre," Donovan said, "not stupid. He has eyes, and he has access when no one's looking. *A priori.*"

Emma held up her hand. "You're not going to believe this part. Ziegler lived alone after a brief shack-up with a woman who fancied herself a Paris fashion doyenne. One day, the same woman ran screaming from his flat that he was threatening to eat her with a fork. She was nude and had a minor stab wound on her upper shoulder."

"Holy shit!"

"But Ziegler flashed his MI5 ID at the investigating officer, and the man abruptly broke off the investigation. It's here in the police report I requested."

33

Ziegler repeatedly returned to the Westminster Station, looking for a thumbtack in the wooden frame around the Arrivals and Departures sign, but was disappointed each time. He then decided Anchev had somehow missed the communique, so he snuck up Anchev's flat again, just after midnight, and folded and inserted a list of Soviet intelligence agents the Brits were recruiting to spy. He peered through the mail slot to confirm his offering had passed through. Then he ran off.

Anchev found the list on his floor the next morning. "My God!" he cried. "Who is this Lana?" It was time to respond.

Anchev appeared at the Buckingham Underground station at five a.m. the following morning. This would be Westminster Circle. He carefully looked around, and when no one was watching, he pinned a single thumbtack into the side of the Arrivals and Departures listing. He quickly shot a glance around again. No one saw; it was too early in the morning for a crowd.

That night, Lana slipped the third message through the mail slot. Lana would meet him at the Coach House the next day at two p.m. He would be wearing a purple waistcoat. Anchev was to wear purple as well.

Anchev dug through his closet. Nothing. So, he sent an aide out shopping that morning for a purple shirt. In 1962, men's shirts were rarely purple. However, the aide returned two hours later, bearing a purple shirt with frills down the front. "Really?" said Anchev with a frown. "This is it? I'll look like a lounge singer in Berlin."

"My apologies, General," the aide said as he backed out of Anchev's office.

With a sigh and a reminder to himself that he was doing it for Party and motherland, Anchev changed into the shirt. Indeed, he did look like a lounge singer, the mirror told him, a lounge singer with a noticeable gut. But purple was purple.

At two p.m., he walked into the bar at the Coach House, went to the end, and eased himself down onto a stool. The bartender came over. Anchev seldom drank during the day, so he ordered a Coke. As if a ghost had insinuated itself next to him, Ziegler appeared.

Anchev assessed the man. The MI5 spook was hollow-eyed from lack of sleep, a desperate look permanently pasted to his face, looking more denizen than human. He was intoxicated, the smell of booze wafting off him as he had difficulty arranging himself on the barstool.

He wasted no time once he was plumb. "I am Lana. You're Anatoly Anchev. We have your picture at MI5. The purple was an afterthought."

"Well, Lana, you have provided some serious information to us. How can we thank you for that?"

"I want five-hundred pounds each month. We'll meet right here. You bring it in a paper bag and leave it on the bar. I'll come over from my table and pick it up. Do it while the bartender is at the other end."

It sounded like a plan with problems already, but Anchev didn't argue. "What might we expect in return?"

"One of your agents is spying for London and turning over huge volumes of sensitive documents every day. I can give you his name. That's the first five-hundred pounds."

Anchev nodded and kept nodding, saying, "I think we have agreed, then. When should we meet again?"

"One week. I will have your spy's name and a list of his most recent documents turned over. You can judge for yourselves."

"That keeps my interest up. What else can we look forward to?"

Lana rolled his eyes and looked up at the ceiling. "You haven't asked about my department yet."

"Based on what you've turned over, I am assuming you're counter-intelligence. You are what we call a spy catcher."

Lana laughed and made a pistol with his fingers. He shot it like a gun as he said, "You nailed me! I love the KGB."

"Please, keep your voice down. We're in a public place."

Lana looked around exaggeratedly as only intoxication would want. "Right-o."

"One week, then. Five-hundred pounds for a name. Until then." The general downed his Coke.

"Don't forget," Lana called to the general's back.

Lana ordered a glass of red wine to celebrate. Then he found a seat just two tables down from the coffee-swilling, sandwich-chewing MI5 agents who had just witnessed the entire transaction. Two other agents pursued Anchev on his trip back to the Soviet Embassy and confirmed who he was. Since the pictures they snapped matched the man's face, it was more ritual than necessity.

"In hindsight," Donovan would be heard to say, "we should have seen him coming. But sometimes one gets through, and it's nobody's fault. It's part of the game, and sometimes the game wins."

Now that Ziegler was confirmed, Donovan's team was anxious to obtain his confession. But MI5 would want the collar, which ULYSSES did not want because of publicity and such. So, Donovan delayed since Ziegler possessed top-secret information that Donovan didn't want to get away from the ULYSSES division inside MI5.

"Let's think this through," Donovan told MI5 when they called to report on Ziegler. "He possesses top-secret information I cannot allow to escape from ULYSSES. "We will debrief him first. And then we will give you a tape-recorded confession when we are finished."

MI5 had no choice but to agree. ULYSSES was off-limits to everyone but the ULYSSES team.

34

Nikolai returned to the safe house on August 10 and requested an update on the Lana search.

"How close are we?" he asked the team.

Bolling said, "We have confirmation."

"Has he been arrested?"

Donovan fielded this one. "It isn't that easy. We must debrief him. He knows enough about our international intelligence operations to ruin us. We're working with the Crown Prosecutor to put him in solitary confinement without access to the outside world for the rest of his life. That's what it's going to take. We're moving in that direction, but it's taking time."

"I understand," Nikolai said, "but that doesn't make me feel any better. I'm walking on eggshells. Every face I see, I ask, is that them coming for me? It's hard to sleep at night."

Donovan nodded. "I get that. But all you can do at this point is to return to your normal duties. If you don't, if you go into hiding or don't show up, it calls attention to you."

"*Chert!*" Nikolai muttered.

"I understand your terror," Donovan said. "I would be terrified, too. Especially if it was jeopardizing you and Sasha."

Bolling broke in. "The poor man has suffered enough. It's time to take action. Not only that, but we also cannot afford to have Nikolai outed. He's the most valuable resource we have on the planet just now. Please don't lose him."

So Donovan took action.

On a pretense, Ziegler was called into Counterintelligence for a discussion about an alleged spy. That perked him up, and he shaved and wore his best suit. Instead of being taken into a new team, however, on his arrival, he was taken to a top floor office and the evidence against him laid out by Donovan—a man whom Ziegler knew and feared. Donovan and his team presented a photograph of Anchev's front door with Ziegler blocking the mailbox with his body. Then they produced a picture taken at the Coach House, Ziegler and Anchev in deep conversation.

"See? We know you were passing documents to Anchev. We know you met with him. It's time to confess and let us help put all this behind you."

But Ziegler played it cool and didn't collapse. He said, "Tell me how I can help nail this bastard, Anchev. Your photograph is the night I was feeding him a phony list. He thought he had recruited me."

The interrogators shared a look. He was wily; they learned that out of the gate.

"We also know you passed him a list of the officers who turned the spies we expelled. That wasn't a phony list."

"Harmless. Chicken feed. It escapes me, but I believe I thought their names were even in the newspapers."

"Come now. You know their names wouldn't be released. You can't really expect us to believe that."

Bugs relayed the conversation to the electronics room one floor down, where MI5 and MI6 officers listened intently, almost without breathing, taking in every word. It was a dangerous time, not only for Nikolai but also for the entire world, with Khrushchev unloading his Operation Anadyr matériel and men almost daily on Cuban shores. Nikolai absolutely could not be lost for what else he might bring across as Soviet intelligence, including war plans. The Brits already knew the plans had changed and changed again since Oleg Penkovsky had come over. New plans were in place. The West was counting on Nikolai Semenov to deliver them. Running Ziegler to the ground and extracting his confession was magnitudes bigger than where it had begun.

It continued all night. In the morning, Ziegler was offered breakfast, still seated at the table where he had sat most of the night, refusing all questions. His resolve seemed unbreakable. Then he dozed, sitting up, for thirty minutes until someone slammed a book on the table, startling him awake. It took several minutes to get his bearings. Then he asked, "Am I under arrest? If I'm not under arrest, I'd like a ride home to bathe."

The interrogators looked at each other. Donovan fielded it. "No, you're not under arrest. We're still investigating."

"The pictures aren't conclusive, are they?" Ziegler said with a smile. He had them, and he knew it.

"We're looking to you for the truth," Donovan replied. "This case has become about more than you and the KGB. There are international implications involving the Soviets and the Americans. Your treatment by the Crown would be greatly remediated were you to cooperate."

"Nonsense. I want to go home. Who's driving?"

He wasn't driven home at all. He was told he was relieved of all duties and to stay away from River House until he heard from MI5. He acknowledged and headed for the door. "Ta." He turned and waved at the door. "See you around the corner." He made a finger pistol, fired it at Donovan, and blew away the smoke.

Then he was gone.

Nikolai demanded a meeting with the ULYSSES team after the interrogation. Donovan and Bolling accommodated him that night at the safe house. He had dry-cleaned his way there for thirty minutes, he said, as the watchers had been very sticky.

"What about Ziegler?" he demanded.

The British officers knew the score. He was worked up and had every right. Lives were counting on MI5 to neutralize the spy.

Donovan answered, "We had to let him go."

Nikolai cried, "What? You have a picture of him with Anchev! What more is there?"

"He said Anchev recruited him and he was passing chickenfeed. It was the smartest thing he's said in years. That's my guess," Franklin Bolling offered. "It raises a serious question of fact for any court. Was he or wasn't he? We wanted his confession and failed to get it."

"Answer me this, then," Nikolai said, fighting to control his anger, "Is he Lana?"

"Absolutely," Donovan said immediately.

"One-hundred-percent," Bolling replied. "There is no doubt."

Nikolai sat back against his chair. "So, what happens next?"

"That's the not-so-good part," Donovan said. "We've let you down. Our hands are tied until he makes another move. Fear not, we have eyes around the clock. He's not going anywhere."

"But how do you get close enough to an Anchev meeting to hear what's said? It seems to me he always gets to claim he was recruiting. Recruiting, hell!"

"We know, Nikolai," Donovan said in a quiet voice, trying to calm him. "And we're damn sorry it went south on us."

"So, that's it?"

"For now."

"Until he identifies me to Anchev. At which point, I die, and Ziegler—nothing happens to Ziegler because, again, you have no proof?"

Donovan and Bolling stared at the tabletop.

"Not so good, gentlemen. Unacceptable."

The meeting broke up. Nikolai walked outside and looked up at the stars. He remembered counting stars when he was young. How simple that time had been when no one was creeping up from behind. Now, the entire world had to be watched. He had complicated his own life, especially now, with Robert John Ziegler, who was two words away from Nikolai's instant death. Sasha and his mother, too. It was the price Masirov back in Moscow would extract.

He had but one choice.

And time had run out.

He must act.

35

Nikolai had a new target that interrupted his days at the Russian Embassy in London. To anyone at the KGB station who might be watching, he was doing KGB work, but he was, in fact, on the trail of Robert John Ziegler.

Through some finagling with Bolling, he obtained a full-face photograph. An ugly little man, so plain looking, yet so dangerous to Nikolai.

Once he had the photograph, he had the man. But it took weeks of surveillance because Ziegler was now *persona non grata* at River House. Then, one day in October, he appeared as he stepped off a double-decker bus in front of the spy house and hurried inside. Nikolai closed in, became invisible, and waited for him to finish his business upstairs and re-emerge.

Which took less than one hour. Later, Nikolai would hear from Bolling that Ziegler had voluntarily come into MI5 for a second interrogation, which was non-productive, so he was again allowed to walk.

Nikolai picked up his trail outside at the bus stop. He slid in behind him, posing as just another passenger. But other passengers most likely did not have a coil of picture-hanging wire in their pocket.

At Piccadilly, Ziegler stole a look around, checking eyes, then hurried off the bus. Nikolai waited until the next corner, keeping an eye on Ziegler the entire time. Then he turned and walked back up the sidewalk, spotting his target at a newsstand, thumbing through a magazine while doing a bit of dry-cleaning himself.

Unfortunately for him, he missed Nikolai entirely.

Satisfied after another twenty pages in the magazine that he wasn't being followed, Ziegler walked ahead two blocks south, then a block west, before stopping in front of one of two identical buildings. He stepped through the entrance of the first and disappeared from Nikolai's view. It didn't matter. Nikolai had him now.

However long it took, there would come a night when Ziegler would leave his flat for some errand, meeting with Anchev, or other, and Nikolai would be waiting.

For now, he turned and walked away.

A week of nights went by. Days, Nikolai was finding it difficult to stay awake at his desk. Which meant he spent many afternoons ostensibly recruiting, so he told Anchev, while he was sleeping on the rickety couch at the safe house.

Late after work, Nikolai finally found a parking space on the street a block down from his flat building. The night was dark and visibility poor with rain. Streetlamps illuminated only patches of the sidewalk and street. As he shifted the car into park, a man walked beneath a halo of light. To Nikolai's surprise, it was Ziegler who was walking up the sidewalk, calling for someone named Esther.

For the first few moments, Nikolai was puzzled, thinking the man had lost his mind. But then he understood when "Here, Esther!" changed into "Kitty, kitty, kitty, kitty!"

And he knew he had him. All this time, Ziegler had been living just around the corner from Nikolai. The irony of life.

He stepped out of his Jaguar and set off toward Ziegler.

"Kitty, kitty!" Ziegler called out again, scanning the bushes and trees staggered along the sidewalk. Like the poor MI5 agent he was, Ziegler wasn't watching his surroundings and didn't see Nikolai approaching.

Just as they passed each other on the sidewalk, it was KGB School 1010 as Nikolai spun on his heel, dropped the picture wire around the target's neck, and pulled. As promised at spy school, the razor-thin wire neatly cut through the jugular veins on either side of Ziegler's neck, and he went down on his knees, then slumped onto his side. Nikolai reached into Ziegler's back pocket and jerked his wallet free.

Silenced.

He casually walked back to his Jaguar and switched on the vehicle's interior light to check his hands and jacket for blood. Seeing just a small amount on the thumb webbing on both hands, he switched off the light and reached for the handkerchief he had thought to bring along. With a bit of saliva and effort, he removed the blood enough that Carolina, babysitting Sasha, wouldn't notice before he made it into the bathroom and finished it off with hot water and soap.

Ziegler hadn't fully bled out, but he would by the time Nikolai entered his flat in less than five minutes.

Nikolai slept that night for ten hours. At midday, Sasha came in to jump on his bed and make sure he was awake.

He was awake, he told her, tossing and catching her.

Awake and very, very free of the fear he'd lived with for weeks on end.

* * *

"Ziegler was garroted," Bolling told him when they next met at the safe house.

"No," said Nikolai. "What a great sense of relief! I'm free!"

Bolling smiled. "It was perfect timing. The police inspector believes it was a simple robbery. His wallet was missing."

"Whoever robbed him, put me down as very, very grateful."

"We thought you would be relieved."

Nikolai's eyes narrowed. "Was it you?"

"It was not," Bolling exclaimed. "Though we discussed it. But in the end, we knew we would be the obvious perpetrators if the police started snooping motives. So we passed."

"How about you?" asked Donovan, who had been nursing a cup of tea.

Nikolai shrugged. "Haven't you heard? The KGB doesn't actually exist."

Donovan nodded. "I won't ask again."

"You can ask, but my answer's the same. I brought documents today. Do you still want them?"

They broke up a half-hour later.

Nikolai drove back to the embassy, ready to go back to work.

Poor Anchev, he thought when he happened to use the men's bathroom while the *rezident* was washing up. His chance for glory at running down the ULYSSES mole kaput.

Poor Anchev. The man would find out soon enough that Lana was now gone, along with the answer to ULYSSES' identity. Nikolai would be taken off the case, but he already got what he'd wanted from it. It was time to move on.

36

Nikita Khrushchev appeared before the KGB personally. He had to deliver his message himself. Notepads, pens, and paper were left at the door to the meeting room. Everyone got searched. Khrushchev's first words to the KGB top staff: America was about to launch a first strike and burn the Soviet Union off the map.

Gasps went up, even among the steely, hardline KGB officers present. The worst had come. But why hadn't they known about this ahead of time? Where was his information coming from?

"Never mind," Sergei Tupolev, the head of the KGB, told his under-bosses. "Our President has spoken. Our job is to take it at face value and do what we can to save our country from destruction."

Khrushchev made it clear what he wanted to be done. "The task of the KGB is to discern that this attack is imminent and give sufficient warning that the Soviet Union might attack the Americans first."

Nikolai and all KGB London were suddenly on red alert. They held meetings and made decisions about the types of information they would look for that might be predictive of war. Nikolai began haunting British seaports and airports. The teams returned empty-handed.

"What other investigations are we to perform?" Nikolai asked Anatoly Anchev at the end of two weeks.

"The President has given us his orders," Anchev replied, a grim set to his jaw. "We must find his evidence of war preparations by the British and save the motherland from annihilation. Look harder!"

With that, the spies in Great Britain roamed far and wide again. Their desperate charge: to turn over rocks until the British plan was revealed. The same KGB hunt was ongoing in America, too.

Nikolai wasted no time taking the witch-hunt news to the ULYSSES team, who passed it onto the MI5 Soviet experts at River House. MI5 reacted with disbelief, but MI6's double-agents confirmed.

On 20 August 1962, the information divulged made the British spies sit up and swallow hard, and their hearts hammer. KGB had learned of the activation of Operation Anadyr just that day as Khrushchev was taking troops and missiles into Cuba. ULYSSES had delivered those war plans to MI5. In what they received, there was no detail omitted.

The six seniors accepted the top-secret information as gospel. MI6 spies inside Russia reported secret troop movements and matériel accumulation at Russian ports. War machinery, tanks, APCs, howitzers, and even missile launchers accumulated seaside.

Then, the final sentences of the report. The Kremlin believed, wrongly, that the West was about to launch a surprise attack on the Soviet Union. The West was about to launch its missiles and drop its bombs from one end of Russia to the other.

Khrushchev meant to strike first.

"What in hell's gotten into the Soviets?" 10 Downing Street asked MI5.

"Unknown," said Lightner. "But this much we do know. ULYSSES has never been wrong with his information to this point. Our only path is to act as if it will happen."

True enough, said 10 Downing Street. The Americans must be notified without delay. Cables crossed the Atlantic that night. The reaction of the Americans was one of disbelief. Astonishment. Requests for re-confirmation. Even a request for confirmation the initial cable was actually from Great Britain. Who was the source? The Brits sent a one-word reply: *ULYSSES*.

Randall Cummings, the leader of ULYSSES in MI5, wondered, "Could KGB Moscow really be so out of touch with the world as to believe this?" When all was said and done, the West decided that a systematic release of British and American plans to spread not war but peace among all nations was necessary. KGB spies would carelessly leak British and American plans for peace. War wasn't coming; peace was coming instead.

37

But the peace plans turned loose in the intelligence field went nowhere with the Soviets.

With no proof in his pocket whatsoever, Khrushchev decided the time to activate Operation Anadyr was at hand. The operational first steps at putting Soviet missiles, machines, and manpower in Cuba revved up. If nothing else, the USSR would demonstrate to the West once and for all that it was ready for war. It would reveal nuclear warheads placed in Cuba, just ninety miles from American soil.

Within the first twenty-four hours of the plan becoming operational, American U-2 spy planes reported unusual Soviet accumulations of troops and war matériel at two Soviet seaports. President Kennedy was stunned. "They're actually planning war," he said to his defense secretary, Robert T. McNamara, and his Secretary of State, Dean Rusk. Frantic meetings with CIA director John McCone followed. At each step of all conferences, the Americans took great care to conceal. They knew the KGB was everywhere and paranoid. If they had even an inkling the CIA was suddenly stepping up its meetings with the White House, they might move to a first-strike posture.

Not without questions about Soviet nuclear missiles' capabilities, the White House instructed the CIA to obtain information about the missiles by, "Whatever means necessary." Upon learning this, the CIA was suddenly scouring all sources for information on Soviet Luna missiles. The KGB, horrified the Americans already had learned about Operation Anadyr, sprinted with the news back to Moscow. This only made Khrushchev speed up his plans.

However, having just activated Operation Anadyr and realizing American preparations were already underway to meet the threat, Khrushchev began having doubts. There were leaks, big leaks. Was Cuba a mistake, a miscalculation? There was a hole in the plan, but he didn't share these doubts with anyone. Still, his staff was walking on eggshells.

The esteemed leader refused to leave his office, demanding updates on the operation almost hourly. American troop and materiel movements were reported.

Washington's suddenly hawkish stance was feeding into the Soviet belief system that nuclear war was imminent and that, forgetting their own first steps in moving men and machines, believed the Americans were gearing up for war. Now Khrushchev knew. Nuclear Armageddon was imminent.

The CIA came back to MI5. More information was needed. Could the CIA meet personally with ULYSSES? At this point, the British hadn't said who or where or what part of the planet the ULYSSES information was coming from. The CIA pushed. How reliable was this information? What dealings did MI5 have with this spy in the past that proved him or her reliable? What were the error parameters? The CIA needed to know. Kennedy even got on a call with

British PM Harold Macmillan. Demands were made and fended off. The spy community would need to settle the matter, Macmillan countered when pushed by Kennedy. "The game," he said, "has its boundaries. We are merely the judges, not the players." The words would rattle around the White House for days. England was refusing to yield.

Jason Donovan called in the ULYSSES team. "Ten Downing Street is under intense pressure. President Kennedy demands a meeting with ULYSSES."

"What about Oleg Penkovsky?" asked Randall Cummings. "He has everything Kennedy needs. Don't we know that?"

Bolling answered. "He's given up missile emplacements, numbers, guidance systems, and fueling systems. I don't know what else he has."

"But Kennedy isn't happy," Donovan said. "It's that simple, and that's why he isn't backing down on ULYSSES. In a way, he's got a point. The whole world could go up in one nuclear flash. If ULYSSES can help avoid that, maybe it's time to disclose."

"Then we cable them the information they want," Bolling said. "No need to disclose ULYSSES' identity."

"No good," Donovan said. "Kennedy insists on meeting him to gauge the weight to be given. He must go to Washington."

"I tend to agree," said Cummings.

"Here's something," Emma Magnuson broke in. "Penkovsky's knowledge is limited when it comes down to Soviet army size, vehicles, and armaments. I sat in on the debriefing. I'm guessing that's what Kennedy is after."

"ULYSSES has that," Donovan said.

All eyes turned to Nikolai. He said he was willing. It would need to be dressed up for the KGB to appear that Nikolai was penetrating the CIA, but it could certainly be done.

Then the Director of MI5 said, "No way." The Americans could ask their questions, and ULYSSES would provide answers by safe telephone connections. Still, there was no way in hell the Brits were going to give up the best spy they'd ever recruited just because Kennedy was demanding an in-person interview.

The Director's decision traveled to Washington.

Then the back and forth went quiet.

38

In early September 1962, Ansel McEnery—known around the CIA halls as Spiderman—was Chief of the CIA's Soviet section. A spy-catcher who made webs for the unwary, Spiderman patiently awaited KGB agents who might blunder in and become stuck while he devoured them with his unrelenting interrogations and secret techniques.

But when it came to ULYSSES and the Brits' refusal, Spiderman was stumped. The British had what the United States desperately needed, and they wouldn't give him up. It was unheard of in Anglo-American relations when existential threats existed. After a final desperate call to Randall Cummings, Spiderman slammed down the phone, then jumped up and double-timed down the hallway to Director John McCone's office. He stormed into the inner sanctum.

"John," he began, "the goddam Brits won't give us ULYSSES."

"You spoke with Cummings?"

"Hell, yes! And Jason Donovan."

"Rusk spoke with Macmillan. He put the bug back on MI5. Mac said it's MI5's decision about what to reveal or not. We're at an impasse."

"Here's what I want to do. I want to launch the biggest spy hunt we've ever launched. I want this man. I need him. Kennedy says he's a must-have. Permission requested to run him to the ground."

"That sounds like something you would do with a fly, McEnery."

McEnery's hackles raised. "They're testing me, and, by God, I will not allow it to stand. They won't cooperate, that's just fine. I'll do it myself."

"Permission granted. You have thirty days. That's the most I can give you. Even now, the Soviets are outfitting the Northern Fleet at the home base at Severomorsk. We're just about out of time."

"A month should suffice. My staff will take it on around the clock." But McEnery needed someone on the ground. He told Director John McCone, "I don't need just *any* spy, I need a spy at the top of his game. Who do we have who catches Russkies and doesn't have a huge rep and poster-boy face the Soviets will see coming from a mile away? That's who I need to catch this damn ULYSSES."

McCone thumbed through his Rolodex. "Rosenkranz?"

"I know where you're going with that, maybe using FBI in CIA business because they won't be recognized. But no. Keep going, sir."

"I like this Oleg Penkovsky. I *know* he knows ULYSSES. Both KGB, both double-agents."

"That one gets really tricky. We know KGB has known for a year that Penkovsky is a double agent. But they've been leaving it alone because they didn't want to out their mole in MI5. It's a mess, and I think we leave him alone."

"Why's that?"

McEnery's eyes narrowed. "Because we don't want Penkovsky taking it back to the Brits we're looking. Worse, we don't want him to take it back to the KGB. He's so twisted, I doubt he even knows who his friends are anymore. No, we leave Penkovsky alone."

"Well, who do you have right here in your Division that no one knows? Pardon me for asking, but who's your greatest under-producer?"

"That would be Henry Stoner."

McCone's gray face lit up. "Then there's your man. Make your silk purse out of your sow's ear."

"John, that's exactly what it would take. But you might be right. He's got the brains, just not much else."

"Tell me about Henry. I've got him here on my Rolodex. Not a nice picture, I daresay."

"He's forty, rotten teeth that he covers with his hand when he talks, highly invisible. Late to work all the damn time."

"How susceptible to being turned?"

"Susceptible as shit to being turned. Close to bankruptcy except for paydays. The wife is a Saks Fifth Avenue baby. Can't keep her out of Manhattan with Henry's checkbook. She got him into trouble when she talked him into borrowing a CIA car for a personal vacation."

"Don't tell me. Henry drives a clunker that wouldn't last past the city limits."

"Bingo."

"Now tell me something negative about Stoner," laughed McCone.

"See? That's just it. But maybe you're right. KGB Moscow will never see him coming."

39

Henry Stoner was a CIA case officer who spoke Russian and specialized in the Russian intelligence services. His initial overseas assignment was in Ankara, Turkey, where he targeted Russian intelligence officers for recruitment. Later, he worked in New York City and Mexico City. On 12 September 1962, while assigned to the CIA's Soviet/ East European Division at CIA Headquarters in Langley, he secretly volunteered to defect to KGB officers at the USSR Embassy in Washington. At the same time, Ansel McEnery was determined to identify ULYSSES and bring him to America. He assigned Henry Stoner to bring it home--the worst possible timing, because KGB had turned Stoner inside out. They had made him their best CIA double agent. Stoner passed the names of double agents. He took money from the Soviets. $10,000, $20,000, even $45,000, depending on the importance and density of the intelligence. He was rolling in it now. The wife was receiving new credit card offers in the daily mail and sending them back ACCEPTED.

The names Stoner turned over to the Soviets got people killed. The CIA and FBI watched Russian officials who they had recruited then arrested and executed by the Soviets.

It was early in the game, however, and the CIA had no suspicions about Stoner. He just wasn't raw double agent material.

So it went ahead. Following his talk with Director McCone, McEnery took Stoner aside and told him it was his ball. He was assigned the critical job of finding the identity of ULYSSES. Stoner was doubly pleased with the assignment. It meant money in the bank, lots of money, when he sold the Soviets' the identity, and it meant a for-sure promotion at the CIA. He bought two new suits of clothes with his Soviet earnings and came to work early on Monday.

"Where do I start?" he asked McEnery.

McEnery touched the side of his head. "Use this, Henry. You received that brain from the good Lord for a reason. I want the name in three weeks, no more."

Stoner exulted, realizing he had the authority to move mountains if necessary.

He booked a flight to London. He scouted the Soviet Embassy and located a point where he could monitor the rear exit. He spent two weeks camped there. While Henry wasn't overly creative, he was tenacious. Sometimes that was the key trait in surveillance.

Over the first two weeks, he followed likely-looking KGB operatives as they came and went from the embassy. He photographed them from a distance. In his hotel room, he pasted their pictures to the wall. One by one, he followed them to their flats, picked their locks, and tossed their homes for ULYSSES. He did this with twenty-five agents, looking for clues, expecting the hint he would find was going to be abstract because ULYSSES was brilliant. He wouldn't leave the obvious lying around. Thus, Stoner was thorough. Every drawer, every cabinet, every nook and cranny—nothing escaped his eye.

On his fourteenth day, he made a discovery. He followed a man home, waited until he left after lunch, and quickly let himself inside. In the man's bedroom, he discovered a sea chest with a large picture frame on top. Combination locks were nothing to CIA agents. He was quickly inside and picking through the contents. Then, on the bottom beneath other books, he found a book by James Joyce. The title: *Ulysses*. Stoner instantly knew. He had located ULYSSES. It was just too coincidental to ignore. With all due haste since the officer could return at any minute, he closed and relocked the chest.

He peered inside the closet and swung some hangers. KGB uniforms, a half dozen. He went into the main room and found where the officer kept his mail. He riffled through the envelopes, confirming the addressee that kept coming up. Then he made his way back outside. Out of all the officers Stoner had pawed through so far, this was the first inkling of a clue. It wasn't conclusive and maybe meant nothing, but Stoner felt the pressure to produce, and he wanted Soviet gold. He boldly decided he was going to claim victory.

He returned to his hotel room and made a secure call to McEnery at Langley. "I've found your spy."

"You've found ULYSSES?"

"It will need verification."

"Return and debrief. That is all."

He flew home and spoke with the spy catchers the following night, telling them what he'd found.

"I'm not convinced," McEnery said. "I think we're close, and I think Stoner here has done an outstanding bit of spying, but we still need to confirm."

"No way," said Andres, the plodding spy catcher known to have shot at least three American spies gone bad. "A fucking book title means shit."

McEnery had huge reservations, but, on the other hand, he had nothing else. The connection between *Ulysses* the novel and ULYSSES the KGB spy, was like smoke mixed with more smoke, but it was all they had.

"What's this man's name?"

"The electric bill said 'Nikolai Semenov.'"

McEnery called in the brains. CIA analysts combed through the intelligence supplied by the Brits over the last three years attributed to ULYSSES. They were trying to pinpoint him by elimination.

The process they used began and ended with Operation Anadyr. The CIA knew the Soviet operator was a KGB officer—MI5 had said as much in confirming the source's reliability at the first exchange of data between MI5 and CIA. Now Stoner had confirmed he was KGB as well. The importance of the data, and its density factor, indicated the source was high-ranking. He had to have access to all documents about the operation. He wasn't, in other words, someone who'd had a peek then drawn conclusions. No, this spy knew the entire operation, front to back. Next, the information was flowing with regularity. Which placed the spy in England, probably London, probably weekly debriefings. So far, so good. Then CIA sleuths really rolled up their sleeves and took the intelligence offerings apart, sentence by sentence. What remained was the inescapable conclusion that the intelligence contained little or no technical or high-grade military intelligence, except Operation Anadyr. He seemed to have that down cold. They reviewed every piece of intel ULYSSES had turned over. The context was always connected to foreign intelligence with a healthy helping of disinformation. They decided that the source was working inside the KGB's PR Line of the First Directorate.

They zeroed in on this perspective and asked themselves, what's the first thing a spy does when he comes over? He fingers other spies he knows to be working for the British but in truth were Soviet spies. So, asked the CIA, what countries had ejected or arrested spies in the last three years? Where had the Soviets recently lost agents? They knew of two men, Lazik and Fermer, who'd been lost to the Soviets in Sweden. But the most dramatic exposure of a Soviet spy in the last three years had taken place in London, with the murder of Robert John Ziegler. Ziegler, they decided, had learned ULYSSES' name.

The CIA understood the structure and personnel of the KGB. The high-traffic flow of intel seemed to point at someone in the KGB's London station. Stoner's London trip only strengthened the supposition that someone was hand-delivering from KGB London to MI5 London. The CIA officers then began combing through their files on known KGB agents in London who had also been in Sweden when Lazik and Fermer were caught and London when Ziegler was murdered. Then an exciting find floated to the surface: SÄPO—Swedish intelligence—had fingered an embassy official named Nikolai Semenov as a KGB officer years before. Before London, Nikolai Semenov had served short periods in Sweden, a month or two at the most. But he had come to know the Soviet Embassy staff and the KGB agents there. Here was the same man whose flat Stoner had entered. The same man who was keeping a copy of *Ulysses* in a trunk in his bedroom.

The CIA also knew the British knew he was KGB and, even knowing he was a spy, the Brits had granted him a visa as a bona fide diplomat. The British would never have done this if the Soviet diplomatic posting was on the up and up. No, the investigators realized, the Brits *wanted* this man in London. They had deliberately created a path into the country for their top spy. It had probably been going on for years.

McEnery was confident he had ULYSSES' identity. It was a satisfying professional victory over the Brits.

"That," McCone told McEnery after a celebratory dinner that night, "is how the spy game is played."

Stoner was praised and thanked for his excellent work; even the Secretary of State dropped a line telling him well done.

40

It was early September 1962. After a dozen calls with Castro, Khrushchev agreed to place strategic nuclear missiles secretly in Cuba. The Soviets kept a steel wall wrapped around their war plans, keeping them only in longhand so that clerk typists wouldn't even know. It was these plans that Nikolai Semenov saw in Moscow. Ships sunk far below their waterlines, loaded with machines, armaments, and missiles. A massive Soviet effort was underway.

"What have our troops been told about Operation Anadyr?" asked son Sergei, referring to its code name.

"Our troops have been told they are heading for a freezing region. We have outfitted them with ski boots, fleece-lined parkas, white coveralls, and skis. Even their guns are carried in white covers. They have no idea and won't until they arrive in Havana and see palm trees and sunny beaches."

"What about the American U-2 overflights?"

"There is nothing we can do about that except work under camouflage and work at night. Chief Marshal Biryhuzov says the palm trees will offer protection from prying eyes. When all is ready, the palm trees will be cleared so that the missiles might launch."

"You must be very proud."

Khrushchev ignored this. Laudatory congratulations were the first step toward gaining a leader's confidence. He made a habit of brushing all such applause aside. A fourth-grade dropout from school, a one-time Commissar in the Party, the leader had learned the hard way never to trust. Not even his own son's plaudits were received. He had no time or affection for them.

Nikita Khrushchev only focused on what was at hand. Preparations for a possible war in Cuba were underway. Plans had been made and re-made. Now, those plans had become more serious, more likely to result in a land war in Cuba between Russian and American forces than ever before.

"Sergei," said Khrushchev to his son, "Kennedy is a weakling. We will warn that if he interferes with our ships or missiles in Cuba, it means all-out war."

"What do you believe from Kennedy?"

Khrushchev brushed away the question as if swatting flies. "He will complain, then he will complain some more, then he will accept reality. We then own the balance of power, East versus West."

Satisfied with what he believed, Khrushchev sat back at his desk. It was seven feet wide and featured a divider in the middle, left to right across the width, eight inches high, so that visitors could not see Khrushchev's side of the desk and possibly get a glimpse of what he was addressing. Along the entire wall behind him was a built-in cabinet, glass front, holding treasures he had acquired during his world travels, including antiques from his parents' peasant home that they had presented to him when he became Premier.

Across from him sat Sergei, his son, and a deputy minister in the Communist Party who almost daily visited with his father. The Party faithful knew this, knew young Sergei had his father's ear and accorded him the respect and deference such a connection called for.

Behind Sergei, stretching the length of that wall, were glass partitions looking into a long conference room with a massive oak table hewn from a single tree two-hundred years old in Siberia, another of Khrushchev's favorite acquisitions. At Khrushchev's far-right was a couch made of tan leather that faced the Premier's desk. Its cover matched the inlaid cowhide along the tops of the divider on the desk. "Nicely done," Khrushchev had said to the artisans who brought it in from Leningrad to create a setting suitable for him.

The man himself was sitting pretty except for one nagging matter of Soviet safety that just would not go away. The U.S. had deployed in Italy and Turkey more than 100 ICBM missiles capable of raining down nuclear warheads on Moscow.

"What of Italy and the missiles in Turkey?" Sergei asked. "When are we planning to remove those? The Party is anxious for answers."

Khrushchev nodded and rubbed his chin. "We will scare the hell out of Kennedy with our Cuba deployment. He cannot allow Soviet Luna missiles ninety miles from Florida. So, when tensions are the highest, we will negotiate the removal of our weapons in Cuba to remove his weapons from Italy and Turkey. Then we are back to detente."

"May I carry this plan back to the leadership?"

Khrushchev thumped the top of his desk, and an inkwell jumped. "Definitely not! Let those beggars suffer in silence. Give them none of this. Not even to Andréa do you repeat our conversation."

"I know that. My wife knows nothing of what I do. She prefers it that way with her flowers and her clubs."

"But we know this failed Catholic, this Kennedy fellow with his half-hearted invasion of Cuba at the Bay of Pigs. That ridiculous effort was nothing more than a college boy's attempt at getting serious attention from his girlfriend. I believe it was Marilyn Monroe who challenged him."

Sergei disagreed with his father's assessment—whimsical as it was—but he couldn't say so. While he was the Premier's son, he was held accountable by his father for his actions and words.

41

On September 12, the Soviet Union publicly warned that a U.S. Attack on Cuba or Soviet ships carrying supplies to the island would mean war. But then the missiles were photographed from 40,000 feet lashed to the decks of the Soviet cargo ships. There was no mistake. Khrushchev was bringing missiles to Cuba. Soviet Ambassador to the United States, Anatoly Dorbrynin, received a thunderous phone call from UN Ambassador Adlai Stevenson.

"What in hell's name are you thinking?" cried Stevenson. "This is a declaration of war!"

"Not at all," Dorbrynin calmly replied. "The weapons are purely defensive. The United States has brought this on itself by its invasion at the Bay of Pigs. Rest assured, none of it is offensive."

"This will not stand!" cried Stevenson.

"It already does. We have two-hundred ships, at least. A good third of them are warships. Nuclear submarines are protecting them even as we speak. We are very confident, Ambassador. Tell your

President Kennedy this is no time to interfere. We are ready if he makes that mistake."

Stevenson carried news of the conversation back to Kennedy, who was spending his days huddled in the situation room with his Chief of Staff, Secretary of Defense, Secretary of State, CIA Director, and a mix of admirals and generals.

"It is not a *fait accompli*," Kennedy declared in a steady voice. "It will not stand."

"Will we go to war?" asked McNamara, the Secretary of Defense. "The Pentagon is winding up."

"It could happen, though I dread that," Kennedy replied. "We will threaten, and we will blockade, but we will not invade Cuba. Another loss there and the West is lost to the Soviets. Plus, we all know the Soviets would use nukes against our troops. At that point, the world is lost forever."

Attorney General Robert Kennedy was shaking his head. "It's going to take more than words this time, Mr. President," he said, straightening his club tie, his sleeves rolled up to his elbows.

"All we have are words, Bobby. Words we can say and missiles we cannot use. It's a strange time and a terrifying time. Americans are about to see the end of civilization roll up to their front doors and park. It is only a matter of days before we have to act."

Said McNamara, "First, I'd like to know the efficiency of the missiles. Do we know what they even are?"

Kennedy nodded. "MI5 says they're Lunas. The Soviet's best and most powerful but also the most untested. They've never been tested with nukes on board."

"Exactly," McNamara continued. "So I need to know their efficiency. How are their guidance systems? What is their range? Are they intermediate-range or intercontinental? We need more data, Mr. President," said McNamara with the wireframe glasses and the cool of an administrator running Ford Motor Company. "Before we do anything, we must have technical specifications."

"Oleg Penkovsky's data wasn't enough?"

McNamara spread his hands. "He believes the guidance systems are corrupt. He also says their fueling systems are questionable. But we need more than that. We need to know their range. And we need to know troop size, type of troops, war machinery. We need to know the matériel coming across. Who do we have for that?"

Kennedy looked at CIA Director John McCone. "John," he said, "care to address what resource we have?"

"The Brits have a source we know as ULYSSES," McCone said, keeping the spy's name under wraps. "We have reason to believe he's a very high-up KGB officer. From what the Brits have been willing to share, this ULYSSES was involved in the Soviet's war security apparatus some time ago. We predict he knows what's headed our way."

"Get him!" demanded Kennedy. "While you're at it, you might tell the goddamn Brits we're not mucking around here. I want this ULYSSES yesterday! Tell that to the PM!"

42

Back at London KGB, Anchev was having his problems. KGB Moscow was unhappy with his handling of the Lana situation. They secretly contacted Nikolai. Was he prepared to take over as *rezident*? He said he was, and he was ready for it to happen at any moment. But then KGB Moscow began dragging its feet. Out of the blue, KGB Moscow put the fear of God in Nikolai. They instructed him to return to Moscow for a *rezidentura* briefing on goals and expectations for the new *rezident*.

"This never happens," Nikolai told Bolling at the safe house. "I fear for my mother. She goes to the gulag if I don't return. I cannot see my own mother breaking rocks in Siberia. I have no choice."

"TINKER is waiting in the wings," Emma Magnuson reminded him needlessly. "If required."

"Please, that's not encouraging," Nikolai said. "You know how I feel about my chances of escape from Russia."

She did know. She didn't push it again.

Bolling took the news back to Randall Cummings and Jason Donovan at MI5. Immediate worry set in, and a debate ensued. Cummings floated the idea it might be a trap, that Nikolai had been outed. Some of them thought Nikolai should defect now rather than risk being branded as a traitor and executed. Others thought it was worth the risk of going and receiving the promotion and return with unfettered resources. Both sides argued late into the night.

Meanwhile, Nikolai had made up his mind to return to Moscow; what MI5 had to say about it was irrelevant. He had all but convinced himself he was safe. The spying had taken place unimpeded and gone undiscovered by London KGB for far too long. It didn't make sense that they were only now discovering his collaboration when he was taking over as *rezident*. Had they found out before, they would have acted. This was Nikolai's ace in the hole, the logic from which he made his decision to follow orders and return to Moscow.

But, more importantly, he was going to try to convince his mother to move to Britain. At one point, the KGB would use her as leverage, but if she lived with him in the UK, it would be that much harder to get to her. He was going to leave Sasha behind with Carolina and Maxim. He only planned to fly in and be in Moscow for one day. No point in making Sasha do those long flights back to back. She'd be miserable.

Still, MI5 offered Nikolai the opportunity to defect with all benefits coming to him from the British government. The resettlement, the house, the car, the schools, and money—it was all there in one package, but Nikolai told them no thanks. His mind was set, and he was going. "We'll do this at some point. But not yet."

He was met at the airport in Moscow, almost with a hero's welcome. Everyone told him he was doing a great job. Luka Solinov, Head of the Third Department, said they'd never seen such outstanding accomplishments by anyone his age. Semenov realized the low-level information he'd been supplying thanks to KGB Moscow Center was paying off handsomely. At a formal ceremony the next afternoon, Nikolai was officially installed as the new London *rezident*.

His business done for the KGB, Nikolai went home to his flat in Moscow, where his mother was now staying. Since he had no longer any use for it as *rezident* of KGB London, and with the money coming in from MI5 for her care, they had decided she'd move back to Moscow where Nikolai had grown up and where his mother's friends still remained.

He entered his flat and hung his jacket and coat on the stand beside the door. He called out, "*Mamochka*, are you here?"

She stepped into the living area while wiping her hands with a towel. She moved to him and engulfed him in a big hug. She was a thin, wiry woman with fully gray hair and gray eyes like Nikolai's.

"I am so proud of you, son. The new Soviet Embassy *rezident*. How did the ceremony go?"

"Good…good." He took her hand and led her to the sofa, where he urged her to sit. "Listen, *Mamochka*…I think you should come back to London with me."

She gasped. "What for, a holiday?"

Nikolai shook his head. "No, to live."

"But why?" She began to fold the towel in her lap. "My life is here. My home is here. I'm happy now I'm back in Moscow."

"I just…" Nikolai didn't know how to word it without raising suspicion with his mother. He didn't want to add to any grief she might already carry regarding the KGB and his father's pension. "It's a good life there—a better life than here. You will be able to buy whatever you want. You can get new clothes and shoes. They have all sorts of appliances you can't imagine! Magical coffee makers and toasters. You can go to musicals and plays, art that isn't censored by any government."

"No, Nikolai, those things don't matter to me anymore. I was happy when the KGB supplied them when you were younger, but I'm older now, and I don't need much. I like my routine. I like what I know."

"Please," Nikolai begged. Without outright saying she could be in danger, he pleaded with her. "You will live a long life there. There is always hot water and the medicines you need."

"I don't speak English. I don't want to learn English."

Nikolai saved his most potent artillery for last. "If you come live in Britain with me, you will see your granddaughter grow up. I don't know when we will be back next. It could be years."

"Nikolai," she said sternly. She turned to face him on the sofa and took his hands. "I want to stay and die in my motherland. I will see Sasha before I do."

He would be going back without her.

Nikolai returned to London, a hero among MI5 ULYSSES agents. They had a party at the safe house in Bayswater at noon. Donovan made a warm, congratulatory speech, and Bolling sat beside him at the table, reminding him several times how proud they all were. Even Cummings attended, solemn, quiet Cummings who held out his hand to shake and told Nikolai that he'd never been so proud of someone at his level before. Nikolai was impressed and just a little embarrassed.

43

Under pressure from President Kennedy to produce ULYSSES in the Oval Office, the CIA made its move on MI5. McEnery cabled London.

WE KNOW ULYSSES. HE READS JAMES JOYCE.

Bolling questioned Nikolai that noon. "Do you keep a copy of *Ulysses* at your flat?"

"In my father's trunk, there is a copy. It's an impossible book to read. I'll give it over to you if you're interested."

"CIA has been inside that trunk. They found the book titled *Ulysses* and made the connection back to our code name ULYSSES. Your identity is now known in Langley."

"Then I'm dead!" cried Nikolai. "My name will get back to Moscow."

"Here's the cable. Reread it. 'He reads James Joyce.' They know, Nikolai. They have you now."

Bolling returned to River House dejected and full of apprehension. He immediately went to Donovan, the head of the ULYSSES mole team. The feeling was that there was an American spy in their midst. How else did the CIA get the name? So Donovan started an inquiry of the ULYSSES team. Who among you, he asked, might have outed our most precious intelligence resource to the Americans?

Everyone looked at the others. No one blinked.

Donovan told Bolling the same afternoon the cable came, "Big Brother wants to debrief ULYSSES. They want him in Washington to meet with Kennedy."

"That will be impossible," Bolling replied. "Too risky. It could get Nikolai killed."

"Agree. I'll notify the CIA. No dice."

McEnery was adamant. "We need him here tomorrow, Donovan. The Soviets are sailing an army to Cuba as we speak. We need vitals. We need what ULYSSES knows about the army, numbers, armament, all of it. We can't take no for an answer this time."

"Impossible. Nikolai is under constant KGB surveillance now, both for his safety and for his integrity. KGB would know in a heartbeat if Nikolai journeyed to Washington."

Nikolai was told of the stalemate, but he replied, "I can do it. I will advise KGB Moscow that I've been approached by a high-ranking CIA agent who is willing to sell American secrets about the military response to the Cuban crisis that Kennedy is preparing."

"That sounds very risky," Donovan said.

"Trust me. I know KGB. They will jump at the chance, and they will leave me alone to do it."

Nikolai called KGB Moscow that evening. KGB Moscow was astonished. "Seriously?" they asked. They wanted to ask who this person was, but they did not. Field officers were never asked to reveal sources to protect those sources who could be outed by anyone working at KGB Moscow who might have a grudge or a need to make some fast money. So, the KGB didn't press Nikolai. There was a shallow discussion. It took twenty-four hours, but he was cleared to go in the end.

He told KGB Moscow he would be flying TWA so as not to draw attention to himself, rather than another carrier commonly used by the KGB for international flights. That was cleared as well.

Two days later, Nikolai stepped off the plane in Washington and went straight to his hotel, where he checked in. But arrangements for him had been made at the Mayflower Hotel instead, four minutes away.

It was prearranged that he would lose his Soviet tail, check into the Mayflower Hotel under a secret name, and meet with Kennedy that afternoon at four p.m.

It went perfectly.

At 3:45, Nikolai was in the small waiting room outside the Oval Office. John McCone, Director of the CIA, was there with him along with Ansel McEnery. Nikolai was never told McEnery's role in it all. Nor was he told about Stoner. The CIA kept its methods secret, too.

Then Nikolai and the CIA agents were escorted into the President's office, the Secret Service having thoroughly searched and confirmed that Nikolai was unarmed.

Kennedy stood from behind his desk. To his right was his rocking chair, as depicted in the photographs Nikolai had seen. Also with him was Robert Kennedy, the Attorney General, and Robert McNamara, Secretary of Defense.

"Mr. Semenov," said Kennedy after introductions, "I need your help."

"I'm ready, however possible, Mr. President," said Nikolai, meaning every word of it. One day, he would head up the Washington KGB office as a general in the service. He had his eye on that plum, and now was a good move toward that outcome, meeting with Kennedy himself.

"We have our sources, and one of them has told us about the Luna missiles en route to Cuba. But he knew very little about the army en route as well. I want to ask you about that. First, how many soldiers are we talking about here? Five-thousand? Ten?"

"Almost forty-five thousand, Mr. President."

"What? Forty-five thousand!" cried Kennedy with a look of horror at defense secretary McNamara. "That's enough for a full-scale land war."

"My impression is that the Premier expects a land war once you demand their removal, and he refuses. He and Castro expect nothing less than a full-on American invasion of Havana."

"How many missiles in all? We need your confirmation of our source's best guess."

"One-hundred missiles. Four squadrons of MiG-21 fighters and a squadron of IL-28 light bombers."

"Ground support bombers," McNamara said softly. "Figures."

"T-75 Dvina surface-to-air missiles, eight different locations, fifty missiles at each site, at least."

"Holy shit," said Bobby in his brother's ear. "Jack—"

"Hush!" snapped the President. "Let's hear him out."

The meeting continued for another thirty minutes. Nikolai turned over everything he knew. His access to the Operation Anadyr documents had continued through its different configurations without letup. If the Americans had questions, he had answers. The right answers.

When he was removed back to his hotel, Nikolai was in disguise provided by the CIA. The next day, he reappeared at TWA, where the KGB finally picked up his trail again. It had gone perfectly, and the KGB had been foiled in its attempts to learn with whom he was meeting. They had no idea where he'd been or to whom he'd spoken.

They could only await his report to KGB Moscow.

44

An urgent telegram from Moscow was hand-delivered to the newly appointed KGB *rezident* in London.

Call him prescient, but Nikolai knew almost immediately what he was about to read. The trip to America had had too many holes. Too many new eyes, too many cameras, too damn many people everywhere they went. At least one of them was unfriendly. He kicked himself for ever agreeing to go. With shaking hands, he unfolded the telegram.

"To confirm your appointment as *rezident*, please come to Moscow urgently in two days for important discussions with Comrades Masirov and Barishsky. Your mother is standing by."

Nikolai told his secretary he had an urgent meeting and rushed outside to the nearest telephone box. Then he stopped before dialing, bent forward, and vomited onto the sidewalk. Passersby stepped around his wet spot. He made his call, wiping his lips with his sleeve, and an emergency meeting was set up with his MI5 handlers.

Over the next forty-eight hours, MI5 and Nikolai would make a life or death decision. Life or death for Nikolai and maybe his mother, life or death for ULYSSES. "Rest assured," they told him, "our lives will go on without ULYSSES. Your life comes first at this moment. You must do what is best for you."

The decision was over and done before it was even considered. They all knew: KGB had his mother. That would again trump every other possibility.

Nikolai shook his head. "Sending my mother to Siberia, to the gulag. She is an old woman. She wouldn't last two weeks."

There was no answer to that.

Then Bolling broke the silence. "It's all there, Nikolai. It's time to move beyond the telegram and think of your choice. Go and perhaps die or stay and live out your years in England with the little girl who loves you."

"While my mother dies a slow starvation death."

Bolling turned away. "I just want the best for you. We've come too far together for it—for it to end badly."

That final night at the safe house, the ULYSSES team served smoked salmon and home-baked bread from Emma Magnuson. They clicked on the tape recorder for later study of precisely what all was said. Charles Lightner summarized where they were.

"No intelligence indicates Nikolai's recall is anything other than routine. Except where they mention his mother. He believes that is the beginning of the end for him."

Lightner continued. "But, if Nikolai wants to defect, he should do it today, tonight, right now. He should leave here accompanied by two agents, go home, get Sasha, pack his overnight bags, and leave now for safety. On the other hand, if he decides to go forward with the return to Moscow, MI5 will be grateful forever, no matter how it turns out. But if he returns from Moscow to London as the newly blessed *rezident*, the world is ours. It's time to decide so we can prepare."

Everyone looked at Nikolai. "My mother. That makes my decision, so I don't have to."

"Then let's review your escape," said mapmaker Emma Magnuson. She jumped into action. She walked Nikolai through all arrangements for Operation TINKER. She provided photographs of the rendezvous site, which, in the final analysis, told Nikolai little beyond it was a church. It had no impact on his view of the operation overall.

"While you have been in London," said Magnuson, "all agents have had hammered into them every last detail of the plan. New agents taken into the ULYSSES fold are instructed in TINKER before any other matter. It could mean the difference between life and death for you, and it will not fail because someone didn't have their assignment right. That much, I can promise you." She reached inside her pocket and removed a glassine envelope. "Now, there's one additional refinement I want to add." Then she handed him two small packets of pills. "One packet will keep you alert; the other packet will put Sasha to sleep. You'll need to crush her pills and put them in milk or ice cream."

She also gave him a tin of snuff from James J. Fox, tobacconist of St. James. "Sprinkle this over yourself in the trunk. It might be enough to throw off the dogs."

"You're trying whatever you can to make this work, however small," Nikolai said with a smile. "I appreciate that."

"Well, the KGB will have sprayed on your clothes and shoes a distinct odor the dogs are trained to find. This might help overcome that. Then our team can pick you up at the rendezvous and spirit you across the border to Finland."

"Nice and tidy. I like that." His heart wasn't in it. That much was clear to everyone. But no one blamed him. The plan was too common, too predictable to fool anyone, much less the KGB. The movies were full of scenes where KGB targets escape capture in the trunks of cars. Hadn't that been around since movies of World War I vintage?

"When you make it to Finland," she finished, "I will be there in person to greet you."

He smiled. "You will be an angel I will see."

Nikolai returned to his office the next day. He had Volusa, his secretary, make the reservations on Aeroflot for the following day. He would arrive earlier than required and show up earlier than required. He meant to impress upon them he had nothing to hide.

On Monday, Nikolai and Sasha climbed up the stairway to the Aeroflot jet. Nikolai felt like he was severing yet another tie with the West and the friends at MI5 and MI6 that he loved. But still, they climbed, higher and higher, entering the jetliner, taking their seat, him opening his copy of *Pravda* to the business section, Sasha firmly planting her doll on her lap beside him.

Viktor Bucharov boarded. Nikolai made him once they were seated, and he could steal a glance around. He cringed. Nikolai immediately realized the next day was Tuesday, the best day to signal at the cathedral. He determined that it was probably a go.

He began reading the Russian newspaper as if catching up on the news before going home as any other visitor might do.

Bucharov saw the paper, noted it was turned to the business section, and smiled.

It won't be that easy, thought the First Directorate Colonel.

Read away.

45

The flight kissed the coast of Sweden just as the stewardess brought a ceramic cup containing shark squares stuffed with Kamchatka crab. Toothpicks stuck out. Nikolai raised an eyebrow and looked at the server as she was moving away. "You sure?"

Smiling the Aeroflot-approved smile, she didn't reply, continuing to make her way along the first-class aisle.

Nikolai sat back against his seat. He eyed the offering. His mouth and jaw clenched in that peculiar way of people in desperate trouble. Then, Nikolai abruptly relaxed. The decision had been made. His hand, manicured in the West, lifted slowly from his knee and grasped one of the toothpicks. He brought the food to his nose and sniffed. He opened his mouth slightly for his KGB teeth to nibble a bit of shark and crab. He held it on his tongue just long enough to decide. Would he proceed? Or would he politely spit the meats into his linen napkin?

Rolling the bite across his tongue, the spy deflated, remembering there were no critical decisions left to make. The critical decisions had already been made for him. He was just a passenger in an aircraft hurtling through the sky at 650 km/h like an arrow aimed at Moscow. Whether he ate the hors d'oeuvres or not wasn't worth any more consideration given all the rest. In three quick bites, he ate them all down and pushed aside the ceramic cup. He looked to his right and smiled at the KGB officer he wasn't supposed to know was there. The man looked down and leafed through his *In-Flight* magazine. Said Nikolai to his counterpart, "Tell KGB Moscow I can recommend it."

Through the night skies, he fought to calm himself in the face of the coming storm. He knew the consequences for a high-ranking KGB officer at the peak of his career caught spying for the British. He knew that when the KGB "called you home," it wasn't to discuss your reading habits. No, there was a reason, and the possibilities frightened him despite his KGB training to resist fear no matter what.

He sat back in his first-class seat and shut his eyes. The pilot had doused the lights above all seats. It was dark enough to sleep—if one weren't worried about one's life. Which he was. And for the lives of his daughter sleeping beside him, and his family yet in Russia. Anything could happen to any of them if Nikolai failed to deceive the KGB.

Another hour of dry-mouth that no amount of water would quell, then they landed with a bump and a squeal to arrive at Moscow's Sheremetyevo airport.

Father and daughter hurried up the jetway and entered the airport, him expecting to be arrested. For the occasion, he had selected a plain black suit, a plain white shirt, and a plain black overcoat, the depressing colors of Moscow, signaling his preference for the East. His tall, athletic body wouldn't resist the angry arms that would handcuff him, gather him in, and spirit him away to the Moscow Station and its dungeon of interrogation rooms. After they had gotten all they could get out of him—and they would get it, for they had fail-proof methods—they would put him on his knees and shoot him in the back of the head. He had witnessed their executions. Against his will, he had even held and fired the gun himself. The state would then raise Sasha. She could be taken to an orphanage at any moment.

Just inside the airport, he was stopped at the Border Guard station. He was a Soviet national and should have passed through quickly. But the officer was flipping through his passport several times without pausing as if skimming a menu. Then he looked to a yellow sheet on his countertop. His fingers traced down a list. Then he looked back at the passport then back at the list again. At that point, he made a telephone call. After another delay, while the officer tapped his fingers on the counter and avoided eye contact, Nikolai could stand it no longer. He lifted Sasha and passed on through the checkpoint, expecting to be grabbed from behind at any second. But no grabbing occurred. He picked up his pace. He knew the drill. The passport officer was to inform the KGB the moment he stepped onto Soviet soil. But what about the KGB officer on the plane? Hadn't he already called them? He didn't understand; it wasn't supposed to work like this.

As he walked through the airport, he looked neither right nor left and fought down the impulse to look around for KGB like the guilty would have done.

Given his rank, the KGB would ordinarily have sent an equal to meet him and welcome him home. But no one stepped forward to shake his hand, greet him, or help with his luggage, which was evidence that he would die. He had even been told that the head of the KGB British section would meet him. But there was no one to be seen. Still, he didn't look around. As he crossed the four-story open area, he remained unmolested in his passage. Which unnerved him, making the skin crawl on the back of his neck.

As well, the cab ride home was uneventful.

Nikolai carried Sasha inside the apartment building on Dobrynsky Prospekt and climbed the stairs to the second floor. He inserted his key. The locks gave way easily. He stepped inside and switched on the overhead light in the dim apartment. He looked up at the fixture. A spy device, colored white like the fixture, listened to his breathing. They were there, and they were everywhere.

He put down his luggage, laid the sleeping Sasha on his bed, and kicked off his shoes. Then he dropped to his knees and reached for the suitcase where he kept his books. He had already explained he kept and read these to meet Westerners on their own ground. He couldn't come across as totally uneducated in Western culture when he trolled for contacts. He knew they had seen the suitcase's books. As well as those in his father's trunk in London. Same rationale. The KGB was looking for evidence of collaboration with the British, not for Dickens and Maugham's literary works.

Nikolai had left the suitcase's flip-locks set, so the first two numbers were already dialed in, and all he had to do was spin it clockwise one time and stop at 12, the final number. The locks should then spring open. He twisted the dial to 12 and pushed the button. Nothing. The clasps didn't flip out. Someone had interfered. Someone had been inside. He suppressed an English curse. It was an easy next step since they knew everything else about him now. It was over.

He returned to the living room and picked up his phone. Dial tone, good. He rang up Masirov at KGB Moscow. Masirov had been very friendly and agreeable whenever they spoke while Nikolai was in London. Now he sounded cold, no warmth or glad-you-called in his voice. Nikolai wanted to ask what had changed but fought down the urge.

"No one met me," Nikolai complained.

"That's strange," said Masirov. "I arranged for Igor to meet you."

"Also, someone's been inside my flat. I assume there are microphones?"

"Please," said Masirov in his coldest voice. "There are protocols."

"What is going on here in Moscow? You owe me an explanation."

"I'm sure I don't know. But you will be contacted soon. Patience, please. Impatience killed the cat."

"That's no help," Nikolai muttered and slammed down the phone. He sat on his bed and then lay back beside Sasha, full of dread. Masirov's voice and flippant words told him everything he needed to know.

Tomorrow he would be drugged and tortured until he told them he was spying for London. Would he tell them that? Could he withhold?

He shut his eyes.

No one ever had.

46

His mother arrived from Leningrad. She had agreed to visit and help with Sasha while he worked. They hugged, and tears were shed while his mother looked incredulously at Sasha, who had doubled in size since last time she'd seen her.

The next morning before dawn, as Sasha and his mother slept, he dressed in sweats and headed outside for his run. Two above freezing, it was cold, even for a Moscow October. He switched on his transistor radio and listened. He twisted the dial, listening then turning again. No news of the Soviet fleet headed for Cuba. BBC had covered it yesterday when President Kennedy announced he was sending the U.S. Navy. Nuclear war had been imminent when he boarded his flight in London. But Russian radio was mum about it.

He stuck the radio in his pocket and looked up and down the street. A Volga parked at the corner could contain eyes. Or the Volga on the other corner. He looked again. There was a man behind the wheel of a Saab. Would they follow in their car? Or would they try to keep up on foot as he ran? He turned to his left and set off.

The first five steps were always the hardest. He settled into a rhythm as he headed for the residential area where the pavement was flat. Without looking behind, he knew another jogger was pacing him, and he knew it was Viktor Bucharov—the flop-flop-flop of his clumsy Russian running shoes gave him away. Nikolai increased his speed. He ran five miles every day, his body trained for long distances. He would test the KGB man's condition. Had Bucharov been one of those who had followed him along the Thames when he jogged before every workday at the Soviet Embassy?

He took in his surroundings as he ran. Everything was gray and disagreeable. Uniforms were everywhere he looked, watching, always watching. Coming to a cross street, he hopped the first curb, turned the corner, and then stopped. Bucharov hadn't kept up; he would round the corner any moment. He waited, and then, sure enough, there was Bucharov. The KGB officer didn't change his expression as he came upon Nikolai. He passed by, breathing normally, running off as if it meant nothing. Nikolai called to him, "Tell KGB Moscow you caught me!"

He ran back to his flat for a quick shower beneath the on-again/off-again hot water before he dressed for work and headed to the Center.

At the office, Masirov met him in the reception. He took Nikolai to his own office. They sat across from each other on two facing couches. A secretary brought coffee and tea. "Care for a cup?"

"No, thank you."

"KGB Moscow has questions for you, Colonel. Let's not act like this is a routine visit."

"I can answer questions. Are they worried about my performance as *rezident*?"

Masirov dipped his finger in his cup before he sucked the coffee off. "Old habits," he said with a smile. "When we were kids, we were made to test all liquids for temperature since there was never money for doctors if we burned ourselves."

"Of course." Nikolai looked down at his own hands. They were trembling, so he stuffed them into his pockets.

"Now, you have just been promoted *rezident* of KGB London. That is an honor and well-deserved. But there are urgent questions."

"About what?"

"I think you know about what. It's not for me to say, anyway. Just be ready."

"Who will I be meeting with?"

"One man you know. That would be General Barishsky, who did your foreign service interview. The other man you know but not as well. That would be Colonel Bucharov. Now, when you answer their questions, keep your responses simple. Answer only what is asked. Do not volunteer. But tell the whole truth. KGB has legitimate questions, and KGB will get its answers." He smiled, letting his words soak in.

"I always answer truthfully to KGB."

"We all do. That's why we're where we are. But know this, Colonel, these men are not your friends. They are not my friends. But they do represent Premier Khrushchev himself, just like you do, or I do."

"Yes."

Another dip of the finger. "Anchev was expelled from London. You were promoted to take his place."

"It was sudden and unexpected," Nikolai said.

"It raises questions. Because it moved you from deputy to *rezident*, my question is, did London want you to be *rezident* instead of Anchev? Is that why they expelled him?"

"You're only just now asking this?"

"It has been discussed previously. I will ask again, why did London expel General Anchev?"

"You would have to ask London."

"General Barishsky will be asking you. Prepare your answer. Everything depends on your answer to this, Colonel."

Nikolai tested the water. "Anchev expelled? He behaved too much like a KGB man. There was no Savile Row about him."

"Savile Row?"

Nikolai found it difficult with Masirov, where it had never been difficult before. "You know," he said, "when in Rome..."

"He wasn't British enough?"

"Wouldn't you have tried?" asked Nikolai.

The man was playing stupid. KGB was way brighter than this. Too many questions were meant to mislead, to distract from what they really wanted to know.

Without explanation, Masirov then returned Nikolai to his own office, a cubicle.

Nothing happened the rest of that day. Or the next. Still, he refined the notes he had brought with him about Britain's economy, politics, key figures, and relations with America. Anything to eat up the time crawling by while he awaited his summons.

47

He knocked and asked the next-door neighbor for help with Sasha that night, then took his mother for dinner.

"How did my father do it?"

He was preparing to leave Russia. Dinner was his way of saying goodbye.

"Do what, Nikolaevich?"

"How did he live with himself, doing the things they made him do?"

"Are you finding it difficult, a KGB officer's life?"

"No—yes, very difficult. There is guilt, mother."

"Of course." She was a very bright woman, at one time a KGB officer herself who had retired to have her children. She was also a graduate of Moscow University with an advanced degree in linguistics. She appeared thoughtful, deciding her answer about his father's guilt. He already respected the answer she hadn't yet given.

"Your father learned early on that despite Party loyalty, guilt was a fact of KGB life, unrelieved by State hero medals. In the world of the KGB, rituals for the relief of guilt don't exist. Votives and robes and incense are for other people. So, for Borya Anton Semenov, his absolution was found in the Kubanskaya vodka he swilled at night after you children were asleep."

"God, how desperate."

She cocked her head. "Not really. Most of the time, he enjoyed the KGB. It was only sometimes."

"I remember some of it. At times, there were raised voices."

"Very rarely. But, yes, I knew his burden. It was part of the reason I started a family. Maybe I was too weak to be an officer any longer." She laughed and jabbed at her potatoes. They were undercooked, and neither continued with them after one bite.

"Maybe you weren't too weak to continue as an officer, Mother. Maybe you were too strong?"

She waggled a finger. "The refrigerator made ice, and the radio played Russian music. Benefits of the KGB officer. So, I survived his guilt with him. But the real question is, how does Nikolai handle *his* guilt?"

Nikolai swept his gaze around the nearby faces. He decided it was safe to tell her. "I took my guilt and released it with the secrets I turned over to MI5. I appeased my monster, Mother."

She stopped talking, stopped eating, too, and sat in the booth across from him, looking down at her hands folded in her lap.

When they rode the bus home together, she didn't speak then, either. Nor did she speak at the flat when she went into Sasha's room and shut the door.

She was a top officer, he realized as he read to Sasha before bedtime. It was the first time he'd understood that about her.

48

The next morning, he took a taxi to Moscow Center. His mother and Sasha were still safely tucked away in bed. There were no rearview mirrors in the back seat, and he wasn't about to turn and look, so he had no idea about any surveillance or lack thereof. But he knew he'd be ignorant as hell to assume there was no watcher. He was like a lamb on its way to the abattoir.

Head of the Third Department, Luka Solinov, met him. He seemed nervous and jerky, even for Solinov, almost out of sorts. He went out of his way to welcome Nikolai and induce him to relax and enjoy his moment of pride at being appointed *rezident* of KGB London. Solinov couldn't stop exclaiming about it, feigning the pride he felt for Nikolai. When they were seated in Solinov's office, his entire demeanor changed. Solinov became deadly serious.

"Kennedy just threatened the Russian navy."

"I hadn't heard."

"Yes, he's been emboldened to interfere with our Premier."

"I didn't know."

"You were in Washington," Solinov said slyly. "You didn't happen to meet with Kennedy perchance?"

"Isn't that outside your job description to ask that?"

Solinov blushed. "It is. I'm only trying to prepare you for in there."

"Well done, then."

An hour later, he was summoned to the office of Viktor Masirov, now deputy head of the First Chief Directorate.

He jogged down one hallway, up one floor of the KGB Moscow building, to Masirov's office. He wasn't breathing hard when he walked in and found Masirov discussing a yellow telegram with his secretary. Masirov turned and gave him a stern look. "We won't be here. We'll be moving to another site. Go back and get your coat."

Nikolai returned to his cubicle and slipped into his overcoat without the liner. Then back upstairs. Masirov's title—gold letters on his door—was impressive, and his direction for Nikolai to get his coat was frightening. Why would they need to leave the building for a conversation? He ran it through his mind and could only come up with one answer: noise. There was going to be pain associated with the meeting, and the bosses didn't want the noise filtering into the KGB offices. Nikolai faltered. He wanted to dig in his heels and remind Masirov he was desperately needed in London. But he did not. It was an order, and he had to obey, so he followed Masirov downstairs to the black KGB Moskvich-402.

They drove less than two kilometers to a multistory building built in an L shape. He had never been there before but was aware it existed for use by visitors of the First Chief Directorate. They parked beneath an overhang. It was blustery, freezing outside for October. Nikolai looked up at the sky, taking in the dodging sun for what, he was terrified, might be the last time. Immediate regret for spying on his own people spilled over into his thoughts, and he loathed what he had done, the ultimate jeopardy to which he had subjected Yulia, yes, but mostly little Sasha. His precious child was in no way responsible for what her overreaching father had done, but she could very well end up paying the price as the sins of the father were visited on the child like never before.

A chain-link fence protected the compound but nothing else. Nothing else but Moscow stretching for twenty kilometers in every direction. There would be no running away, no chance for escape. He drew a deep breath and followed Masirov inside.

The furniture was dark, ponderous, and the walls were stained where moisture had seeped. There was but one long central room with a long table and nothing on the walls. A bank of fluorescent lights lit the tabletop, lending a bluish tint to the room. Two lesser agents, two men, stood obsequiously to the side. They nodded at Masirov and ignored Nikolai. Masirov told the older of the two he would have sandwiches and Armenian brandy.

"So," Masirov began and then sorrowfully shook his head. "This is a dark day for us, Nikolai Semenov. A sorrowful moment."

Nikolai had no answer to that. He drew a deep breath, trying to avoid hyperventilation, which took all of his concentration. At that moment, he wanted only to jump up and run, but run where? Outside was only Russia and more Russia and more. He looked at his surroundings, trying to get a feel for what might happen in such a place as this. There were no obvious signs of torture devices or tools to be used against him. But that could be in another room or even another building. He had no idea, and he was panicked.

Masirov spoke again, "We have heard things. We will need answers from you. Do you feel you are ready to cooperate like a proper KGB officer?"

"I'm ready. I will help you any way I can. I only want to help and then return to London and make the KGB proud of its son."

"That is commendable. We will keep that in mind."

The servants brought plates of sandwiches and one bottle of Shakmat. Nikolai knew the drink well. It was over twenty years old and costly. No expense was to be spared. But why?

They drank a double shot of brandy.

"Winston Churchill drank only Armenian brandy," Masirov offered.

Then two other men arrived. Nikolai knew Bucharov as soon as he entered. He was the more robust one, the one who made eye contact coming in, the postcard KGB officer with the steely eyes and ice water in his veins—that one.

"We officially meet, Colonel Semenov," Bucharov said, "officially." Bucharov had been following Nikolai over the last month.

"Yes," said Nikolai. "I would know you anywhere."

Bucharov's dead-pan expression didn't change. "So you would." He gave Nikolai a sinister glare that said it didn't matter how Nikolai danced around the ring and tried to defend himself; it wouldn't change what was about to happen.

The older man wasn't smiling. "You have met me. Let me refresh you. I am General Barishsky, GRU. My job is to interrogate rogue intelligence officers. Are you one of those, Semenov? Have you crossed over since I let you go to London?"

Nikolai swallowed hard, wanting to shout out that he wasn't a rogue officer. Instead, he said calmly, "I am a loyal KGB officer. I am ready for your questions, General." His training as a toughened KGB officer kicked in, and now he was upset with himself for weakening. He was frightened, but his training required him to fight back against it, to ward off his fear and overcome. This hour was an exercise to see if they could break him. He resolved he would not let that happen. He also had on his person the pills Emma Magnuson had given him. When the others weren't speaking to him or looking to him, he removed one of two pills from his shirt pocket and popped it into his mouth. He swallowed hard.

All right, he thought, *let's get to the questions.*

The senior questioner, wearing a rumpled blue suit, looked to be sixty, ten years older now. His face was lined and gray, showing the apparent effects of too much smoke and drink. Still, his eyes did not meet Nikolai's, so no chance to take his emotional temperature.

Masirov, shuffling his feet and looking sorely uncomfortable, said, "These men want to talk about London in preparation for your new job there. But first, let's have lunch. We'll have another drink together before we eat."

The servant poured more brandies. Nikolai watched as the bottle came around to him. The servant turned it on end to serve, but it was empty. He left the room and returned with another bottle and served Nikolai.

Nikolai drank the brandy straight down. In a matter of seconds, the old Nikolai was gone, and someone new occupied his chair. Someone still calling himself Nikolai. But he was transformed.

* * *

Dimly, he heard one of them saying, "Remember one thing. We've got irrefutable evidence of your guilt. We know you are a British agent. You'd better confess. *Priznaysya!* Confess!" Then there was a pause. He remembered Barishsky went out and then reappeared. His movements all seemed abrupt, but probably because Nikolai was half asleep. *"Priznaysya!"* he repeated hypnotically. "Confess!"

Bucharov was colder, more measured. He didn't yell or pound the table. "You confessed very well a few minutes ago. Now please go through it again and confirm what you said."

"Confess again?"

"Yes," Bucharov said. "Then, we can sign a paper and go to sleep."

Bucharov was talking slowly and emphatically, as if to a child who forgets what he heard five minutes ago.

Nikolai kept saying, "No, I've nothing to confess. I've done nothing."

And so it went on. Reconstructing events after, Nikolai guessed that the interrogation lasted more than one day. At one stage, he went to the bathroom where he might have been sick. As he went, he saw the two servants staring at him most unpleasantly. Later, he heard that he made several visits to the bathroom and drank large quantities of water. The interrogators concluded that he had been trained by the British in techniques of combating drugs and was trying to clear the poison out of his system. But really, he just had a great thirst.

On the other hand, it might well have been the single British pep-pill he had taken that morning, which had helped him hold out as well as he did. That was about all he could remember, yet the key question was unanswered: had he or had he not given himself away irrevocably? He could not tell what the KGB had or had not found out, but it was clear that he was, in effect, under sentence of death, even if that sentence was suspended pending further investigations.

It took days to recover from the drug he'd been given.

But when he did, he understood Barishsky's bottom line: they did not have proof positive about him or he would have been dead.

And, so far, he was still very much alive.

49

Which was the time Henry Stoner went for broke. The KGB had offered him one million dollars in cash for the names of all spies against the Soviet Union. Stoner took the bait and made a list. Stoner had decided to turn over all Soviet spies as a defensive matter as well so they couldn't expose him first. They would know from the inside, at some point, that he was the leak the Soviets had developed and paid. He wanted the Soviets to clean them out and execute them all before they had his name. It was all about protection for him. Protection and the matter of one million dollars.

On 12 October 1962, Stoner made his move. That afternoon, he met Sergey Nikintov in Chadwick's, a popular Georgetown restaurant. He handed him a briefcase stuffed with MI5 intelligence, classified cables, reports, and the names of twenty-five Soviet spies working for the United States. And one working for the UK. He had referred to this spy in their earlier meeting. But this time, he had a name. MI5 referred to him as ULYSSES, but Stoner didn't stop there. He opened the McCone memo listing the name. "Your British spy is named Nikolai Semenov. He is the new *rezident* of KGB London."

The intelligence was in Moscow's hands one hour later. All of it, including the name of Nikolai Semenov. The message was referred to General Barishsky. *Here is your smoking gun,* the memo said to him.

They sent a car for Nikolai.

General Barishsky had the Stoner evidence face-up on his desk. He showed Nikolai the report. Nikolai read slowly, then looked up.

"Well," said Barishsky, "I will keep it short. You will return to London as *rezident*. You are a smart, smart man. You already know what comes next."

"I'm to spy for the KGB while MI5 believes I'm helping them."

"I have people outside your house at this moment. If you refuse me this, your mother dies. Then your daughter dies."

"And if I agree to spy for you?"

Barishsky smiled and turned the report face down. "Then you go to London and little Sasha stays here with the State. She will remain in a State orphanage until she is old enough to go to school. She will be sent to a top private school and receive the best education Russia has to offer. Same for middle school and college. After college, she can rejoin you in London if she wishes, for we shall be finished with you."

"And if I refuse?"

Masirov reached for his phone and lifted it, ready to dial. "Don't dare me."

"I am your spy in London."

"Tell her goodbye. You won't see her again until she's a young woman, a graduate of Moscow University."

Nikolai's eyes filled with tears, overflowing down his cheeks. "I understand."

"You will be the best spy we've ever run."

"I know I will. Thank you."

"Now listen closely. You have hurt your country irreparably. You have given me a mess right in my lap. I have to clean up after you. You're going on a special assignment for one week. You will be posted to a dacha. You are directed to write out your history up to when you began spying for Britain and all the years while working for the MI5. We are going to need to track down every agent you've jeopardized and bring them home. We'll have to do the same with every military installation you have compromised. Every politician, every business. Your contamination is endless. But now you are ordered to write it all down so we know where to begin."

Nikolai looked at the tabletop. At one time, he had told the English he wouldn't reveal the names of KGB officers. But even that wall had come down.

He shuddered to think about the coming deaths because he was a traitor. "I will write down everything. I will do whatever I can to save lives."

Barishsky sat back and pushed his glasses to his forehead. He rubbed his eyes with his fingers. "No one survives this in the end. Carry that with you every day."

"I will, General."

"Now write down your time in London. Tell us what you have done and said. Tell us how our people will die because of you."

"Yes, General."

"Now leave my sight. I cannot stand you another minute."

"Yes, General."

He waved a hand at the door. "Now. Leave. We are finished."

50

His mother again stepped up and said she would stay with Sasha. "You are an angel," he told her. She smiled and shooed him away. They were okay again. Then he left.

The dacha was remote, fenced all around, a forest north of Moscow in the mountains. The country house itself was one of four, set in a glade and backed by a pine forest. The skies were blue, the songbirds filled the grasses and trees, and he felt very welcome there. Inside the house, it was rustic but well-furnished with comfortable couches and beds, a well-stocked kitchen fit for a special guest, all of which made him feel he was receiving special treatment because of his KGB station—not a reward, never that in any sense.

He looked around the six bedrooms, found one with good afternoon light for writing, and moved his duffel in here. He removed what few items of clothing he'd brought and put those into drawers. He laid out his writing tablet and pens and moved a desk lamp from another room onto his desk to write at night. He was determined to reform himself, tell what he'd done, and undo as much damage as possible. His new shame was boundless, and his guilt was overwhelming. He regretted every secret, every word he'd ever given to the British. *Lord,* he thought, *if I can only save lives, even one, it's a beginning.*

His first night alone, a dread arose inside of him, unlike anything he'd ever felt. Sasha. Young. Beautiful. Innocent. What he dreaded was how she would be treated after this. She would be an outcast and never get a good job, education, or any semblance of autonomy. Nikolai didn't believe a word the general had promised about Sasha. She would become dependent on Carolina and Maxim for everything, even as an adult. He had seen it too many times. Nikolai paced the floor all night, wrestling with his devils. When the sun came up, and he was drained, he had moved beyond brokenness. It was a new, slow death he was marching toward. Hereafter, he was serving time.

He made coffee, sat down, rolled up his sleeves, and then put pen to paper on the kitchen table where he had cleared a space to write. They had supplied yellow pads and ballpoint pens, which were a luxury at that time. So he felt amply provided for. Then he began thinking back to his first posting in Britain. He remembered it like yesterday. He remembered their arrival in London, the shock of seeing the West for the first time. Had he crossed a line during that first posting?

He wrote: *I was recruited by a British MI5 agent named Jason Donovan. He was assisted by Franklin Bolling, Charles Lightner, Emma Magnuson...*

Then he stopped mid-sentence and read what he'd written. He read it a second time.

He couldn't do it. Those people trusted him, and he was going to betray them, maybe get them killed? But on the other hand, what about Sasha? If he didn't divulge, they would kill him and Sasha, too.

He was stuck.

He shut his eyes, and he thought. He'd seen a movie once, a Russian Jew escaping across two-thousand miles of the frozen Siberian tundra. The images flashed in his mind, the running, the pitting oneself against every conceivable odd to escape. Yet, the Russian Jew, dressed only in a light coat and without food and fire, struggled to freedom. How could Nikolai do any less? How could he sentence his baby girl to damnation? Wasn't a run across the tundra with her father the better choice?

He tore the first page from his pad and set it ablaze with matches from the kitchen. Then he opened the front door and sprinkled the ashes into the breeze.

A new page was begun. He was going to find out how creative he was.

The next day, a roommate came to stay with him at the dacha, clearly put there to keep an eye on him. In his mid-sixties, he was a pensioner, very active and orthodox in his ideas, who tried to follow Nikolai everywhere before he tired of that restless occupation. He put in a bad report on Nikolai for sitting on the balcony and listening through headphones to foreign stations on his shortwave radio, but Nikolai was past caring by that stage. Little did the KGB know that the BBC's World Service Programme Outlook nearly made him cry with nostalgia. The good old English tunes they played represented a world he might never see again.

Three days later, he was finished with his testimony. Eleven pages of lies, falsehoods, and fabrications. He had invented an entire world of imaginary people, places, secrets, and meetings. He had created precisely what Barishsky and Masirov and Bucharov wanted to hear—action items that could be addressed. He would turn it into them and feign good faith and fair dealing. He would tell them he hadn't left anything out. The parts about Soviet shipments of soldiers into East Germany, the planting of KGB spies in Poland, France, Germany, and Scandinavia, the strength of the Soviets' nuclear arsenal on the fringes of Eastern Europe, Soviet plans for economic interruption of the West's booming Capitalist take over—all of it was made up, put down on paper and populated with will-o'-the-wisps and ghosts. He would solemnly turn it in and go home.

Then he would run.

For the second half of his stay, the pensioner was replaced by a lieutenant colonel of the Border Troops, Mikhail Mashky, a typical Soviet officer whose aim in coming to the dacha was to drink and pick up a woman, at both of which he succeeded. In some ways, he was an attractive character and talked openly about his problems. He also told Nikolai a good deal about borders and frontier defenses, in which Nikolai had a rapidly growing interest.

"Where do the Border Troops get their uniforms?" Nikolai casually asked the lieutenant while the man was knee-walking drunk.

"Where?" The man wrote in the air with one hand, trying to remember. "Ah, yes, Sergey's Uniforms on Lenin Prospekt just off Red Square. We all get our uniforms there."

While the man was off wooing some woman or other at night, Nikolai studied his Border Troops' uniform. He noted insignia, the name tag, the collar, and ribbons. He even took a picture with his tourist camera.

One day, the lieutenant colonel told Nikolai that he found it hard to believe what the Soviet propaganda claimed about spies and infiltrators who were continually trying to violate the country's borders and penetrate the frontiers from outside. "That's not true," he said. "I work there. All the border defenses must be against something else. What do you reckon it is?"

Nikolai said, "Well, it's to stop Soviet people trying to flee to the West."

Then he told Nikolai about the woman he had picked up, and she, too, was an interesting character. She worked in the KGB watching department in Novosibirsk, spying on people through peepholes and hidden television cameras. When he had asked her if that wasn't rather amusing, she replied, "Not at all. I spend my life watching wild, raw sex, violence, drunks beating up their mistresses, and so on. It's all incredibly depressing."

One night, the lieutenant colonel asked Nikolai for money. It turned out he had spent all he arrived with on the woman of his dreams.

"How much do you need?" Nikolai asked.

"Enough to make her crazy with love," the lieutenant colonel replied, for he had started drinking early that afternoon and was feeling no pain when they talked.

"Would that be one-thousand rubles?"

The lieutenant colonel's eyes widened like bottle caps.

"But how would you pay me back?" Nikolai wanted to know. "You can't earn that much in a month."

The lieutenant colonel's face fell. He didn't have a way to repay.

"I know what," Nikolai said suddenly with a snap of his fingers. "Sell me your Border Troops uniform, ribbon and medals and all of it."

"Really? Would you pay me for my uniform? How much are we talking about?" While the lieutenant colonel was hidebound in some areas—believing, for instance, that shortages of material goods crippled America, that life there was as difficult as in Russia—he also had a streak of capitalism when it came to his property.

In the end, Nikolai paid one-thousand rubles and now owned a reasonably new official Border Troops uniform.

Standing between bookcases in the dacha library where no one could see him, Nikolai secretly studied maps of the Soviet Union and Finland's border area. Now his study of the Soviet-Finnish border was more inspired than ever.

Outside, the weather remained cold without freezing, sunny and dry. Nikolai enjoyed jogging through the woods, where several times, he spotted surveillance men hastily pretending to urinate into the undergrowth as he appeared. Twice he walked the ten kilometers to the railway station, partly to increase his fitness in case he had to make a long trek during his escape.

He returned to Moscow with his testimony. Masirov collected it and turned it over to General Barishsky. One day later, Lieutenant General Masirov told him the history was accepted. "Now, you may leave for London."

"And Sasha?"

"Really? Do we have to discuss the daughter again?"

"I'm begging this time. I promise immense loyalty. Only let her come along with me."

"She has already been removed to her new home. Now get out!"

51

He left Barishsky and drove home at breakneck speed, terrified for Sasha. He let himself inside his apartment, only to find his mother sitting alone on the sofa, weeping.

"They were just here. They took our Sasha!" She could scarcely get the words out between sobs.

An icicle pierced his heart. "Say that again?"

"KGB knocked. I was in the kitchen cleaning up after our little meal. I was putting plates away when I heard them. I went to the door and pulled it open. Two KGB men swooped in without a word and muscled past me. 'She's in the bedroom,' one man said. They went to the bedroom and returned with Sasha. He held her under his arm like a sack of potatoes. Poor Sasha! She was crying and screaming to be put down, but they didn't. Instead, they pushed by me because I was trying to block the door. One of them put his hand on my chest and shoved me out of the way. 'Don't ever get in our way again.'

"'Where are you taking her?' I cried. I knew I had to get some idea of where she would be taken. I knew I needed something to tell you, Nikolai. Oh, my God, I am so *so* sorry!"

He was in shock and couldn't speak. His mind had shut off, and now he was trying to swim through the mire, swim toward the light of logic and action. "Where does KGB take children? Who do we ask?"

"Let me call a friend. Her son works for the oblast." She dialed the phone. "Hello?" She held the handset out from her ear so Nikolai could hear what the friend said. "One question, Annalisa. KGB came here and kidnapped my only granddaughter away."

"No!"

"Oh, yes. I was hoping you could tell me where KGB takes children they take away from home. Can you ask Nazik?"

Annalisa called out to her son, repeated the question, then said to Nikolai's mother, "To Moscow Oblast Family and Child Protection Service. It is located on Popov Boulevard."

Nikolai shouted at the phone, "Nazik, how do I get into this place and get her out?"

On the other end, Nazik picked up the phone and spoke. "Sure, that's the question—armed guards at the door, armed guards at the gate. I'm sorry to report that I have taken children there before. There is no way in and out without written orders from the judge."

"I need a court order?"

"You will find out they had a court order to get Sasha away from you."

"That makes no sense. But I must trust what you say. All right. You have no ideas for me?"

"I'll be thinking about it. I'll call back if I think of something."

"Thank you, Nazik."

His mother replaced the handset in its cradle and looked at Nikolai. He held up a hand, indicating she should let him finish his thoughts.

He wrote on the notepad used for private talks. *I have to get inside. There has to be a way.*

His mother wrote, *You could watch to see who drives in and out of the gate. When they come out, follow and steal their vehicle and go back yourself.*

"KGB knows best," he said for the benefit of the electronic ears listening to their every word. "I can only leave it alone."

She understood why he was talking like that. "The Party is always right. Maybe you can visit her there. With permission."

"All right, then. I have been ordered to London by General Masirov. I need to pack my clothes and things."

"Will Sasha be going to London with you?"

"No, she will stay here. KGB is going to take excellent care of her. I'm very pleased."

She didn't hesitate. "I'm sorry, Nikolai, but the Party is right."

"It will be difficult, but life always is. First comes duty. She will remain here, and I will try to visit. Eventually, they will let me. Thank you for watching her while I was away on business," he told her. "It's time for you to return home. The bus comes in thirty minutes downstairs."

"I'm already packed." She leaned in and kissed his cheek. "Goodbye," she whispered and left with her suitcase.

He shut the door behind her and looked around the room. He wouldn't say another word after that. He could only hope that his feeble attempt at convincing them he was acquiescent would work.

52

The ULYSSES team was on high alert in London.

"Whatever has happened?" Charles Lightner asked at a short meeting.

"No news isn't good news," Bolling said. "If all were well, he would have let us know. If all were bad, he couldn't let us know. I'm apprehensive we've lost him, team."

Emma Magnuson wasn't so sure he was lost. Of all the team members, Magnuson tended to be the most optimistic at such times as this. "There's also the possibility all is well. Maybe he's back at work or in training, and they're watching him too closely, so he hasn't been able to signal."

Jason Donovan stood and stuffed his hands into his jacket pockets. He walked to the windows and looked down on the sidewalk in front of River House. "Here's what I think. I think we have Moscow Station contact him somehow."

"How would we do that?" Lightner asked.

Donovan shook his head. "Not sure. Ideas? Anyone?"

"Do we know he hasn't signaled he's in trouble?" said Bolling, one of Nikolai's handlers. "I've been reading and re-reading every document and call memos and pouch contents from Moscow. What about illegals?"

"No one's seen anything," Donovan said. "At least not that I've been told."

Cummings finally spoke up. "I've sent an urgent cable to MI6 Moscow and instructed them to be on the highest lookout for the activation of Operation TINKER. But I'm very doubtful. I can instruct them all I want, but if there is nothing from Nikolai, the highest alerts in the world are meaningless."

A pall of pessimism settled over the team. Meanwhile, on the world stage, Kennedy had just steamed for the Russian fleet 500 miles from Havana. The world was on the verge of all-out nuclear war. Which was when MI5 received a cable from CIA Washington. The cable was short and sweet. "Overseer needs to talk with ULYSSES. Request an immediate call." The "Overseer" was President Kennedy himself, needing additional information from Nikolai.

Randall Cummings said to cable back that ULYSSES would call.

"How's that?" asked Donovan. "KGB has him under constant surveillance. The odds of him shaking free and making a phone call on a secure line are non-existent. We need him the hell out of Russia."

"Agree," Cummings said through gritted teeth. "We're going to get him the hell out of Russia. Then he's going to get Kennedy on the phone and save this world before it blows itself apart. That's an order!"

53

Roy Longfellow, a distant relative of Henry Wadsworth Longfellow, the American poet, was MI6 station chief in Moscow. Bluer blood never flowed through English veins—the monarchy excepted. He received the cable from MI5 London and immediately dropped what he was doing. The President of the United States needed a word with Nikolai Semenov. Kennedy's next chess move in the Cuban Missile Crisis depended on a missing piece from Kennedy's chessboard. Semenov held that piece.

Longfellow also understood the problem. Semenov had been removed from the streets. No one had a clue about how to make contact. He was gone, kaput. Longfellow called his second, Rodney Mallard, into his office mid-morning, minutes after the cable arrived. Mallard was an experienced officer who was soon due to take over from Longfellow as head of the station. Everyone agreed he was the best field agent in Russia.

"We must remove Semenov from Russia. President Kennedy must talk to him. There is no failure possible."

"TINKER, then. It's all we have."

Thirty minutes later, Longfellow received a call from MI6 London from the Director. He was to meet with his staff and rehearse TINKER immediately.

"TINKER is at level four. Full rehearsal is ordered. This means the signal could come at any minute. Pass the most recent full face to the team," Longfellow ordered Mallard. They needed the most recent headshot. "We start full rehearsal on my call."

"Photographs were updated as of six this morning. ULYSSES was in there. But it's grainy as hell. It could be anyone in the snap."

Longfellow and Mallard reviewed TINKER top to bottom.

For two years, now, the Longfellows—the chief and his wife, Sue Ellen—had traveled by car and ferry from Moscow to Tallinn to Helsinki several times to familiarize themselves with the escape route rendezvous point. Each time, they shook their heads in fear the plan would ever conclude with a happy ending.

"I'm torched, Rodney," Longfellow said, collapsing into his executive chair behind his desk. "There's no way a car with diplomatic plates will leave Moscow without KGB escort."

"Agreed," said Mallard. "Arriving without surveillance at the rendezvous point is laughable."

"But no one's laughing. It's a bitter pill to see that TINKER is the best London can do. The several times Sue Ellen and I practiced the trip, she egged me on to improve on the plan. Honestly? I couldn't come up with any alternatives. Fleeing Moscow, where KGB agents smother the city, is all but impossible. If I knew of a better way, I would've flown it. As it is...zero. I've got zero to offer."

Just six people in Moscow knew of the escape plan: Longfellow and his wife; his deputy, Rodney Mallard and his wife, Cindy; Nikolai; and the MI6 secretary, Missy Anders. The six MI6 staff lived in the expatriate compound on Diruvsky Prospekt. Every month, one of the officers headed off to the Red Square and Saint Basil's. When Nikolai was in Moscow, the chapel was checked twice each day for the hymnal. Whether in snow up to their hips or pouring rain or a bright and sunny evening, failure wasn't an option. They monitored the cathedral, looking for the signal day and night.

As it turned out, Cindy could leave their flat, walk to the corner, and peek around north to see Saint Basil's and the people passing by. Sometimes she would walk there and check. Longfellow and Mallard usually manned their turns in driving home, always going past the landmark and keeping the same routes for the KGB following behind. Sometimes they broke it up by entering the church and taking pictures. It was known by the bugs inside Longfellow's flat that Sue Ellen's mother painted religious paintings. She wanted interior photographs of Saint Basil's.

Still, whenever Sue Ellen went out shopping, she had a three-car convoy of KGB cars following close behind, so close the targets understood the KGB didn't care whether they were noticed or not. The job was going to get done, and secrecy be damned.

Nikolai would signal with the hymnal, and the team would acknowledge by calling his Soviet number and leave a message that Somerset Maugham had called.

"It's a complex plan," Longfellow said to Mallard, "and full of holes. I see failure nine times out of ten."

"Likewise," Mallard told him. "Why not just disguise and paper him and fly him out on British Airlines? Wouldn't that be simpler?"

"Could very well be," Longfellow had to admit. "Maybe they've passed on that plan for some reason. For once, I'm glad I'm not in the driver's seat on this one. I don't see a happy ending at all."

"What about the vehicle search at the Tallinn ferry? Are they sure the Border Troops won't demand an open trunk? What then? Take him out and shoot him? It sickens me to think."

"It calls for the exfiltration of his child, too, not just ULYSSES the spy. He's bringing his young daughter, just two years old. How will a kid behave when stuffed in the trunk of a car? It's going to be horrifying for her. She's likely to cry out at any moment, drugged or not."

Mallard shook his head. "The KGB is all over us. When I evacuate my bladder, they know the ounces."

"Diplomats, diplomatic cars, all of it bugged."

The garage doing the maintenance on embassy automobiles was a KGB front. "No vehicle left unbugged" was the joke around the embassy when cars were checked out on business. It was true. You just didn't talk in the car except maybe to call a stop for lunch or to share directions to some destination. Otherwise, nothing else got said. The vehicles of suspected MI6 officers were sprayed with the same radioactive dust put on Nikolai's clothes and shoes. Additionally, there was a chemical odor the KGB German shepherds were trained to sniff out. So each MI6 officer kept two pairs of shoes, one for everyday wear and one for secret missions.

Longfellow and Mallard sat and stared out the embassy's top floor windows opening onto the Moscow streets below. Nothing was said. They were helpless and could only wait for Nikolai's signal.

54

Nikolai locked himself in the bathroom with *A Tale of Two Cities*. He thought of those two cities as London and Moscow. And what a tale it was.

He slit open the specially bound novel, brought out the sheet bearing the copy of his exfiltration plan, and studied it. The document would have meant little to anyone else, for it appeared to refer to places in France, but it contained detailed instructions for reaching the rendezvous in the city of Tallinn on the border between Estonia and Finland. The distances were all real. For security, the names of French towns had been substituted for Russian originals—Paris for Moscow, Marseilles for Leningrad, and so on.

He read the escape plan for the last time in the bathroom then struck a match. He watched the cellophane sheet flare up with an acrid flash before he flushed it down the toilet. Then he went into the kitchen and poured himself a half glass of vodka. He drank it straight down, then poured the rest of what was in the bottle into the sink. He washed it out with cold water, then splashed water into his eyes and drew a deep breath. "So. I'm ready."

The telephone rang. It was Yulia's father, Jana Valerov, the retired KGB general.

"Nikolai! It's Yulia's old man, the man who's going to inherit you one million rubles!"

"We can wait on that," Nikolai chided back, "no rush."

"Come for supper at seven tonight," said Valerov. "I'll cook a nice chicken in garlic."

Nikolai thought fast. The invitation for 7 p.m. clashed with the escape preparation. The KGB eavesdroppers listening in on the bugged telephone would be suspicious if he turned it down. If he accepted, they would be expecting him at his father-in-law's home at Davitkova on the city outskirts at the very moment when, with luck, he would be free of surveillance. "Thank you," he said, "I'll look forward to it."

The phone rang again. It was Mikhail Mashky, urging him to come and stay at his dacha for a few days the following week. Nikolai, again thinking quickly, accepted the invitation. He would come on next Tuesday, he said, catch the train arriving at Zvenigorod at 11:13 p.m., and travel in the last carriage. On the notebook by his telephone, he wrote, *Zvenigorod 11:13*. Here was another false trail for the KGB.

Nikolai wanted to look smart for his rendezvous with MI6, even if the KGB was waiting. He dressed in suit and tie, put on shoes that were probably radioactive, and picked up his English leather cap. At the last minute, he took along his Border Troops uniform in a Tesco shopping bag.

He walked two blocks and withdrew money. There were no ordinary banks in Moscow, only primitive savings banks, and he knew that the most he could draw from his account without attracting notice was three hundred rubles. He intended to leave most of this for his mother. Eighty rubles would be plenty for his train ticket, a couple of taxis, and meals during his journey. At the end of it, rubles would be of no further use to him. He would either be out of the Soviet Union or dead.

He walked two kilometers to the row of shops closest to home, taking care never to look behind for the agents trailing him. He stepped inside a dry cleaner and stood at the front window, watching. He saw no other eyes. Upstairs he went on an interior stairway to a real estate office. Now he had a view of the street below. Then he ducked into a busy food shop where he walked along in a line. The employees assembled a sandwich while he watched from the other side of the counter. After ducking down a rear stairway, he ran down two alleyways and into a public restroom. He went inside and waited in a stall for a full hour. Then he exited the building and hailed a taxi. He had the driver make a U-turn while he watched behind for the same maneuver—the classic moment when a spy knows whether he's been successful at his dry-cleaning. At Teatralnaya, he boarded a Metro train, jumped off at the first lurch forward, and jumped onto a train heading opposite. He exited that car and ran to the farthest carriage where he re-entered the station. He jogged up the stairs, and once on the street, hailed a taxi to Red Square and Saint Basil's.

Once there, he darted inside the cathedral and removed a hymnal from the back of the first pew. He went forward and placed the book beneath the open bible on the lectern. Then he ducked out a side door and hurried to the cover of a bus stop.

It was Rodney Mallard's turn to monitor the signal site since Roy and Sue Ellen Longfellow were going out to an embassy party with a Russian acquaintance, a former diplomat. As they pulled onto Diruvsky Prospekt in their embassy car and headed east, a surveillance car slotted in behind as usual. It was easy to spot the KGB vehicles since the brushes of the KGB carwash, for reasons unknown, could not quite reach a spot in the middle of the hood, so each car had a telltale triangle of dirt on the front. Longfellow glanced across the wide avenue and froze. A man resembling Nikolai's grainy picture was entering Saint Basil's. The time was 6:40. Nikolai's instructions were to leave immediately after placing the hymnal.

Rodney's missed him, thought Longfellow, swearing under his breath. His heart went straight to his toes. He poked Sue Ellen in the ribs, pointed across the road, and drew on the dashboard the letter T for TINKER. Sue Ellen resisted the urge to swivel in her seat and stare; she knew exactly what he meant.

Longfellow had ten seconds to decide if he should swing the car around and go inside the church, but the KGB was already tight on his bumper, and any change of behavior would instantly arouse suspicion. The KGB would know, from bugging the telephone, that they were going out to a dinner party, and suddenly performing a U-turn, jumping out of the car, and running into the cathedral would lead the KGB straight to TINKER. He drove on, feeling as if the world had fallen in, and he had done the wrong thing for the right reasons.

The party was hellish. Their host was an unreconstructed Communist apparatchik who spent the whole meal talking about how great Stalin was. All Longfellow could think about was the spy waiting for a call from Somerset Maugham. He was unaware, of course, that Nikolai no longer even visited that office.

While Longfellow had driven east on Diruvsky, Rodney Mallard passed the cathedral in his Peugeot, slowed a little, and scanned the sidewalk. There seemed to be lots of people milling around, noticeably more than usual for a weekday evening. And there, on the edge of the sidewalk, he was almost certain, was a man wearing a peaked cap like the man in the picture. The man had hurried inside the cathedral.

Mallard drove home, adrenaline racing, made a U-turn at the end of the avenue, entered the compound, and parked in the garage. Trying to appear unhurried, he took the elevator to the flat, dropped his briefcase, and loudly called to Cindy, "I need to see our priest." She immediately knew what was happening.

The elevator took an eternity. He walked to the cathedral, fighting the urge to run. The man had gone. He wondered if he would recognize him anyway since he had only ever seen one grainy photograph of ULYSSES that morning.

"I was so convinced I had seen someone," Mallard recalled later. He queued at the chemist's, keeping one eye on the street, which seemed even more crowded than before. Mallard decided to make another pass by the cathedral then go inside. That's when he saw him. A man of about 6'1 around 80 kilograms, held a Tesco bag on the sidewalk near a bus stop outside Saint Basil's. He appeared to be enjoying the light breeze and a cigar.

Nikolai spotted Mallard at the same moment. On the point of leaving, he had drawn back from the sidewalk edge. It was the man's demeanor. To Nikolai's hungry eyes, the man walking toward him, whistling, looked wholly, unmistakably, British.

Their eyes locked for less than a second. Nikolai heard himself silently shout at the top of his voice, "Yes! It's me!" Mallard took another deliberate step then turned inside the cathedral. He found the hymnal on the pulpit just minutes later and came back outside. The man had vanished.

General Valerov was annoyed when Nikolai finally arrived at his flat, sweaty and apologetic, nearly two hours late. His special garlic chicken was overcooked. Yet his son-in-law seemed strangely elated and devoured the burned meal with gusto.

Roy and Sue Ellen Longfellow returned from their excruciating dinner party around midnight, accompanied by five surveillance cars. Beside the telephone was a note from the nanny saying that Rodney Mallard had called and left a message.

Longfellow knew, from the dinner party conversation, that President Kennedy had ordered Cuba's naval quarantine. The naval blockade was possible at any time. That would be the moment when the world either exploded or someone backed down. The clock was ticking toward a nuclear meltdown. *Would you like a recording of those wonderful Russian hymns?* read Mallard's message.

Grinning, Longfellow showed the message to his wife. Mallard had picked up the escape signal after all. He whispered to her, "I'm relieved he's seen it. But it's like the coming of Armageddon."

TINKER had been triggered.

55

Charles Lightner was on leave. Semenov's case officer was still coming to terms with the grim situation: one of the most effective agents ever recruited by British intelligence had been sent back to Moscow and straight into a KGB ambush. He couldn't stop rolling the how-did-it-happen scenarios through his head over and over while he was at home on his patio, reading the newspapers and talking with his wife, Mary Anne. "How," he asked his wife, "was Nikolai found out?"

"Do you have a mole inside MI5? Isn't that a great worry for you people?"

"Oh, it's a tremendous fear. It's something we worry about every day. An insider turning our secrets into money from the other side is our single greatest worry."

"Plus, I know you take it personally since you're his handler."

"We are very close. He depends on me. It's like I've agreed to protect him no matter what. The feelings that I'm having right now are like I've let down my best friend. He's been arrested—or worse—and I can't be there to help because he's in the Soviet Union. It's maddening, Mary Anne."

"You've worked so hard with the man. I wish I knew his name so I could say a prayer."

Lightner smiled. "Try generalizing when you pray. Your friend in the sky will know who you're talking about unless I miss my guess."

"Well, you've done all you can for him. It's just something you can't control."

She was right. A good agent, which Charles Lightner was, provided stability amid uproar and enormous stress. Even when not asked, he would help financially and procure a well-thought-out plan of escape alternative if there was an upset in the original plan. The best that could be done with Nikolai was TINKER, and everyone in ULYSSES felt terrible about that, including Emma Magnuson, who had schemed it out. The consensus was they should be able to offer Nikolai, who would be helpless if discovered, something more likely to work with than TINKER. Lightner felt he had let Nikolai down by not insisting on more. So he spent his days reading and re-reading the same paragraph of his spy novel while thoughts of Nikolai's well-being intruded upon his mind.

But things were about to explode.

P5, the head of the Soviet operational section, was in his River House office early Wednesday morning when the phone call came. A double-encrypted telegram had been sent overnight by the Moscow office. It read: TINKER FLOWN. HEAVY SURVEILLANCE. EXFILTRATION UNDERWAY. ADVISE. P5 dashed downstairs to Baxter Kelly's office. He was the charge officer when the others weren't around. "Do we have a TINKER plan?" he asked.

"Yes, sir," said Kelly. "We do have a TINKER plan. Make the calls!"

Lightner was still wrestling with his book in the garden when P5 called. He went inside and picked up the kitchen phone. "Hello?"

"It has begun. Please drop in."

Lightner put down the phone, his mind racing. It was Wednesday. Something happened yesterday, Tuesday, which could only mean one thing since Magnuson had made it clear a Tuesday was her preferred choice. Nikolai must still be alive!

The train to London took forever, but in reality, only thirty minutes. On the tenth floor of River House, he found a scene of pandemonium. The plan had electrified Team ULYSSES.

First came a series of meetings. Then Jason Donovan started in with the orders. First to Martin Crawford, MI5 overseas liaison. "You'll fly to Copenhagen and update our team there. All Danish intelligence needs to have ears and coordinate plans for when he sets foot on Finnish soil. Then we need you in Helsinki to sandpaper the Finns. Explain that this isn't just another escapee but a critical person, and he's not to be returned to the Soviets for any reason. Should they ignore us, it won't be good for them. Let their people know that in no uncertain terms. You are also charged with laying any groundwork for their crossing of the razor wire to the Finnish side. One more thing, Martin. I'll want you to drive down to the rendezvous point. Make sure the Russian army hasn't suddenly encamped there for maneuvers this weekend."

"Got it," said Crawford. "And how long do I have to pull all this off?"

Donovan smiled a grim smile. "Twenty-four hours. Not a minute longer."

Crawford jumped up and all but ran from the meeting. There wasn't a minute to spare.

Lightner spoke up. "How do we guarantee the Finns don't send him back across the border?" The others also knew the unthinkable could happen because the Finns had an agreement with the Russians to turn over Russian fugitives on Finnish soil. The underlying rationale was the Soviets promised not to invade Finland as long as the Finns cooperated in this manner. Who could blame the Finns? Still, it was a systemic knot that had to be addressed.

"In addition to Crawford settling them down, I plan to call the Chief of Station in Helsinki. He'll listen to me, especially when I suggest that Big Brother is backing us up."

Lightner knew Donovan was right. The Finns would listen, especially if they thought the CIA was in on the play. No one doublecrossed the CIA. While Finland had declared itself neutral in the Cold War—much to Washington's disgust—they couldn't be allowed to take sides and suddenly return Nikolai to the Russians. That would be anything but neutral.

"Listen up, everyone. Here's where we are with the Finns." He explained how, a few months before, MI6 Sovbloc controller had paid a visit to Finland to meet up with Rudo Zeppa, the Chief of the Finnish Intelligence Service (SUPO). The visit was in preparation for Operation TINKER and Nikolai escaping to Finland. "If we had a defector that we needed to bring through Finland, would you turn your head?"

"Quite right. We don't need to know."

The controller had fixed the Chief with his eyes. "SUPO wouldn't want the Soviets to learn the names of all SUPO agents operating in Moscow, now would it?"

"Is that a threat?"

"You're goddam right; it's a threat. We're not asking on this one. We're demanding. And enough of your goddam supposed neutrality that has you sending poor people back to Russia. How the hell is that neutral? You're bordering on seeing your country overrun with CIA and MI6 agents watching every last fucking thing you do. How's that for neutral?"

"Message received. No interference from us."

"Just so long as we understand each other."

"Loud and clear. We're out on this one."

"So, that's where we stand with the Finns," Donovan finished.

"What about Crawford?"

"The Finns don't want to know anything in advance. Crawford knows that."

Lightner asked, "So if Nikolai is intercepted in Finland by Finnish authorities, they will immediately turn him loose without a word?"

"Oh, they know to tell us. They also know to tell the Soviets nothing."

"What about flying Nikolai out of Finland then? Why send him to Stockholm for his flight?"

"The Finns know the Soviets are quite capable of sending a *Spetsnaz*, a special forces squad, to take down the airport should that happen. Helsinki airport is crawling with KGB."

"All right, everyone," Donovan continued. " Emma and Franklin here will transport Nikolai west to Turku from Helsinki. From Turku, they will take the ferry to Stockholm. A regular airline flight will take them to London."

For weeks, the ULYSSES team, which was now TINKER—the escape operation having superseded the spy operation—had grimly waited for something, *anything*, to happen. Now they were energized, and the entire room was buzzing.

56

MI6's Moscow safe house lay just a kilometer from the British Embassy. It was part of an apartment complex that catered mostly to tourists on a one-week ticket to Moscow, but one of the units had been rented under a Russian name using a fake ID. Rarely was anyone home. The few permanent neighbors minded their own business. All of the other units were occupied from one night to fourteen with vacancies in-between. MI6 safe house and its occupancy, or lack of, went unnoticed. Nikolai arrived by taxi after a thirty-minute circuitous ride. The dry-cleaning had been a success.

Nikolai had a key to the safe house. It was prearranged that he would not return to his flat once he gave the Saint Basil's signal. From then on, he would remain at the safe house, sleeping on the cot and not going out during the day except when the TINKER plan required it.

He sat on the sofa and lit a cigar.

He would steal Sasha from the orphanage. Then it would be time to decide. Did he take Sasha with him? Or should he leave her with the Longfellows to bring to Tallinn as one of their own? He weighed both in his mind. Logic seemed to indicate he should leave her with the Longfellows, but his heart was heavy when he thought of that. What if they couldn't get through? Or what if the KGB refused to allow them to leave Moscow? He would never see his baby girl again, a risk he could not take.

So the next morning early, Nikolai sat at the window table in Misha's Cafe, directly across the street from the orphanage, Moscow Oblast Family and Child Protection Service. He watched the ancient building where Sasha had been taken. It was one-hundred years old, constructed of red brick, in serious need of tuck-pointing and paint along the white wood trim, and contained all the way around by a six-foot-high fence topped by razor wire. He knew because he had already walked around it, two times now, looking to spot an opening, which had been unsuccessful.

As he watched the building and accepted the third refill on his coffee, a blue van swung up into the orphanage driveway and stopped at the guardhouse. The gate was down as the driver spoke through his lowered window to the guard. Nikolai could hear none of the exchange, of course, but he guessed the driver was giving the reason for his appearance. Along the side of the van in yellow block letters read ISHKON PLUMBING.

After a short exchange, the gate lifted, and the van rolled through. It parked just in front of the building.

So, even orphanages had stopped-up toilets. But it was no time to smile at the thought. Instead, it was time to watch and follow precisely what happened next.

The door opened, and the driver stepped out. He was wearing gray coveralls and smoking a stubby pipe. He came around to the van's rear and removed a large box of what could only be plumbing tools. Nikolai watched him climb four steps up to the front double doors and then go inside the orphanage.

Thirty minutes later, the man emerged. He climbed into his van, made a U-turn, drove through the gate, and made a left before speeding away.

"A left and tromp it," he whispered. "Got it."

The waitress, exasperated with the customer who had long ago overstayed his welcome, brought the coffee pot to Nikolai once again. "Refill?"

He smiled and put twenty rubles on the table. "No and keep it. You've earned it—a couple of things. First, if anyone comes here asking about me, ever, you never saw me. Second, do you know where Ishkon Plumbing is?"

"They are just around the corner, Svobodnyy Prospekt."

"Number?"

"Thirty-nine."

"Thank you. Remember, you never saw me."

"For twenty rubles, of course. Thank you, sir."

He walked out.

The plumbing company's name was written on his palm. He went up a block and hailed a taxi. "Take me to this company," he said and told the driver the name of the plumber and address.

Nikolai had the driver stop the taxi a block away. He climbed out, paid, and left a handsome tip. "You never saw me, okay?"

"You've got it, comrade. I never tell them nothing anyway, so you're good."

"Thank you."

He walked up the block to a storefront painted shocking yellow. In huge black letters, the sign said ISHKON PLUMBING. Nikolai walked on by, checking out where the vehicles were kept, which was surprising because the plumbing company was in the middle of the block and had no parking except the street. The van he had his eyes on was parked in front of the building. Nikolai went down to the end of the block, crossed the road, and came back up the other side until directly across from the van. He then made a beeline across, moving neither fast nor slow, but crouching when he got to the driver's door as if he were bent and inserting his key.

Except he didn't have a key. He picked the lock in seconds and was inside the van and cross-wiring the ignition in one easy flow. His KGB training made vehicle theft as easy as downing a shot of vodka.

He pulled away from the curb, obeying all traffic laws, and drove down to the corner of Svobodnyy Prospekt. He carefully activated his indicator; it was no time to get pulled over by the police for failure to signal.

He completed his turn and sped up to the traffic flow, merged and heading west. Ten minutes later, he turned into the orphanage driveway and rolled down his window.

The guard spoke first. "Called you right back, did they? Where is the other guy?"

Nikolai shrugged. "It happened again, but Adrik is on his lunch."

"Oh," the guard commiserated. "They need to replace the pipes in there. Old is old, and this place is ancient."

Nikolai pulled forward into the same parking slot used earlier by the real plumber. After turning off the ignition by separating two wires, Nikolai climbed out and then opened the rear doors. He lifted out the same box of tools. Along with a courtesy tarp to keep water spills off the floor where he was working, off he went.

"Not again," said the guard at the top of the stairs.

"Someone needs to learn how to wipe with single-ply tissues. This double-ply toilet paper is making me wealthy with service calls."

"Go on ahead. You're clear."

Nikolai entered the building. Hallways proceeded straight ahead and both left and right. Which way to go?

A first-floor map was attached to the wall inside a frame. Nikolai stepped up and looked it over. A fire evacuation map. *You are here*, it read, and an X marked his map location. The office was dead ahead, end of the hallway on the right. So he struck off in that direction. He didn't know what he would say to them to find out where they had his daughter. But he had to try, even if it meant getting caught and arrested by the armed guards and hauled off to jail. He had to try.

A single glass door marked the office with hours of operation and phone numbers in black letters. Before entering, he looked both ways. No one was coming from either direction, which he saw as a good sign, so he went inside.

Up to the counter, he walked. "I'm looking for Sasha Semenov. She was brought in last night."

The clerk was a woman of about thirty, chewing gum, a pencil stuck in her hair, indicating a substantial lack of interest in her job or the people who came to her desk.

"Let me see." She went to a clipboard and examined it. "Purpose of visit?"

"I'm her uncle. As long as I'm here for the plumbing, I just wanted to wave to her."

"Second floor, first room on your right. It's a playroom for one-to-three-year-olds. Your niece is right there."

"Thank you."

She nodded at his toolbox. "Stopped up again?"

"What is this, fourth time this month?"

She waved him off. "Ha! Don't we wish? I'll bet you guys have been here ten times if you've been here once. And it's only the twentieth of October. We have another eleven days. That should be another eleven visits, uncle."

"For your sake, I hope not. But we'll see. Thank you now."

"Good luck."

Sasha, when he opened the door, didn't look up. She was sitting on the floor in a circle with young toddlers. They were singing and clapping their hands at the end of each verse an older woman read out of a book. When it was Sasha's turn, she shook her head "no" violently. She was having none of it. Two young female staff were at the other end of the room, working with a movie projector. Nikolai strode right up to his daughter, picked her up from the group, and left the room with her.

"Don't be scared," he whispered to his daughter. "Papa is going to play hide-and-seek. You're going to get inside this tarp while we play, all right?"

"I'm hungry, Papa. Pancakes!" But Sasha still couldn't pronounce "hungry" so it came out clipped, half a word.

"All right. Let's go home and see."

He unwrapped the tarp and placed it beside Sasha. Then he wrapped it around her, scooped her up under his arm, and ran for the stairs. Downstairs they went two steps at a time, then into the hallway. He headed for the front door and, minutes later, they were in the van. Nikolai made a U-turn and pulled through the guard station. The gate was up. Nikolai and the guard saluted one another, and Nikolai pulled through.

"Hungry!"

"Soon. I promise."

* * *

Lieutenant General Masirov dialed the extension for Viktor Bucharov. Major Victor Bucharov of Directorate K was the most difficult KGB officer known to Masirov. He was challenging to be thrown off the track by deceit or dry-cleaning or threats. Difficult in being dissuaded from his mission by guns or knives or money. He could be counted on to run any target to the ground, so Masirov called him now.

He came into Masirov's office wearing a top of the line suit made in Russia. He walked like someone whose body was accustomed to being tested in dangerous situations or tea rooms. He looked like someone equally comfortable in either case. His hair was black and cut very short in a Caesar cut. Sunglasses were tucked into his suit pocket, where a pocket square was meant to peek out. He was chewing gum, which he removed from his mouth with a tissue and hid away inside a waist pocket. His posture in the chair he was offered was very erect and confident--the same pose the KGB taught its youth in KGB School 1010.

"Colonel, the time has come."

"Colonel Semenov?"

"Colonel Semenov kidnapped his daughter today from Moscow Oblast Family and Child Protection Service. You are to find him, kill him, and return the daughter there."

"And his remains?"

"I don't want to know."

"Very good, sir."

"Go now. Make it quick. Do it so the little girl doesn't see her father die. We're not animals, Colonel."

"Yes, sir."

57

Roy and Sue Ellen Longfellow met in the sound-proof room below the British Embassy's ground level in Moscow. They had to concoct a cover story that KGB ears would fall for. The embassy car needed at the rendezvous point would have to arrive precisely at 5:30 p.m. tomorrow. But KGB suspicions would immediately shoot off the charts when an embassy car headed out of town. The car would be carrying Longfellow, a senior "diplomat." Longfellow decided he would be leaving on a family emergency involving the law.

First, Sue Ellen would receive a telegram from her sister. The KGB couldn't intercept a telegram. The sister, Linda, would contact her from Helsinki and be in jail on drug charges.

Sue Ellen would fly into a panic and outrage over her sister's arrest, and she would curse the Finns into every microphone at the flat that she could find. She would beg her husband to help get her sister released from jail. He would wring his hands, wondering if Russian lawyers could help. Sue Ellen would say Russian lawyers couldn't help. She had called two of them from the mall, and they all but laughed at her. But the third one, the nice one, had said she needed to go to Helsinki and hire a lawyer there.

She said they should leave at once, that Helsinki jails were notorious for assaults and sex attacks on prisoners. At first, Longfellow didn't want to make the journey and resisted, insisting that it was against embassy policy to use embassy vehicles for personal reasons. But Sue Ellen threatened him as only wives could threaten husbands, and he finally relented and said the embassy would make an exception just this one time.

Again, all of this discussion, including Roy's reluctance, would be played to convince the eavesdropping KGB that the trip was legitimately a legal mission of mercy. It was decided they would also bring along their fifteen-month-old daughter rather than rely on a babysitter overnight. They felt better doing it this way. The group would leave first thing in the morning.

That same afternoon, Sue Ellen Longfellow received a telegram from her purported sister from Helsinki. It was a plea for help, just as planned. The telegram was followed up by a call from Emma Magnuson in Helsinki. She was posing as Sue Ellen's sister.

"Sue Ellen, it's Linda! They gave me one phone call. Randy and I were arrested by the Helsinki police on our way to see you."

"My God, what happened?"

"I was waiting in the car while Randy went into the drugstore for aspirin. He came out with an electric razor inside his shirt. They arrested him and me, too!"

"But you didn't do anything wrong!"

"I know, I know. Please, Sue Ellen, get me out of jail! I need a lawyer, too. Please hurry. It's horrible here. Drunks and addicts and insane people all around me. Come now!"

Of course, their flat was bugged, so Roy and Sue Ellen were heard discussing the trip to Helsinki to get Linda out of jail and hire a lawyer. Longfellow then made two calls to two different attorneys in Helsinki for appointments. He tried speaking Russian with them at first because he wanted the eavesdroppers to have no trouble understanding his plan. But the lawyers only spoke Finnish, so he hung up without an appointment. Now KGB was searching out the lawyers to interrogate them in Helsinki.

Longfellow next called an English-speaking lawyer in Helsinki and made an appointment for the following day on an urgent basis. The lawyer himself came on the phone, suggesting they bring along one-hundred pounds. They would need at least that much to pay him and to get the sister released.

Rodney Mallard and Roy Longfellow went to a café for tea that night.

"Tomorrow, you make your pick up and run like hell for Vyborg," Longfellow told Mallard. "I'll be headed for Leningrad."

"It doesn't feel like this is going to work at all," Mallard said. "How in God's name do you shake loose from your KGB escort tomorrow so you can make the church and pick up poor Nikolai?"

Longfellow slowly shook his head. There was a grim set to his mouth. "I don't honestly know," he finally said. "I've played it over and over in my brain hundreds of times. We're going to have to pray, I suppose."

Mallard wasn't satisfied. "No, you need a plan. Some way of throwing them off." Then he scoffed. "I'm not even sure the hymnal was put there by TINKER. Do you know how many hymnals I saw in that church?"

"No. But that troubles me, too."

"I counted three hymnals up front where the priests sit. Scares the hell out of me that maybe we've triggered this whole thing, and it isn't even TINKER."

"What if the KGB tortured Nikolai and made him give up the plan, and it was KGB who signaled? Have you worked that scenario through your head yet?"

"Only a hundred times. It's entirely possible."

"This could blow up into a horrendous mess. It could result in us getting expelled from Russia and bringing great condemnation to Britain. That, alone, worries the hell out of me. Not to even mention poor Nikolai. For all we know, he's lying in some unmarked grave this minute. What in the hell are we doing? Aren't we supposed to be spies and have the upper hand?"

"If only," Mallard said. Another pot of tea arrived, and the men poured milk into their cups.

"Plus, am I going off the deep end, or is there more KGB surveillance around the embassy the past few days? I feel like ants are crawling all over us."

"I've noticed it, too. Ordinarily, I ignore them, but this feels like they're on to something."

"And we don't even know his identity or what he looks like. The man I saw outside the church might not have been him, just some random guy smoking a cigar. But I couldn't describe him now. It was only a split second our eyes met."

"London has told me he is a KGB colonel, a long-time agent dating back to his London days, a man so important to the UK that they're willing to take losses to save him."

"Take losses?" asked Mallard. "What in the hell does 'take losses' mean?"

"Go figure. It startled me, too," Longfellow agreed. "I've never seen that before."

"Sounds like we have Khrushchev himself in our net."

"Might be easier to smuggle out of Russia. He's bland as hell."

They laughed at that. Sometimes the laughter helped when things were ominous, and there was unknown meaning in every stranger's face and untold danger behind every corner.

MI6 Moscow kept MI6 London apprised of its preparations. But in MI6 London, too, there was new worry that a failure could compromise Anglo-Soviet relations at the exact moment the world was balancing on the precipice of war. The Cuban Missile Crisis was growing more frightening every day.

58

Nikolai's most urgent task was to buy railway tickets to Leningrad for him and Sasha, which meant a trip to the Leningradsky Station on Komsomolskaya Square. Proof positive habitual dry-cleaning was fundamental to survival.

But right now, Sasha was dirty and wet. Potty-training was underway but wasn't perfect, and mealtime was always a disaster. Her needs came first.

"Dirty diaper? You must be very upset. You're a big girl, and big girls use the potty."

"Mama?"

Here we go again, he thought. But it had to be done each time until she understood.

"Mama went to heaven. She's with God." He believed none of that, but until someone found a better alternative to give toddlers, it was what he knew to say.

"I want Mama!" she demanded and banged her sippy cup down on the table.

"Yes, I want Mama, too. I wish we had her with us right now."

"Mama, come home!"

"That's right. But Mama went away. She's in heaven."

"Where?"

Nikolai shrugged. "You know, heaven."

Nikolai wasn't all that comfortable with his answers for Sasha. At the safe house table, he teased her into a spoonful of food and a swallow from her cup while his mind roamed over the man he would have to anticipate.

It would be Bucharov, their best.

Bucharov would be a handful. Who killed who depended on who saw who first. If he saw Bucharov before Bucharov saw him, then Bucharov would die. Nikolai was at least that much of a warrior. He felt grateful he had been in the war and fought hand-to-hand. He was thankful he had killed and learned to keep going.

He picked up the baby's meal things, washed them in the sink, and then washed the table where Sasha had pounded spaghetti into the placemat.

He went around the safe house and loaded a few items he would need, including a short length of chain and a padlock. Then he packed their gear into one bag.

He washed her hands and mouth and lifted her out of her kitchen chair. "Hang on. We're almost ready to go."

He dug out a spare set of clothes for Sasha and packed diapers in his bag. She was potty trained but was accident-prone if stressed.

Nikolai's old soldier knapsack let him carry her on his back, swaddled in her footsies and winter coat. Even though it was only October, it was freezing. She fit perfectly in the knapsack, the top of her head just peeking out from the canvas, and she was safely away from the wind and snow. If needed, he could even close the knapsack flap over her head, but that would be only in an emergency.

But before he set off, he had to ask himself one last time, was he sure this was the best thing to do for her? Meaning, might it be safer if Longfellow transported her? Each time he asked, he knew he would take her with him. It was the only way, for he loved her too much to risk losing her forever. Besides, she was all he had left of Yulia. "Come along, little Sasha."

He called a taxi. When it arrived, he loaded the knapsack first and then followed. He told the driver to go to the end of the street and make a U-turn. The driver complied, and Nikolai told him to stop. Now they faced the two-way road with a view of all oncoming traffic. Nikolai then had the driver move ahead at a high rate of speed. At the next corner was a stoplight that Nikolai asked the driver to turn right on red. He drove down two blocks and stopped at the north corner of the shopping center, GUM, or Main Universal Store, facing the Red Square.

At that point, just as they rocked to a stop, Nikolai and Sasha climbed out and caught the bus just coming up from behind. The bus took them down a block, stopped, turned right, then another block, and stopped. He was now on the south end of the shopping mall. Nikolai climbed down out of the bus and began walking back toward the south entrance. He entered through the department store and immediately made his way to the public bathrooms on the basement level. By his wristwatch, he timed off fifteen minutes before reappearing outside. He found a phone by the entrance and called a taxi. When they climbed into the cab, he felt he'd made a good start. He had the cab take them downtown, pull into a parking garage, and stop. Nikolai walked to the stairwell and entered. The steps were concrete, and the door had a handle. Perfect. He pulled the chain from his bag and twisted it around the handle so it wouldn't turn. Then he attached his padlock. Now it was time to take the elevator and disappear.

He left the parking garage with Sasha tucked safely in his knapsack. He set off on foot and made for nearby Albat Street. After ducking into a couple of shops, he then jogged along the sidewalk and up to a small block of flats. Once around the corner and out of sight, he sprinted thirty yards, Sasha banging against his back. She cried out, but he quieted her with a "shoosh!"

He leaped into the first passing bus, rode it for a couple of stops, took a taxi to the traffic police station, went in, came out, made sure no one was behind him, and then dodged block by block to the Leningradsky Station where he bought a reserved fourth-class ticket for a train due to leave Moscow at 5:30 a.m. tomorrow. The ticket was purchased in the name of Mikhail Mashky, the same name that decorated his Border Guards uniform.

He returned to the safe house, all the while dry-cleaning, and fed Sasha again. Then he got down on the floor with her and played hide and seek until she bored of it. Alligator River came next, where he was on all fours, and she climbed onto his back. They crawled throughout the flat, on the lookout for alligators, which they inevitably found with a roar and laughter. Afterward, she climbed up onto the couch, turned onto her side, stuck her thumb in her mouth, and shut her eyes for a nap. Nikolai dropped his jacket over her and pulled her blond hair away from her face. Then he leaned in and kissed her forehead. At that moment, she looked just like Yulia. He sat down beside her and quietly wept.

The rest of that day, they played, talked nonsense words, and watched TV. He made up stories. A new tale starred Benny Belka (Benny the squirrel) but lacked sound effects to hold her attention. She fell asleep listening. He put her beside him on the bed, and they both slept until sometime in the night when she awoke to cry for Mama. He did what he could to soothe her, and, when she'd finally gone back to sleep, he followed.

59

It was, after all, the CIA's ballgame, CIA Moscow station chief, Wendell Ranski, told Roy Longfellow late at night in a parking garage meeting. It was the CIA's ballgame because the United States and nuclear war hung in the balance. It only made tactical sense that the CIA would meet Longfellow and help expedite the escape of Nikolai Semenov into the West, where he could immediately contact the American President and answer the questions the President needed to be answered in the next forty-eight hours to deal with the Soviet fleet steaming for Cuba. In a word, said Ranski, the CIA had more skin in the game than even the British at this point, more of a vested interest in seeing Semenov successfully escape than its little brother, MI6.

Longfellow couldn't argue. Rodney Mallard would head north toward Vyborg, along with Captain John Winters, USMC. Winters would be loaned from the American Embassy. This was a diversion trip.

The CIA would then meet Longfellow in Leningrad and try to run interference with the KGB parade of vehicles following the MI6 officer. The CIA would then load onto the Helsinki ferry with him in Tallinn. The CIA officer was a man named Daniel Danbury. Nikolai Semenov had met him at The Flamingo Club in London, and they had exchanged intelligence for a time. The CIA said Nikolai's talk with the American President was so crucial to national security that two things would happen. One, Danbury would interfere to spring Longfellow from the KGB cars pursuing him. Two, the U-2 spy plane from Ramstein AFB in Germany was going to overfly the Helsinki-Stockholm portion of the trip. CIA would also monitor the journey with a vehicle of its own driving behind the vehicle transporting Nikolai.

In Stockholm, Danbury would facilitate the call between Nikolai Semenov and President Kennedy through the CIA switchboard in Langley. Passcodes were required; Danbury would come prepared to provide them.

60

October 20, 1962

4:00 a.m. MI6 Safe House, Moscow

In the morning, they were up at four a.m. Sasha fought the early wakeup call, but he bribed her with pancakes he'd made out of the cupboard mixes, dressed in butter and honey, and cut into small pieces for Sasha's fingers. While she ate what quickly turned into a lump of sticky goo, he made coffee and thought about the day. It came to him, then, to contemplate what might happen to Sasha if Bucharov killed him. Would he also kill the baby? Sell her into white slavery? Return her to her aunt? Walk away and leave her crying? The process of working it through his mind only made him that much stronger. Those things couldn't be allowed to happen.

He turned on the TV and sat Sasha on the floor to watch. Then he changed into the Border Troops uniform with the name of the original owner, Lieutenant Colonel Mikhail Mashky. He put it in the bottom of his knapsack, his favorite anorak, English cap, and essentials for washing and shaving. He had to laugh—he had abandoned his own KGB uniforms at his old flat.

At the bottom of his KGB knapsack, he also placed as much as he could for Sasha: a change of clothes, sippy cup, bottle of milk, diapers, crackers, and a set of pajamas. He dressed her into her winter coat, boots, and mittens.

Before lowering Sasha into the bag, he dropped in a small road atlas covering the Estonia-Finnish crossing area. Knowing that Soviet maps were deliberately falsified in border regions to confuse and mislead runners, he was unsure how much use the MI6 rendering would be, but it was all he had. Everything else he left behind, and when he closed the door, the knapsack securely on his back, he knew that he was closing it not only on his home and his possessions but on his family and his Russian life.

He went down from the eighth floor in the lift. Sure enough, the concierge was at her desk, but he didn't stop to check if she noticed him. He swept through the lobby and out the door.

Outside on the street, it was still dark. Only 5 a.m. and below freezing, his breath like locomotive smoke billowing out of the funnel. He trudged on, classically dry-cleaning his way to the Leningradsky Station via the early bus, then jogging again, and another couple of busses. It was too early for many shops to be open, but any that were, he popped in and out, one a bakery that smelled like heaven. Even Sasha squawked when he turned away from the pastries. By the time he arrived at the station, he was so nervous that everything appeared highly sinister.

He shivered, shifted Sasha into a better position in the knapsack, and walked inside. Bucharov was either waiting for him with his gun or he wasn't.

He took a deep breath and plunged ahead.

61

5:05 a.m. Kinovov City Park, Moscow

Captain John Winters, USMC, left his flat two blocks from Moscow's British embassy, just before dawn. Dry-cleaning the KGB from his tail was no problem for the Marine whose tactics had been blocked out with Roy Longfellow, MI6, the night before at the embassy.

When the lone KGB officer assigned to follow Winters had been lost in the lobby of the Luxembourg Hotel on Valyaa Prospekt, just off Red Square, Winters then proceeded by taxi to the jogging route used every morning by Nikolai Semenov. The taxi let him out at a wooded area just inside the Kinovov City Park that made up one-half of the jogging route. Winters proceeded into a stand of trees and sat down. He was wearing jogging clothes consisting of sweatpants, running shoes, two heavy undershirts—it was cold that morning—and a hooded sweatshirt with a towel around his neck.

Then, he waited.

62

5:25 a.m., Leningradsky Station

No shot rang out as Nikolai crossed the cavernous station. Sasha said several words about "pretty" something, but he wasn't paying all that much attention as his gaze darted from face to face.

They had their tickets. He studied the Departures board, figuring out their gate. Then off he headed for Gate 4 at the far end of the station.

Leningradsky Station was crawling with men in uniform. He felt threatened by this totalitarian display, and, for a moment, his overheated imagination made him think they were looking for him. Then he remembered that young people from all over the world were pouring into the city for an international youth festival due to open that day. The first event of that kind, held in 1957, had seemed to him a marvelous occasion, lit up by the spontaneous excitement of mysterious new music by a man named Elvis

Presley whose records everyone had hoped might come to Soviet black-market record stores.

Today's crowd was double the size judging from the tourist queues. He saw that it might work to his advantage. Creating confusion, the mass of foreigners going back across to Scandinavia would surely help distract the frontier officials when the outbound lines queued at the border for permission to leave the Soviet Union. But it was impossible to predict what might happen.

They waited at the train for the doors to slide open. Just as he turned his back to the train and studied the oncoming passengers, Nikolai caught a glimpse of a face he thought belonged to Bucharov. The face was dodging through the crowd, trying to get a look back at Nikolai.

At that moment the doors parted, and Nikolai leaped onto the train. Sasha squealed with delight as he hurried into the aisle and started searching for their seats. Nikolai quickly set Sasha down onto the train seat and then loaded his knapsack above his head. He looked out the window at the crowd down below. The face he had seen wasn't Bucharov after all.

He settled Sasha with her doll and covered her with a blanket, her head on his lap, and bought a newspaper from a vendor walking through the car. Now his face was blocked by the paper to passersby.

The train whistled and slowly pulled away from the platform. Nikolai lowered the newspaper and inventoried the faces he could see around him. He began to get the feeling they had made it onboard without Bucharov in hot pursuit. As he looked outside, he saw Moscow receding behind. His heart fell as he thought about Yulia and the happiness they'd known here. But that was slowly lessening as the train picked up speed.

Hours passed. Sasha slept soundly; he even managed to doze to the clackety-clack under the floor.

Three hours out of Moscow, he breathed a sigh of relief and played with Sasha, walking her through the cars. People smiled and touched her on the head and gave her a cookie or sweet. Then the father and child returned to their seats.

They devoured lunch with a hungry traveler's appetite and then napped, Nikolai lightly.

Nikolai's newspaper was again a shield against curious eyes when he resumed reading. He was ready if suddenly confronted. He now had Sasha positioned so that he could leap from his seat and engage. Relaxation might come later. For now, he was ready to die to protect his daughter.

And so, he waited.

63

5:30 a.m., Dobrinsky Prospekt, Moscow

Colonel Bucharov was late because Masirov waited too long. He should have sent Bucharov to shoot Nikolai as soon as they knew his secret. Which angered Bucharov so that he would shoot Semenov on sight.

He arrived at Nikolai's flat and pounded on the door with his gloved hand. He called out Nikolai's name, demanding he open up. When there was no answer, he opened the small case containing his lock picks. He let himself in and immediately scouted room to room. He picked up a clock radio from the bedside and threw it at the wall. He was in a rage—both at Masirov and Nikolai.

At that point, he forced himself to calm down and think. He needed to know what kind of weapons Nikolai might have on him.

He began in the kitchen, looking under the sink for chemicals the KGB fugitive could use to blind or burn. He saw drain cleaner, an abrasive white powder for stubborn grease, vinegar, and turpentine.

He nodded and moved into the bathroom, where he opened the medicine cabinet and found analgesics and prescription pain relievers. Two pill bottles, mostly used up, one of aspirin and the other an antacid. He was doubtful any of it was along for the run. There was missing, however, no plastic bottles capable of spraying. So noted.

He opened drawers throughout the flat, looking for the junk drawer. He found it and began pawing. No picture wire meant to watch for garrotes. No cigarette lighters ensured the runner would have the ability to light fuses, bombs, Molotovs, flammables. No blades, not foldable, not fixed.

He wasn't necessarily hurrying as he snooped. He reasoned Colonel Semenov was already aboard the Leningrad train, snuggled down into a seat with his daughter, maybe hidden beneath a blanket, perhaps a newspaper blocking out the world and passing eyes. So be it. His Volga would outrun the train, for it made many stops along its tracks, while Bucharov's Volga was on a straight shot through. He turned and decided where he might focus next.

He took inventory of knives, kitchen utensils, automobile tools, box openers, wires, and chains. There was a gun hanging in the closet inside its holster. Extra magazines on a strap. Wasn't conclusive. Most KGB carried a .380 hidden on their ankle or an inner pocket.

He cast an eye over baby paraphernalia. She would be with him since the wife was dead. Plus, he wouldn't leave her in Russia. He might not make it just because of her, but he wasn't going to try it without her, regardless. He pursed his lips then let go. Had to admire the guy, but she would slow him considerably and all but take away his ability to flee on foot.

He assessed what he saw—and what he didn't see, maybe more importantly. The turpentine was extremely volatile. Squirted through a flame, it could be deadly. He might have a squeeze bottle along full of it. There might be a second gun. There might be a blade or straight razor since Bucharov had found no shaving items. Enough pain meds pulverized and sprinkled into a drink could be deadly, too. Screwdrivers and box cutters—killers.

He stepped out onto the walkway. Officers would be checking the railroad for passenger lists. He expected to receive news at any moment. So he went downstairs to his car, climbed inside, and waited. Someone would be along.

64

5:50 a.m., KGB Headquarters, KGB Moscow

A very frustrated and angry Bucharov called in. Any news from the train station? The bus station? Car rental outlets?

He learned Masirov had ordered a manhunt. A messenger was on the way with news since the phones were tapped.

65

6 a.m., British Embassy, Moscow

First Assistant British Ambassador Adam Staples pulled his green Saab into the sally port at the British Embassy. The steel-reinforced door closed behind him. He was alone in his car and had with him a thermos of Colombian coffee, the good stuff you couldn't buy off the shelves in Moscow.

He took the elevator two floors up where he checked the 24-hour clock on the wall: 0600. He entered his office and buzzed Sidney Browning, his First Assistant Deputy Ambassador. "I'm here."

"On my way."

Staples was angry, given what a terrible situation London had left him to sort out. A spy about to die, an escape plan that leaked terribly, a KGB net tightening even then. He fully expected to have one deceased double-agent on his hands before the sun went down.

Browning came in with a flowery pink mug of his Darjeeling.

"See you couldn't find your own in the lunchroom," Staples said, indicating the mug.

"Ginny McWherter's. What she doesn't know won't hurt her."

"Holiday?"

"Yep, lucky girl."

They spread a map on the desktop. Yellow highlight traced the spies' route from Moscow to Tallinn. It also highlighted travel to Vyborg and Bialystok and several other jumping-off places just in case prying eyes happened to spot it in the bin of rolled-up maps Staples kept beside his desk.

Then they looked at the route MI6 would drive that day. From Moscow to Tallinn, a trip of about twelve hours that Longfellow intended to cover in eleven. Why not? He would have a KGB escort to keep him company and probably even lead the high-speed chase.

Staples rubbed his hands together as he sometimes did when he was frightened while alone in Russia, an embassy island with a foreign flag, outnumbered 280 million to 60.

"All right, let's get down to KGB watchers."

"They'll be out in force," said Browning, stating the obvious.

"All we have is a protest we might file. That will obtain nothing. Still, we'll have to do it at the very least. Our chaps are out and about on embassy business, and they have a right to privacy."

"Privacy?" scoffed Browning. "What's that in Russia?"

"There's no such right in Russia," Staples agreed. "We're not in London. But it won't hurt to try. If KGB is smothering our people, this whole thing gets stuck in the mud up to its hubs before it even begins."

"Agree. If we can coerce them to pen up their hounds, there's one for the Queen."

Staples called the Soviet Foreign Ministry. No one he spoke to had any idea what he was talking about. Said one junior Soviet officer, "KGB drives everywhere. The road belongs to everyone."

Staples hung up, shaking his head. "All I've accomplished is to guarantee they will follow our men for sure."

"They would anyway. It was worth a try."

"Point."

Sidney had been thinking. "Hold on, Mr. Ambassador. What if MI6 rented cars with Russian license plates? Why do we have to drive diplomat cars? Just use Russian plates and fit in with the traffic."

Staples pointed a finger at his deputy. "Bingo! Call them now. Wait, haven't they already thought of that?"

"I'll call."

66

6:05 a.m. Dobrinsky Prospekt, Moscow

Bucharov was anxious to set out after Nikolai when KGB agent Borodokovich tracked him down. "We've found where he was fifty minutes ago! He's left the city. We've canvassed the train and bus stations. It appears he's taken the Leningrad train just this morning."

"You showed his picture?"

"The station master is sure it was him. He had a fourth-class ticket to Leningrad. Am I driving or you?"

"Never mind. I'm traveling alone. What time did his train leave?"

"Maybe thirty minutes ago, give or take. It was five-thirty on the schedule, but the station master said it always leaves fifteen minutes late."

"Why did you wait so long to tell me?"

"Masirov thought you had gone on ahead. We looked here last."

"I called in fifteen minutes ago."

"We just found this out. We received a call from our agent at the train station."

Bucharov didn't try to hide his disgust. Now he was more determined than ever to find the target. "What's the running time to Leningrad?"

"I didn't ask."

"Of course, you didn't. Now you know why I travel alone."

With that, Bucharov climbed into his Volga and squealed away from the curb. Bucharov knew the answer to his question. The distance between the two cities could be covered in about seven hours at emergency speed. Calls would be made to clear all traffic. The train had a head start, but Bucharov knew he could overtake it and be waiting for Nikolai inside the Leningradsky Station. He knew the precise location where he would shoot the traitor.

His foot pressed the accelerator almost to the floor, and the Volga jumped up to 155 km/h. He switched on the radio and roamed the dial, looking for classical. He chose Rimsky-Korsakov's *Scheherazade* at the bottom end of the dial, increased the volume, and lay a hand against the gun inside his jacket.

The gun warmed to his body heat.

67

6:15 a.m., British embassy, Moscow

The deputy ambassador called the chief of MI6. Both the deputy and the chief knew the call was tapped, that everything they said was also heard by the KGB listening a block away from the embassy.

"Longfellow, Sidney Browning here."

"We're swamped, Brownie. I hope this is important," said Roy Longfellow.

"Have your boys considered renting Russian cars? The hell with diplomatic license plates the KGB will follow?"

"Certainly, we've thought of that. But the diplomatic license plates are our only hope the Border Troops don't open the trunks. If we rent and show up without Russian plates, we get searched. Never fear, we're wracking our brains down here, figuring out how to keep them out of our trunks. Now, if you have any good ideas about that, call me back in the next five minutes. Otherwise, I'm busy, Browning."

68

6:25 a.m., Helsinki Herttoniemi, Finland

MI6's Martin Crawford had patiently stepped through TINKER with the Finns. They were smart people he was dealing with at the agency, and they immediately understood their role. Moreover, they were eager to help with such important exfiltration.

Traveling under false passports, Emma Magnuson and Franklin Bolling had arrived in Helsinki the night before. They checked into the Helsinki Herttoniemi Hotel down by the seaport, and early the next morning, drove to the ferry landing. Acclimating themselves as to what to expect there, they then went to the rendezvous point.

That rendezvous, a city park one block off the main thoroughfare, had been chosen—and visited and photographed—when Emma Magnuson first formulated the TINKER escape plan. It was a mile away from the seaport.

The park wasn't visible from the main road and yet was close enough that Longfellow and Mallard could get Nikolai and Sasha out of the automobile trunk as soon as possible after crossing.

The MI6-SUPO team searched the area. Emma Magnuson referred to her coded notes and photographs in confirming the location when they located the park, the rendezvous.

"I like it here," she said. "The park's in a nice, quiet neighborhood. We might see at most two or three mothers watching their kids on the swings or slides during the day."

Bolling nodded his agreement. "Well done to whoever chose this park. It works perfectly, plus it's only a block off the main road. Simple to find."

"Okay," Emma continued, "we'll meet right here and break into two groups. Nikolai and Sasha will come with Bolling and me. The other car will be our security team. Our SUPO guys."

The two SUPO agents nodded. They were quiet but ready.

Bolling recounted how they would then drive three miles west and stop. "We'll have a physician waiting there to check on Nikolai and Sasha. Dehydration is our main worry. But that depends on how long they've been inside the trunk. All we know is that it will be hotter than Hades in there and suck the water right out of them."

"Then we make our way to Stockholm. The call will be placed to Washington, and Nikolai will speak with the American President. The call will be automatically routed through to our Sovbloc controller, waiting with the P5 team in River House, which will route the call to the President's secure line in Washington."

"All of which assumes the KGB broke off the chase at the water," Bolling said. "We can't promise that, but we do have the security team with us at that point. Just in case."

"We've then got a two-hour drive to Turku," Emma said.

"And Longfellow and Sue Ellen go to meet a lawyer the next day in Helsinki. After that, they return to Moscow."

"Where they'll probably be arrested," Bolling chimed in. "God forbid that, but knowing the Soviets, they will come down hard on the British Embassy for this."

69

6:40 a.m. Dobrinsky Prospekt, Moscow

Roy Longfellow's dog decided to ride along. Her name was Lucky, and her favorite pastime was riding in the car. She came inside the house just as his wife, Sue Ellen, was packing a Helsinki trip bag.

"C'mere, Lucky," Sue Ellen said. She reached down and scratched her dog in the way dogs enjoyed. Lucky's hair was long and very thick. She was a Russian dog, a Caucasian Shepherd Dog that the Russians' bred as guard dogs for their prisons and bear hunting in the Siberian wilderness. Tradition said the dog would wade into a bear twenty times its size without hesitation and kill the bear. Lucky pawed at Sue Ellen's leg. "What?" she said. "Do you suspect a car ride upcoming? Want to go?"

Lucky sat on her haunches and watched the fevered packing. Sue Ellen ignored her. Bored, Lucky walked to her water bowl, took a drink, then headed again for the backyard through her waist-high doggy door.

While they packed and moved about their flat, Sue Ellen and Roy Longfellow kept up an ongoing discussion of Linda's legal needs and how long the trip would take and how fast they needed to get there and post the sister's bail money. The microphones in their flat reported all of it.

The British MI6 agent knew the Soviets would be using sniffing dogs, infamous German Shepherds, capable of quickly locating concealed bodies at the ferry landing. Longfellow could only hope they went past without sniffing. It was a long shot, because why else did they have the dogs? Still, there was nothing they could do to throw them off the scent.

The day was cold. Sue Ellen wore a wool skirt with a white blouse and padded jacket. She armed herself because her trust in Soviet agreements had been broken too many times during their stay in Russia. Then she went into the kitchen where she put together a picnic basket full of sandwiches and carrots to be brought out at the church parking lot in Tallinn if Nikolai wasn't there and they had no choice but to wait for him. A picnic would provide some cover. She also packed spare diapers, baby food, and a change of clothes for Angie, her daughter, and Sasha. At the last minute, she tossed in Lucky's bowl, a bag of dog food, and a couple of rawhide bones.

They put Lucky on her leash, loaded Angie and her diaper bag and spare supplies, and went to the elevator in their building. Longfellow himself punched the ground floor button.

On a different floor of the same building, Rodney Mallard and Cindy likewise made preparations for a long drive.

The Technical Services engineers had specially modified the Citroën awaiting them in the parking lot down below their building at the British Embassy. Now, its backseat was removable from the trunk, a simple modification involving the unfastening of four L-brackets designed to hold the upright portion of the seat in place.

The Mallards climbed into the Citroën and then waited until the Longfellows in their Saab pulled up alongside, waved, and then drove ahead, leading the way while the Mallards followed.

70

6:45 a.m. Kinovov City Park, Moscow

The Longfellow-Mallard vehicles were paced by two KGB vehicles, one assigned to the Longfellow Saab, one to the Mallard Citroën.

Oleg Medeved, Lieutenant, KGB, drove the KGB vehicle on Longfellow's rear bumper. He was a stout, heavily muscled man who wore wireframe eyeglasses and chain-smoked. He was a weightlifter and a runner—his 10K times worsening the longer he smoked—always armed with two guns, one in a shoulder holster, the other in an ankle holster. As they said at KGB stations, he was always ready to make a Westerner die for the Soviet homeland.

Longfellow—followed by Medeved with Mallard just behind—drove a circuitous route around Moscow, ever-widening his way from Red Square, as if trying, unsuccessfully, to shake his tail. Medeved accommodated Longfellow, eventually backing off and running parallel to Longfellow's Saab so that he might believe he had dry-cleaned the KGB vehicle. Mallard's tail also dropped away as agreed between Medeved and the other KGB drivers on their two-way radios.

Longfellow and Mallard broke off the evasive maneuvers fifteen minutes later and began driving straight to Nikolai's jogging route.

At the city park where Captain John Winters had hidden, Longfellow and Mallard abruptly turned in and followed the jogging path until coming upon a lone jogger, his face hidden inside his hooded sweatshirt, wearing the same brand of jogging shoes that Nikolai wore, head down, arms pumping.

Longfellow and Mallard pulled up beside Winters, who suddenly stopped his run and double-timed it to the Mallard's Citroën. Mallard swerved to the shoulder, pulled the key from the ignition, stepped out into the freezing morning air, and opened his trunk.

Winters climbed into the trunk and lay down on his side. Mallard slammed the trunk shut.

None of this was lost on Oleg Medeved, who observed the entire pickup and sequester from a half a mile away with his Kenko binoculars.

Once inside the trunk, Captain Winters, lying on his left side, so he was facing toward the Citroën's engine in the front of the car, pushed free the backseat's upright portion and wiggled his body into the rear passenger compartment where he continued to lie flat in the backseat.

Then he was ready for a long, comfortable drive.

At the park entrance, Longfellow turned left, and Mallard turned right. They threaded their way back through Moscow until, on the other side of the city, Mallard turned north to Vyborg, while Longfellow turned west toward Leningrad.

The KGB Volga car radios erupted around Moscow. Mallard was broadcast to be headed for Vyborg with Nikolai Semenov in his trunk. The decision was made to allow him to proceed to Vyborg because the Soviets couldn't be seen randomly searching an embassy's official vehicle somewhere in between. At Vyborg, the car would be searched. Everyone inside would be arrested and taken to Lubyanka and thrown into the dungeon for interrogation.

Oleg Medeved, meanwhile, was ordered to keep after the Longfellow vehicle.

Upon hearing all this, Colonel Viktor Bucharov, traveling at top speed toward Leningrad, broke in with his car radio. "It is a ruse," he warned KGB Moscow and the other drivers. "That's not Nikolai in the trunk of the Mallard vehicle. Stop it now, and you will see."

General Masirov, monitoring the radio traffic from his office, picked up his transceiver, and issued an order contravening what Bucharov said. "Nonsense," he said in his command voice. "It is Nikolai Semenov in that trunk. I want four officers to follow him to Vyborg and intercept him there. Arrests are to be made, and the criminals brought here and chained in the dungeon. Then I will interrogate them with the aid of General Barishsky. That is all."

Bucharov switched off his KGB radio. He had heard all the KGB nonsense he could stand for one day. He knew Masirov was wrong, that he had fallen for a classic bait-and-switch. More than ever, he knew Nikolai was on the Leningrad train as reported by the stationmaster. Bucharov planned on meeting him there, shooting both him and his daughter, and returning to Moscow a hero. He shook his head at Masirov's stupidity, yet again dumbfounded how the KGB continued to support the General and follow his lead.

Bucharov turned up the volume on his classical music station and roared on toward Leningrad.

71

12:00 p.m., Neighborhood Park, Helsinki Finland

Magnuson and Bolling unwrapped the sandwiches they had brought along and ate their lunch. They were only hours away from greeting Nikolai on Finnish soil if all went according to plan.

72

1:30 p.m., Leningrad Churnicha Cafe

The Longfellows had prearranged to meet a contact. It had been decided it would look best if Roy and Sue Ellen and Angie stopped for lunch. They found the cafe the CIA had chosen in Leningrad and parked in front. A single KGB Saab parked beside them. The Brits piled out of their vehicle, carelessly opening their trunk, retrieving baby things, to show they had nothing to hide. They took the necessary baby items for a diaper change and feed for Angie and went inside for lunch. The KGB didn't follow.

Inside, they headed for the third booth on the right and joined the single man waiting there. His name was Daniel Danbury, and he was CIA out of Estonia. The waitress brought menus. Following the small talk, the table fell silent. Longfellow, appearing to study the menu, said from the side of his mouth to Danbury, "I'm guessing Tallinn is about four hours up the road."

Danbury replied, "Unless we get pulled over, I'm thinking six o'clock."

"That's a big unless. What about the thug outside?"

"Thug? You mean thugs."

Longfellow looked out to see that the one KGB trailing car had become two. Three agents leaned against their car, smoking and laughing.

Danbury said, "It's time for me to help you lose them."

Longfellow's eyes widened. "That's a great attitude, but what does it mean?"

"It means we're going to outfox these bastards."

Longfellow looked from the window to Danbury across the table. "They're going to follow us to the church in Tallinn unless our cars can outrun the Volgas. Maybe we can get far enough ahead to swerve into the church street while they go tearing past."

"That's our plan? To outrun them and hope they don't see us turn off? That sounds like some Walt Disney cartoon. We have to do better than that."

Longfellow nodded grimly. "Unless you have something better."

"I say we pull off the road and lead them into the forest."

"Really? And then? This is very thin ice. We could be murdered confronting them."

Danbury shrugged. "I could cause an accident and delay them."

"They would only call ahead and tell the border to stop us."

"And Nikolai?"

"We pray he can make his way to the ferry and somehow cross over. I don't have an answer for that."

"You're right, what a terrible plan. I don't see anything except a dead KGB fugitive at the end. I'm sorry to be so negative."

"I know. You're reading my mind."

Longfellow poked disinterestedly at his hamburger patty. He administered a plop of mustard out of the plastic bottle. He took a tasteless bite.

Then they were loading in and pulling away from the cafe. On the outskirts of Leningrad, they passed a large GAI police post with a watchtower. Moments later, a blue Volga with two male passengers and a tall radio aerial tucked behind them.

"No," said Longfellow.

"We're finished, then," Danbury said in his car.

They could only drive on to the rendezvous, both drivers trying not to panic and make a premature run for it.

Still, the KGB followed.

73

2:15 p.m., Main railway station, Leningrad

He placed Sasha into the knapsack and stood. This time, he put the top flap loosely over her sleepy head, secured the straps, and hoisted the pack onto his back. Nikolai and Sasha were first off the train when it pulled in and rocked to a stop. Afraid to look behind, he walked swiftly down the elevated platform to the station entrance. It was dark on the platform, the enormous structure covered to keep the rain and snow outside. He was wearing the Soviet Border Troops' uniform with a soldier's knapsack on his back and drew no looks or double-takes as he made his way along the platform.

Waiting just inside, his hand clutching the hidden gun inside his pocket, Colonel Victor Bucharov was scanning the faces milling around. Then he saw the train pull in and, from a distance, saw the man who he thought looked like Nikolai Semenov. But he wore a Border Troop uniform, so he kept looking. There must have been seventy or eighty people walking up the platform all at once. Bucharov was bobbing and weaving and trying to keep his head above to spot Nikolai.

Nikolai knew Bucharov's face and picked it up just ten paces away from the station's doors. He averted his face and looked away as he stepped inside. However, it did not escape his notice that Bucharov was gripping his gun inside his coat pocket and meant to shoot as soon as his target was spotted. Nikolai stepped to the side of an older woman, slowed, and was abreast of her as they passed by Bucharov. She shielded him from view as he grasped her arm and offered to help with her bag. She refused to release the bag, jerking it away, but by now, they were beyond Bucharov, so Nikolai hurried in a slow trot for the exits.

Bucharov stood planted in the doorway, forcing passengers to pass around him, and once they were considerably thinned out, he decided he would board and search the entire train himself. It was better anyway because, when he fired his gun, there would be less chance of hitting a bystander and creating the kind of stew that always made. It had happened to him before, and he would just as soon avoid the red tape an inadvertent shooting would spark.

Nikolai hurried outside to the taxi stand. Except there were no taxis in the area. But several private cars circled, their drivers leaning toward the crowd, looking for fares. Nikolai climbed into one. "To the bus station," he said.

Bucharov by now had reached the lead engine and stood, waiting, until the final passenger had passed him. Still no Semenov. He boarded the train, expecting to find his quarry hiding in a bathroom. He ran car to car, banging bathroom doors open, brandishing his weapon. When he finished with the last car, he climbed back down to the platform. He shut his eyes and forced his mind to go over it. He had no doubt the traitor was headed either for the border at Tallinn in Soviet Estonia or Vyborg in Soviet Russia. He ran for the train station, passed through, and then out to where he'd parked earlier. He decided on Vyborg by instinct and decided to go that route instead of Tallinn. He jumped into his Volga and headed out of Leningrad.

Meanwhile, Nikolai arrived at the bus station at 2:30. To Nikolai, it only represented the second step to freedom from everything Russian once he got on a bus. He hurried inside, this time shooting a look back over his shoulder. Then he took a seat in the waiting area before proceeding to the ticket counter.

He was going to scan the arrivals for the face of Viktor Bucharov. If he saw him, he would try to surprise the man and kill him with his hands. He had attended the same school as all KGB officers who knew that tactic. He set Sasha beside him on the bench and gave her a half-pint of milk in a carton. While she dribbled milk down her chin, Nikolai fought to control his frightened breathing and prepared to do battle.

74

2:30 p.m., Leningrad

Nikolai walked up to the ticket counter. He had most of his eighty rubles left, the notes folded in his right pants pocket. The escape plan called for him to catch the bus to Tallinn and get off at the city limits and flag down a taxi for the church. When it was his turn at the counter, he bought two bus tickets to Tallinn.

The old bus was half full as it wheezed out of Zelenogorsk. Dense woods soon lined the road with birch and aspen, broken by the occasional clearing with picnic tables. He saw several places where a running spy could hide. For several minutes, he wished he was anyplace but here. Was it too late to return to Moscow and turn himself in and beg for mercy? Would there be mercy for him? What if they knew his name from inside London MI5? Or even from the American CIA? Then he would be taken out and summarily shot and buried in a shallow hole outside Moscow by the river. Maybe Sasha with him.

75

6:10 p.m., Tallinn highway, twenty kilometers east

Longfellow tried speeding up. The KGB cars stayed right with him. He tried slowing down. They slowed down. Then he grew frustrated and angry. At a forest service road turnout, he slowed and turned onto the forest service road. He drove into the forest two kilometers before coming to a turn-around. He abruptly swung around with Daniel Danbury following on his bumper. Now they were staring head-on at the KGB cars. Longfellow threw the car into park and got out. He walked up to the black Volga and knocked on the window. The driver rolled it down.

In Russian, Longfellow said. "I need your name."

The driver smiled his crooked Russian smile and said nothing.

"Your name, sir!"

"Why my name? You are writing a letter to London?"

"No, I'm filing a formal complaint with Foreign Service. You are harassing us as we're on private business. I demand you back off, turn around, and leave us alone now."

The driver's smile faded. "Or you what?"

"Or I'll file a complaint!"

"Should we follow you back to Moscow while you file this complaint?"

"All right, then, dammit. It's your head on the block. I'm going to have my people follow your people even when they have to pee in the middle of the night. Count on it!"

"Get in your car, Mr. Longfellow. So lonely out here. Anything could happen. Is that your wife with you? May I see?"

Longfellow stepped back. "Sweet Jesus," he muttered and retreated to his car, shaken. He made Sue Ellen lock her door, and he did as well. "Animals," he shouted into the microphones. "KGB are bastards!"

He then started up the embassy vehicle and went roaring back up the forest service road in the highway's direction, Danbury close behind.

"What did you tell them?" Sue Ellen asked, no longer caring about the eavesdropping.

"I told them the United Kingdom was going to follow their spies even when they got up to pee in the middle of the night. And we will, by God!"

Back on the highway, the kilometer marker posts were counting up. Roy Longfellow had no plan in mind at all as he drove at a high rate, drawing ever nearer to Tallinn city limits. With one car in front and three behind, it was developing into a sorely lost cause. He would be unable to turn in at St. Nicholas Church, leaving poor Nikolai on his own. He knew if the KGB were still with them at the church, he could only fly by and continue to the ferry and make their crossing to avoid any further suspicion. Nikolai and Sasha would be left in the city on their own, on foot, without means to cross the ferry as they had no departure papers. They would easily be captured and returned to Moscow.

Coming around a long curve, he saw Danbury's car suddenly flit across the rearview mirror. He turned to see, and there was Danbury, crosswise on the road, blocking the following vehicles. Longfellow tromped down on the gas. He was pulling away and putting distance between them. One hundred meters, 300, 350. He kept accelerating. Then he drove around a long sweeping curve with a terrible blind spot. He was overdriving his sight distance and, suddenly, coming out of the turn, he ran up behind a green farm tractor pulling a wagonload of hay. A large lory was approaching from the opposite direction. Longfellow slammed on his brakes, and his car swerved sideways, making a power stop before hitting the tractor from behind. He watched in his rearview. Just as quickly, the black Volga came running up on him but didn't totally slow, instead flying around him, cutting in ahead between Longfellow and the tractor. The Saab's driver tossed off a wave and threw his head back.

Longfellow pounded his steering wheel. "Damn it all!" he cried.

He looked behind for Danbury, who caught up to him several kilometers later. It was only at that moment that Longfellow's mind cleared enough to wonder how Daniel Danbury knew about the cross-road maneuver that only the British had discussed on the phone before leaving Moscow. Then it came to him. Of course, the

CIA was listening in on British calls. He had to stop and shake his head. Of course they would; they were the CIA.

They cut their speed and glided past the mile markers, boxed in front and rear by the KGB.

The last hope had gone nowhere.

76

6:15 p.m. East of Tallinn

Four hours later, Nikolai and Sasha were two kilometers east of Tallinn. Sasha had slept most of the journey. Nikolai had read two magazines the bus company had placed inside the chair backs. One of them extolled the virtues of travel on that particular bus line; the other was dedicated to Leningrad's nightspots. As he read, he dozed intermittently.

They soon found themselves among a large number of military vehicles, including armored personnel carriers. The border area was heavily militarized, as were all Russian border areas. He wondered whether his uniform would work here.

Would he make it to the port in the trunk of a car? Or would he miss the rendezvous with Longfellow and have to make his way to the ferry and try to talk his way across as a lieutenant colonel in the Border Troops? A colonel with a child? The knapsack helped, but it wasn't wartime, so why would he be wearing such a thing?

The road curved to the right. Nikolai increasingly recognized bits and pieces of the passing countryside from photographs Emma Magnuson had provided at London's safe house. He sat upright in his seat. The time was nearing when he would have to make a decision. He would either climb down from the bus and take a taxi to the church or take the bus to the ferry where he could try to cross as an officer on official business. Or perhaps, climb down, mix with the crowd, and wait for Longfellow while acting as a Border guard on duty at the ferry. But what of Sasha? What would he do with her in that case? The ideas for what he might try, thanks to the uniform, were beginning to form in his mind. But a border guard with a baby? How suspicious did that look? He would be arrested on the spot and maybe gunned down by the guards with their automatic weapons. No, he had to climb down off the bus inside the city limits and make his way to the church.

He shuddered in his bus seat. A bead of sweat glistened on his forehead. He recognized more signs, petrol stations, turnouts, and curves in the road as places he had visited before in photographs.

Soon they entered the city limits. Jumping to his feet, he took a final view out the window and knew. He had arrived, and it was time. He hurried forward to the driver. "Sorry, I'm feeling sick. I'm going to vomit. Can you let me off?"

Irritated, the bus driver pulled to the side of the road, stopped, and opened the accordion door. Nikolai climbed down with the knapsack on his back and Sasha in his arms, hurried to the rear of the bus, bent over, and made vomiting noises as if he were quite ill. He hated the moment because everyone on the bus watched him and could identify him when the KGB started asking about him at the ferry landing. They would remember him getting off here within several hundred meters of the city limits.

The roadside was dark. He started walking, passing the bus's front as it waited for him to get back on. Then he was ahead of it and waving the bus to pass him. Once he loaded Sasha into his knapsack, he didn't look back and walked boldly along as if on duty. The bus wheezed on by. Nikolai didn't look up so as not to give any backward-looking passengers a chance to see and remember his face. Then it was gone, out of sight around the next curve.

After walking a kilometer, he reached the petrol station's phone booth. He checked his watch. Time to call a taxi and head for the church. It would be at least two hours before Longfellow arrived.

A lone KGB car crept past, studying customers inside the fuel stations and cafes. Nikolai was inside the men's room in the petrol station at that time with Sasha, her trying to pee into the toilet. They came out, and he purchased a Coke and fresh milk but didn't see a thing, for the KGB car was long gone. But Nikolai knew Bucharov wasn't far behind. He played the scenario in his head as they rode in the taxi to St. Nicholas Church. Bucharov would locate the point where Nikolai had climbed down from the bus—the bus driver would remember. Bucharov would then begin searching the area where Nikolai met the taxi. He would locate the taxis working the area and find out where Nikolai exited the cab at the Church. About that time, the Brits should arrive. Who would get to him first? He shuddered and poured the fresh milk into Sasha's bottle. While she drank, he took the milk carton and Coke bottle to the trash container just outside the church and made a deposit.

His mind started playing tricks. He knew the embassy vehicles driven by Longfellow would have to be diplomatically licensed, and all adults would need papers permitting them to leave the Soviet Union. Such documents were signed without comment when diplomats came and went by airplane out of Sheremetyevo

Airport. But when they left the country by motor vehicle, it was a much more involved process. Who was going? For how long? Purpose of the trip? Returning when? Embassy orders permitting to leave? Any of the red tape could have snarled and prevented his pickup vehicle from even leaving Moscow. They had no way of telling him that, either, as all communications had gone black. He was terrified, more so maybe than he had ever been.

He decided he would hitchhike to a cafe and have a drink.

Sasha wouldn't mind, and he needed one.

77

6:35 p.m., A cafe south of St. Nicholas Church

Night had fallen. A Saab pulled over when the driver saw Nikolai hitchhiking. *Avtostop* was common in Russia and encouraged by Soviet authorities. The young driver was carefully dressed in the latest style of civilian clothes. Possibly military or KGB, thought Nikolai, as he climbed inside the vehicle with Sasha and took a seat. He thanked the driver without making eye contact, staring straight ahead. Luckily, the young driver couldn't have cared less about Nikolai's identity and drove on without a word. He did, however, play loud Russian folk music through the radio. Not the choice of any KGB officer.

He had the young man let him out at a cafe downtown and offered him three rubles. The young man took the money, tucked it in his breast pocket, and winked at his passenger. "Enjoy your meal," he said and roared off in a smoke cloud from the car's tailpipe. A few minutes later, Nikolai was sitting down with two bottles of beer and a plate of Russian cabbage rolls with gravy. Sasha had finger food: a hard-boiled egg and a blini. She touched very little, preferring to bang her spoon on the table instead. The waitress stopped to ask how everything was. He told her excellent and meant it; the cabbage rolls were delicious, and he was ravenous.

Then he asked, "How far to the ferry?"

It was easy. "Two kilometers on the nose."

"Do militia men stop here often?"

She rolled her eyes. "Ugly Russian soldiers always coming and going and always asking me to go in their cars. Oh, yes, they come too often."

"When—I mean, will they be by yet today?"

"Of course. They eat at all hours." At a bell ringing, she said, "I must get a plate. That's my order."

He heard the bell ringing for her again. He dug back into his cabbage rolls and swilled a bottle of beer. He helped Sasha with a forkful of blini. She resisted, turning her head side to side and refusing to eat. He gave up and sat back. The relaxation was almost instant with the first one-half beer and cabbage rolls. A plan formed in his head, the head of a lieutenant colonel of the Border Troops, or so his uniform said.

Twenty minutes later, he paid, and they left the restaurant. He held Sasha's hand, and they walked up alongside the road and stopped. He looked both ways, trying to make up his mind: back to the church or on to the ferry? Sasha pulled against his hand and pointed. He looked in her direction, along the road ahead. "There's a sign," he said, following her eyes.

A military vehicle was heading their way on the road.

78

6:40 p.m., Leningrad to Tallinn highway

Longfellow looked down at the dashboard. He was doing 120 kilometers per hour, and the KGB cars were right on his rear. Two police vehicles had joined the convoy, and a third KGB car was following behind even farther back. Longfellow decided it was now or never.

He took his foot off the accelerator. As he slowed, so did the rest of the convoy. At kilometer 340, he slowed again, until they were rolling at barely 50 kilometers per hour. Other cars farther back began to stack up and began swerving into the oncoming lane to look at what the holdup was.

Then gradually, Longfellow increased his speed. So did Danbury, hanging just behind. The road again was straight and clear. Longfellow pressed the gas pedal further down, and the Saab smoothly accelerated to 140 kilometers per hour. More than 2400 meters opened up between Danbury and the closest KGB car behind him. Kilometer post 345 shot past. The rendezvous point was just ten kilometers ahead.

Longfellow swung around a bend and hit the brakes. An army column was crossing the road with its howitzers, rocket launchers, and armored personnel carriers. A bakery van was stopped ahead of Longfellow, already waiting.

"That's it," Longfellow said to the bugs. "We're done."

79

6:40 p.m., City of Tallinn

Bucharov wasted no time interrogating bus drivers who arrived in Tallinn that day from Leningrad. The afternoon bus had been driven by Igor Stravinsky, an Estonian who had been making the run between Leningrad and Estonia for over fifteen years. Bucharov showed him Nikolai's picture—the formal file photo of Nikolai in his KGB uniform.

Stravinsky viewed the photo and instantly spoke. "He became ill at the city limits on the way into town. I had to pull over the bus and let him off."

"Was he traveling with a child?"

"Yes, I think it was a girl maybe a year or two at most. She boarded my bus in his backpack, which I found odd."

"It was outside the city limits where you dropped them? What is there in that part of town where you might go to meet someone? Some well-known meeting place?"

The bus driver scratched his head. "There's nothing on that end of the city. No landmarks, no ancient buildings. Some old churches, but no one goes there anymore."

"Most popular church in the area?"

"That would be Saint Nicholas."

"All right, thank you," Bucharov said. "I'm leaving now. If you think of anything else, you will call KGB Moscow and give me a message. Do you understand?"

The bus driver was frightened. "I will call if anything else comes back. Thank you, Colonel."

Bucharov turned on his heel and left.

His next stop was the taxi barn, two blocks over from the bus barn. All drivers were out picking up fares, he learned. Two drivers in between shifts were questioned. Neither recognized the man in the photograph.

Minutes later, Igor Stravinsky called KGB Moscow from the bus station office. He'd remembered something just after the colonel had left. "This is Igor Stravinsky calling from Tallinn. I have an important message for Colonel Bucharov."

The clerk in Moscow smacked his gum, waiting. "Go on."

"Tell the Colonel the man he is looking for was wearing a uniform."

"What kind of uniform?"

"Not KGB but Border Troops. He was high-up, I believe."

"And who is Colonel Bucharov looking for?"

"I don't have a name. He was on my bus, and he was wearing a uniform."

The call ended. The Moscow clerk took the pink phone message and crammed it into a pigeon hole, one of twenty-five above his desk. The hole was marked *Bucharov*.

Bucharov found Saint Nicholas Church on Tallinn's edge, within two kilometers of where the bus driver Stravinsky said he'd stopped his bus and allowed the passenger to climb down with the child on his back.

He parked and approached the main door on the front of the church. He lifted the handle and pulled.

Locked. So, he walked around to the rear of the church and looked there. No clues, no discarded snack wrappers, or drink cups. No discarded containers once holding a pint of milk.

There were other churches in the immediate area. He had torn the page out of the phone book and intended to visit those within three kilometers of the bus's stopping point.

He walked around to the front of Saint Nicholas and knocked loudly and tried the handle again on the off-chance that someone inside had heard him trying a few minutes ago and had come to see who was there.

To the side was a trash receptacle. He tipped the lid and looked inside. A single half-pint milk carton and Coke bottle. He reached inside and touched the milk container with his fingertip. Cool to the touch...maybe.

He jogged back to his Volga.

He knew he couldn't be more than minutes behind. Believing he had found a clue in the milk carton, he headed directly for the border crossing at the ferry.

80

7:00 p.m., Zerzatasky road at cafe

The militia vehicle had stopped at the side of the road where Nikolai stood with Sasha lashed on his back in the knapsack, hitchhiking.

"Where is your unit, sir?" asked the passenger, leaning out the window.

"Gone off without me. I've been on watch out here for an escaped British officer."

"Where are you headed?"

"Ferry, same as you."

"Then climb on inside. I'll make room."

Nikolai climbed into the truck.

"Welcome aboard, sir."

"Thank you," Nikolai said. "Let's give it the gas, shall we?"

At Sasha's cry from inside the knapsack, the soldier asked, "Whose baby?"

"Mine. We're meeting her mother. We're divorced."

No other questions were asked, and the small truck shot on down the road, headed for the ferry crossing.

81

7:10 p.m. 106th Tallinn Border Detachment

They arrived at the border crossing station at seven. It was good because Sasha was getting fussy and needed to get out and walk.

Nikolai waited until his ride had pulled into the expansive parking area to the checkpoint station's right. Then he climbed out, thanked the driver, and walked along beside the vehicle as it pulled away, shielding him from anyone who might be watching, which nobody was. Now he stood there in full view once the militia truck pulled away, wearing a lieutenant colonel's uniform, a baby strapped to his back, going to meet his ex-wife.

Along the station's outer wall was a bench. Nikolai sat down on the bench and lit a cigar. He placed Sasha beside him, still inside his army knapsack, which he then unbundled. He put her on the ground and told her to stay with him. For once, she obeyed, playing at his feet with her doll. He would smoke and get his bearings. He picked Sasha up and offered her the evening bottle of milk.

Five minutes after Nikolai sat down, he spotted the British embassy car pull into the lane for border inspections, and he immediately knew. Then he looked again. The car just behind the British embassy car was an American embassy car. Were both for him? What would they do if he approached? He didn't know them, and they didn't know him. He doubted they even had his photograph. He looked behind the second car, knowing what he would see. Sure enough, KGB. Now four of them. He leaned back against the wall, hiding his face in shadows.

Suddenly, Bucharov climbed out of a Volga idling directly behind Daniel Danbury and walked forward. "Unlock this trunk!" he shouted at Danbury. Danbury jumped out and unlocked the trunk. Bucharov looked inside. "Where have you hidden Semenov?"

"I don't know who you're talking about," Danbury said. "I'm on official American Embassy business in Helsinki."

Bucharov walked around Danbury's car and went ahead. He walked around to the lead embassy vehicle and knocked on the glass with his knuckles.

"Open up!" he called.

Longfellow climbed out.

"Open your trunk immediately!"

Longfellow reached inside, removed his key from the ignition, and went around and opened his trunk.

Bucharov leaned in and looked inside. "Where is Semenov?" he demanded.

"Who?"

Bucharov cursed and turned. He stormed back to his Volga and climbed inside. Suddenly, he pulled out of line and made a squealing U-turn. The other KGB drivers and police followed their leader, squealing U-turns, and heading back the direction they had just come at breakneck speeds.

Nikolai stood. He gently placed Sasha and her doll back in the knapsack and lifted her like a bundle of luggage. Then he walked over to the vehicles being inspected before they were checked at the actual crossing gate.

At the second embassy vehicle, he knocked on the glass. "Please open your trunk again."

Danbury got out of his vehicle and opened his trunk a second time. Nikolai bent forward and looked in the trunk, lifting small bags and examining them as a border guard would. "TINKER," he whispered. Then loudly, "Leave it open, thank you," he told Danbury. Now he was blocking the view of the cars behind with the American's trunk lid.

Nikolai went forward. Longfellow's glass was down. "Open your trunk again, please," Nikolai told Longfellow.

Longfellow again reached inside and retrieved his keys, then proceeded to the car's trunk and inserted the key. He twisted, and the trunk flew open.

"What do we have here?" Nikolai asked, and then he bent double, leaning forward as if inspecting the trunk. He then handed his knapsack and Sasha to Longfellow. Longfellow then witnessed the border officer bend down and turn onto his side and draw his knees to his chest. He said, "I am Colonel Nikolai Semenov. Close the trunk, please."

Astounded, Longfellow slammed the trunk shut. He turned and looked around. Sasha's hair barely showed above the top of the knapsack. All officers were busy with other vehicles, dogs here and there, sniffing, agents looking inside and out. Longfellow's hands were shaking as he climbed back inside the car. He handed the knapsack and baby to Sue Ellen.

"What is it?" Sue Ellen asked, no longer considering that the KGB would be listening in.

"Twisted my back, that's all," said Longfellow. "Had to open the trunk for the officer. My back is on fire."

"Goodness. We'll find a back doctor."

"Indeed."

82

7:15 p.m. 106th Tallinn Border Detachment

Danbury shut his trunk and climbed back inside his car. He started the engine. Longfellow and Danbury then pulled forward into a car park. They went inside the Border Troops station. They joined the queue at the customs and immigration counter. Filling out paperwork for leaving the Soviet Union could take a long time. Sue Ellen prepared for a ten-minute delay, at least.

Nikolai, his eyes growing accustomed to the dark, held perfectly still, so the vehicle didn't sway on its suspension. Angie was awake and grumpy, crying out and wanting her bottle. The soldiers ignored it. Babies always wanted something.

Finally, Sue Ellen picked her up and walked between her car and the next. The woman in that car also had a small child, so the women began chatting while Sue Ellen rocked the baby and patted her on the diaper. She then looked back into their Saab and was relieved to see Sasha was taking a late nap. Lucky was happily working on a rawhide bone.

Border guards passed between the lines of cars, looking right and left. Sue Ellen braced herself to suddenly become violently ill if they tried to search the trunk. She would demand that all searches stop under the Geneva Convention. At that point, they would probably all be arrested.

"Get back in your car, please," said a young border guard passing by.

Sue Ellen nodded and placed Angie into her child seat before she climbed into the passenger seat. Lucky was next to Angie, gnawing her bone and taking up way more than her share of the back seat. Next to Lucky was Sasha.

Longfellow made Russian small talk with the woman working the customs kiosk. He had to control the impulse to hurry her as she looked over the dozen or more student visas that had preceded him into the station as the Finnish students headed back to Helsinki. The other cars searched were mostly Finnish visitors heading home from Moscow. Drugs would be the target ever since the Moscow Mafia had flooded the streets with illegal drugs.

Inside the trunk, it was sweltering from the vehicle's transmission and high-speed run. Nikolai shifted his weight, causing the car to rock ever so slightly.

Sue Ellen turned in her seat. A Soviet dog handler appeared and stood eight yards away, looking intently at the British and American embassy cars and stroking his German Shepherd.

Further back, she saw a second sniffer dog inspecting a container truck. The first dog approached, eager and panting, straining at its chain. Sue Ellen reached casually for the second rawhide bone with its distinctive meaty flavor. She pushed open the door and held the bone out for the dog, bobbing it under his nose. He quickly snatched the rawhide up in his mouth. His handler commanded him to drop it. The dog only looked at him. His handler commanded again in his harshest voice, but the dog still ignored him and turned and began walking away. He would have continued, except he hit the end of his chain. Yet he wouldn't drop the bone, no matter the threats from the Soviet guard. At that moment, his unsmiling handler yanked him away. But when he stooped to remove the bone from the dog's mouth, it growled, baring its teeth, and the handler came upright, red-faced. He continued with his dog back down the line of cars.

The other dog had closed in on the car and was sniffing at the trunk, inches away from Nikolai. The fugitive heard the muffled sound of Soviet voices.

As the dog circled the car, sniffing as it went, Sue Ellen knew it was time to walk Lucky. Lucky hated when other dogs sniffed around her family. She was very possessive and wouldn't hesitate to bare her fangs. Sue Ellen let Lucky head for the rear of the car, where she encountered the German Shepherd aching to get inside the trunk. Sue Ellen loosened her grip on Lucky's chain, which Lucky took as a signal. Instantly, Lucky headed for the German Shepherd, whose handler saw her coming. He knew all about the breed —they were Russian and used to guard the meanest prisoners in the world inside Soviet prisons. Alas, they were also used by the Russians to hunt bears. He jerked with all his strength at the German Shepherd's chain, removing it from Lucky's immediate danger.

"Oh, I'm so sorry!" Sue Ellen cried in Russian. She caught up and seized Lucky's collar.

Having had enough and caring too much about his dog's welfare, the guard moved along the line to the next car, Danbury's car. It was unoccupied, so the officer headed for the car next to Danbury's. After Lucky went to the bathroom on a swatch of grass, Sue Ellen and Lucky climbed back inside their vehicle, where Lucky resumed gnawing her rawhide bone. Sue Ellen's heart was thumping in her chest.

It had been too close.

The men returned with the completed paperwork. They re-entered their vehicles and began waiting with the others.

Fifteen minutes later, a border guard came casually strolling outside the guard station, holding up the three consents to leave the Soviet Union. He leaned inside Longfellow's car and checked the signed clearances against the adults. Same thing with Danbury's car. Satisfied with the matching faces and photos, he smiled and wished all a safe trip.

A line of seven cars had formed at the last barrier, consisting of a razor-wire fence with two elevated lookout posts and machine guns.

For the next twenty minutes, the vehicles inched forward, submitting passports a final time, then driving onto the ferry. Longfellow broke out in a drenching sweat though the outside air was freezing in late October. The line was taking forever, and he was about to lose it, even for a veteran spy. They had to be careful since they were scrutinized every few seconds by guards with binoculars in the towers.

When they finally inched forward to the gate, the Soviet Border officials examined the British diplomatic passports, turning them over and back and talking amongst themselves. They looked at the occupants again and then at the official documents. Finally, the passports were stamped, and simultaneously the barrier was raised.

83

7:25 p.m. East of Tallinn

Colonel Bucharov wasted no time calling by radio to KGB Moscow.

"Semenov is not at Tallinn. Update me on Vyborg."

"You've had your radio turned off!" cried the dispatcher. "We've been calling and calling you!"

"What?"

"The MI6 car that went to Vyborg. The stowaway in the trunk was a United States Marine!"

Bucharov immediately understood. He slammed on his brakes while signaling and swung a high-speed U-turn back toward Tallinn.

This couldn't be allowed to stand. Somehow, Semenov was already there. He was suddenly sure of it. And most likely, he was now inside the trunk of the British Embassy vehicle.

He picked up his microphone and called ahead to the Tallinn Border Guard station. "Stop the British Embassy vehicle! There's a fugitive inside!"

The line went dead for several minutes. Then the border guard came back online. "Where are you, Colonel?"

"Ten minutes east!"

"The embassy vehicles are no longer here. We're unable to locate."

Bucharov threw his transceiver's hand microphone at the dashboard. His rage overcame him. Pushing the accelerator to the floorboard, he drove wildly toward Tallinn.

But he was missing one piece of the puzzle. While KGB had shut down the scheduled Tallinn ferry crossing, the Sunday night ferry was a local custom, unscheduled on Soviet records.

Bucharov was unaware.

84

7:40 p.m. 106th Tallinnskiy Border Detachment

Longfellow drove onto the waiting ferry and parked on the sea level. By that point, it had filled, so Danbury went up one deck.

Longfellow switched off the engine as directed by the signage. Nobody spoke. He couldn't take his eyes from the review mirror, expecting the sudden return of Colonel Bucharov. He wiped sweat and more sweat from his face with a diaper, unable to control his terror.

At that second, the captain of the ferry announced over the loudspeaker, "*Ole hyvä ja pysy autoissasi!*" Please stay in your car!

The ferry moved away from the pier one foot, two feet, three.

Almost unbelievably, a Volga roared up to the pier. The driver's door flew open, and Bucharov leaped out, drawing his gun from his shoulder holster and aiming at Longfellow's car on the ferry's stern. The ferry was moving away in the water, so Bucharov tried jumping onto the stern but fell short, plunging off the pier and underwater. He surfaced and immediately twisted onto his side and took to side-stroking with one arm while pointing his gun with the other, crying out in Russian, demanding that the captain stop the vessel. Nothing. Like yelling at a mountain.

He put his face down in the water and swam, both arms and legs, propelling himself through the water faster than the ferry's sluggish pace.

Longfellow stood alongside his Saab, shocked to see the KGB officer still coming on. He ran to the trunk and unlocked it, all the while keeping one eye out for Bucharov.

A bewildered Nikolai sat up in the trunk.

"Bucharov!" Longfellow cried, pointing wildly at the stern. "He's coming!"

Nikolai's forearm lay across his eyes as he adjusted to the brilliant overhead parking lights. He sat up, shaking his head. "What?"

"Bucharov is coming up the stern ladder! I don't have a gun!"

Nikolai clambered out of the trunk and ran for the stern. He had to get there before Bucharov was aboard.

He just made the stern ladder as Bucharov's shoulders leveled with the railing. Nikolai chopped at the gun hand, sending the pistol spinning into the foamy sea as Bucharov brought his right hand up from his waist and chopped Nikolai in the throat, staggering him. He went down on one knee, violently choking and fighting for air. Bucharov lunged up and over the railing and kicked a heavy boot at Nikolai's head. Nikolai grabbed the boot just as it came at him and twisted with his full upper body,

Bucharov rotating violently to the side and slamming down on the deck, cracking his head on the steel plating. He moaned and tried sitting up, then fell back.

Nikolai was gasping for air yet, clutching at his throat. Slowly, he clung to the last car's bumper and climbed to his feet and was about to deliver a death blow to Bucharov when the KGB officer suddenly jumped upright using tremendous leg muscles and jerked Nikolai's legs out from under him. Nikolai flew backward, his head slamming against the metal flooring where it bounced once. Then he fell back and was still.

Bucharov bent and felt inside his right boot. He withdrew a long hunting knife and moved for Nikolai's throat. His arm swept closer and closer, but a small-caliber pistol barked just as the blade was at his throat. Bucharov started to turn around. "What—?" he managed to say before he fell forward, shot behind the ear by the .380 semiautomatic Sue Ellen had worn in her garter holster. The enormous roar of the ferry's engines had covered the noise. She approached Bucharov gingerly and looked at his death face. Then she turned her head away and shot him between the eyes.

Nikolai recovered and was struggling to sit up. Longfellow slipped his hands under his arms and helped him to his feet. Nikolai shook his head, focusing his eyes, and looked around for Bucharov, whom he found lying behind him, his head within a widening pool of blood. Then he looked at Sue Ellen.

Her gun had slipped around on her trigger finger so it was hanging upside down. The other hand covered her mouth. Then she spoke in a muffled tone. "My first kill."

Longfellow went to her and wrapped her in his arms. Nikolai came and tried to take the gun, but she jerked it away, saying, "It belongs in my holster. I'm not home in my own bed yet." She turned her back to Nikolai, lifted her skirt, and replaced her pistol in its garter holster. "Got to check the babies," she said solemnly and headed for the car.

Nikolai nodded appreciatively. "You know what's best. Thank you, madam," he called after her. Then, to Longfellow, "I am Nikolai Semenov, formerly a KGB Colonel. And you are MI6 Longfellow. We met when I gave you my baby, sir. How is she?"

"She was sleeping minutes ago. So was ours."

"I see."

Nikolai went to Bucharov and wrapped his arms around his midsection. To the dead body, he said, "Swimming, is it? All right, then." Then he lifted him up and over the stern rail and watched as he cartwheeled into the ferry's screws below. He went under and didn't float back up.

"We're not home free yet," Longfellow said and motioned toward his car's trunk. At the embassy car, Nikolai took a quick peek at Sasha, then sat down backward in the trunk, swung his legs up and over, and gave a thumbs-up sign.

Before Nikolai closed the lid, Longfellow said, "We have Finnish customs and immigration, then Finnish passport control. Then I can let you out, Colonel."

Nikolai, lying again inside the dark, knew the hurdle ahead. It would only require a single phone call from the Soviets in Tallinn to the Finns in Helsinki to turn them around.

Longfellow wiped his face with yet another diaper as the ferry plunged powerfully on its journey across the water. Beyond was Helsinki, Finland, its lights like diamonds on a hill. He sat back and shut his eyes. Sue Ellen fed crackers to the children. He reached and squeezed her shoulder. "Just wow," he whispered.

"I know," she said. "It wasn't your wife out there."

The crossing took two hours. Then the ferry unloaded in reverse-order, level by level, and a line of vehicles formed at Finnish customs beyond the pier. Ever so slowly, the embassy vehicles crept along. At last, they approached the lowered gate and came to a halt.

Passports were requested. Longfellow and Sue Ellen supplied theirs. The Finnish officer slowly examined the passports, then handed them back and came out of the kiosk to raise the barrier. But his phone rang. So he went back inside and talked forever on the phone.

Longfellow sank lower and lower in his seat, his eyes glued to his rearview mirror. He had no doubt the Soviets were on the other end of the phone line and that Finnish border guards would soon appear brandishing their machine guns. He caught a glimpse of the guard inside the station, talking animatedly on the phone while staring directly at his car.

The guard returned minutes later, yawning, and said to Longfellow. "Wife wants a fish for dinner. I told her I'm sick of fish. You would be too after three straight nights. You're free to go. Enjoy Finland."

Danbury followed just after.

It was 9:50p.m. Moscow time, 8:50 in Finland.

Inside the trunk, Nikolai felt the Saab pick up speed and then reach full highway velocity. Losing all thought of time and place, he suddenly tried to stand and cry out with joy, banging his head on the trunk in the process. Western rock and roll music poured from the front of the car back into the trunk.

He was free. Tears came to his eyes, and he turned his face to his shoulder, sobbing. It was all he could do not to shrivel up and die from joy.

85

9:15 p.m. (Finnish Time) City Park, Helsinki

Twenty minutes later, the British and American diplomatic cars turned off the main thoroughfare, their headlights searching through the night. Ahead was the park. Longfellow's headlights played across two rough-looking thugs he hadn't expected, only to find out that he was viewing the Finnish SUPO officers, Koskinen and Virtanen. They were huge, and they were armed, ready for whatever came pulling up the road they guarded.

Longfellow parked, Danbury just behind. Longfellow ran back to the trunk, where he inserted the key and lifted the lid. The light came on. A dazed, sweat-soaked ex-Soviet spy met his gaze. "Good of you to let me out," said Nikolai, closing his eyes and sinking back, exhausted.

Nikolai was helped out of the car by the SUPO officers. He stood to his feet, wobbly for a moment, then went and retrieved Sasha from the backseat, waking her up. He kissed both cheeks and held her aloft. "Welcome to the West," he told her.

Emma Magnuson came over and held out her arms for the baby. As she took Sasha, her lips pecked Nikolai on both cheeks. He flushed. "There's my angel. I'm back in the West, surely."

Then Franklin Bolling came and hugged him, the last thing Nikolai ever expected out of the diminutive genius MI6 officer. Then the Brit backed off. "You're home. Now you're a subject of the Queen from this moment on." He handed over two passports, one for Nikolai, one for Sasha.

"God save the spy." Emma laughed.

Against everything he considered strong and manly, tears formed in Nikolai's eyes as he realized what Bolling was saying was true. He was now a Brit. Even his new official passport, brought along by Bolling and Magnuson, said British.

Lucky leaped out, rawhide bone clamped purposefully in her teeth, and peed on a yellow pine tree.

Sue Ellen took Nikolai's radioactive shoes, tied them in a plastic bag, and deposited them in a trash can. She outfitted him with a pair of shoes of his own, and Danbury handed him a change of clothes and helped Nikolai into the Bolling/Magnuson backseat. Emma gave him Sasha through the open door. He dug a finger inside her diaper. Poor Sasha had had no chance to go to the bathroom. "How long since she was changed?" he asked Sue Ellen.

"Why, is she wet?"

He smiled. "I'm shaking so bad, I can't tell."

Sue Ellen passed him a diaper bag. "Here. Change her for good luck. Just don't stab the poor thing with those pins."

The Longfellows came and hugged and told him how brave he was. Tears were shed. The Longfellows would be driving to downtown Helsinki where they would stay overnight and visit the lawyer tomorrow. Then they would take the ferry and go back to Moscow, where they would be arrested and expelled from the Soviet Union. Their job was finished. Now it was time to hear from the Soviets.

"Everyone in?" called Bolling from the driver's seat. "We're off!"

Five minutes later, Sasha said, "Waddo." Time for water.

Nikolai dug through his new diaper bag and found it. He slid the sippy cup handle into her one hand and laid his head back, holding her free hand in his.

Sasha sipped water as the little car roared west, the American CIA's Danbury close behind.

It was a leisurely drive to Turku. Bolling drove slowly, ensuring they weren't pulled over for exceeding the speed limit. Nikolai and Sasha dozed in the backseat.

Shortly after midnight, they reached Turku. They would take the Turku ferry to Stockholm in the morning and then fly to London. It was time to find a hotel for the night.

No calls were placed to Washington that night or the next day until the Turku-Stockholm ferry docked in Sweden. The Finns were too closely allied with the Soviets, not out of choice but out of fear. So the President was made to wait for team TINKER to clear Finland.

86

October 22, 1962

9 p.m. Stockholm, Sweden

The ferry ride took all day, but it was a peaceful day with team TINKER wandering the decks, drinking tea and hot chocolate, eating a filling lunch, watching the ferry's screws boil the water off the stern, and sleeping.

It was dark by the time the ferry groaned up to the dock in Stockholm.

CIA officer Daniel Danbury placed the call through the CIA's Washington switchboard within minutes. It was only a short wait before President John F. Kennedy was on the phone in Washington.

"Mr. President, this is Nikolai Semenov calling from Stockholm. I know you wanted to hear from me. I hope I'm not too late."

"Thank you for calling, Colonel," said the President. "I have one question for you that only you can answer."

"I can only try, Mr. President. I'm all ears."

"Colonel, are the Soviets ready for nuclear war?"

Nikolai looked out of the booth, out across the petrol station parking lot, thinking. What about Khrushchev? Was Russia ready for nuclear war? He remembered his training: there was a war readiness plan for KGB officers when war was imminent. That readiness plan had not been activated.

"Mr. President, Khrushchev will not go to war. He will not launch his Luna missiles."

"Thank you, Colonel. I look forward to seeing you again one day. And thank you for your call."

Upon hanging up, President Kennedy blockaded the Russian fleet, refusing to allow it passage to Cuba. The date was October 22, 1962. The time was 3:00 p.m. Eastern Standard Time.

Missiles bristled in both countries. A half-hour passed, then an hour.

Finally, a call was made from Moscow to Washington. The Soviets were turning their fleet around. Khrushchev wanted his act conditioned on Kennedy's promise not to invade Cuba. Kennedy agreed. The next day, Khrushchev demanded the U.S. remove its missiles from Turkey. The U.S. removed the Turkey missiles, even though it wasn't part of Kennedy's original deal.

The Russian fleet sailed for their home base at Severomorsk.

Franklin Bolling placed a call to the MI5 team in London. "We are pleased to report we have two guests with us tonight," was all he said.

. . .

Shouts went up all over River House. P5 called the Director, who called Downing Street and spoke with PM Macmillan. Semenov had crossed the Soviet border with his daughter. Father and child were healthy and well and on their way to Britain.

87

11:00 a.m., Next Day, Petrol Station, Helsinki

In Helsinki, Roy Longfellow pulled into a carwash and made every effort to remove any signs from his car and trunk that Nikolai had been there. The Longfellows had earlier gone to a confused lawyer's office and begged a walk-in appointment. The lawyer was kind and listened to the Longfellows talk about the weather and Helsinki sports for a half-hour. Then they left in a rush and left one hundred pounds with his receptionist. The Longfellows then drove back to the car wash, finished up there, and then drove on to Moscow, where, with Rodney and Cindy Ballard, they were promptly put under Embassy arrest by the KGB and two days later thrown out of the Soviet Union as spies. They returned to London the next day.

Mikhail Mashky was waiting at Zvenigorod Station to meet the 11:13 train, but Nikolai was not in the last carriage. Mashky waited until the platform cleared, then drove back to his dacha, disappointed but trusting that Nikolai had done something excellent for his predicament. Deep down, he knew it had been a ruse. He only wished his friend the best. And he could keep the uniform, which he had acquired for a steal.

Numerous KGB officers returned to Directorate K defeated. They reported the loss of Colonel Bucharov, and they reported their failure to find Nikolai Semenov. Boats were dragging the channel and shoreline for Bucharov's body even then. KGB agents were ordered to search Moscow, and men were dispatched everywhere, searching lakes and rivers and train and railway stations. Nikolai's flat was watched night and day, for only Bucharov knew the truth.

88

MI5 moved Nikolai and Sasha to a private British estate outside London, where they remained for four months. It was like a five-star resort, complete with butlers, any food they could desire, posh bedding and furniture, London TV with all the kiddie shows for Sasha and real news for Nikolai. Eventually, they were visited by the team from ULYSSES. Nikolai was encouraged to begin writing his memoirs. His story was guaranteed to be a bestseller. Random House in New York called to talk about his book, as did Penguin in London.

One day, walking in the woods at the back of the property, he remembered when Anchev had assigned him the task of discovering ULYSSES's true identity. He had never reported back on that. So…Nikolai wrote a letter to Anatoly Anchev, KGB Moscow, Soviet Union, and put it in the mail.

The letter said: *Dear General Anchev. I have discovered the identity of your mole. Unfortunately, you no longer have top-secret clearance since you were demoted as rezident and therefore cannot hear the name. Truly, Nikolai Semenov.* On a darker note, Nikolai hadn't forgotten it was Anchev who'd ordered Yulia's murder. There would come a time when they would come face to face over that. Nikolai had sworn to his wife's memory that he would settle up with Anchev. Her death would be avenged.

He repeatedly asked for news of his mother in Moscow. Would they send her to the gulag to punish him? So far, they had not. But Great Britain was prepared to exchange prisoners for obtaining her freedom to Great Britain. This was his new country's promise to him. Nikolai struck up correspondence with her and kept it up biweekly, continually checking on her well-being.

MI6 reported that Lieutenant Makov had been returned to Moscow and summarily dismissed from the service. He was now driving a taxi. Was there anything else MI6 could help him with regarding Makov? Nikolai declined the offer of assassination. He would deal with Makov himself one day.

And he would see Makov first.

EPILOGUE

Nikolai Semenov traveled the world for the next six months. Sasha was always right beside him as he flew. He briefed intelligence agencies worldwide on the KGB, its structure, tactics, and last known strategies. He traveled to New Zealand, South Africa, Australia, Canada, France, West Germany, Israel, Saudi Arabia, and Scandinavia.

Six months later, MI5 bought a house in the London suburbs for Nikolai, who took up living there as John F. Johannsen, with his daughter, now Susan. He gave his child most of his time and attention after school until bedtime. During his off-hours, he would read and write. Sketches of Soviet life began appearing in monthlies and journals under his new name. A following developed, and he finally wrote that book London and New York had been clamoring for, with an anonymous byline. Now he was fixed financially for life, as was Susan.

General Viktor Masirov of KGB Moscow continued to thrive. Two years after Nikolai's escape, he was appointed head of Directorate K and rose to the full general rank. After the collapse of Communism, Masirov founded Worldwide Security. In 1992, it was announced that Worldwide Security of Moscow won a $3.1 million contract to guard the U.S. Embassy in Moscow. Nikolai read the press release and scratched his head. He assailed his soft-boiled egg in a cup—an English breakfast custom he had embraced—with a rap of his spoon and turned back to his paper with a sigh. It was never-ending.

England was pleasant, but for the rain. Still, compared to Moscow snow, it meant nothing.

One day, he was tapped on the shoulder. How would he feel about serving his country? The people at MI6 wanted to know.

Russia and Anchev and Makov? Yulia deserved no less.

Yes.

THE END

QUESTIONS TO JOHN ELLSWORTH
(MOST COMMONLY ASKED BY READERS IN THEIR EMAILS)

Question: Before writing *God Save the Spy*, you had written thirty-some legal thrillers. What prompted you to move over to spy fiction?

Answer: The first book I read after high school was *Seven Days in May*. When I fell in love with writing, I had just read *Eye of the Needle,* followed by *The Day of the Jackal*. When I fell in love with storytelling as something maybe I could do, I had just read John Grisham's *The Firm*. (John still does the lawyer genre better than any of us.)

Sandwiched somewhere among these great reads and true inspirations were college and then law school, with stints here and there in post-graduate writing seminars, summer schools, and even a brief fling in an MFA program (where I and my twelve-string closed the local bar just about every night. Maybe the real reason I'm such a late bloomer). But I always keep coming back to this: I want the last 100 pages of *whatever* I'm writing to keep me up all night. If a book doesn't do that, put it on the shelf and find another. Legal thrillers don't much do that for me, logical as they must be, though they have given me a new life and I'm forever grateful. But spy thrillers, especially the one spy against the world, maybe on the run, perhaps trying to save the world by herself, this is the story that keeps me coming back to blank pages, wondering what I'll write today. So, this time out, I decided to draw on everything I know I like, add to it, and see what happened. As it turns out, we have *God Save the Spy*. By the way, as I write these words, I'm at work on a second Nikolai Semenov book I've titled *Red, White, and Spy*. It will be coming in 2021.

Question: Why a Soviet Union hero? Why not a Brit or American or any country but Russia?

Answer: My heroes have always been people who grow up in a system advocated to them, forced on them is maybe truer, by their parents and schools. We all have to rebel against "everything," so we all have that story in common. My hero, Nikolai Semenov, is a youth who hungers to be a KGB officer by blindly following in the footsteps of his father and uncles, all KGB officers. Plus, there's his wife, Yulia, the daughter of a KGB officer. The challenge for *God Save the Spy* was to construct a world where a KGB officer such as Nikolai, who knew only KGB, would even want to cross over. Could decide to "become" British. These are the stories that move me, the stories about people who overcome a set of beliefs to become something better. Our beliefs are more challenging to overcome even than some terrible diseases, because one is about "I" or our essence, while the disease is just physical. Is being British better than being Russian? I didn't say that. But being free, in my experience, is something I would never give up for ideology. Would you?

Question: Why should God save the spy?

Answer: Because we need to know what our enemy is thinking.

Question: What was the most challenging part of writing this book?

Answer: First, I lived through the Cuban Missile Crisis. It scared the living hell out of all of us. TV was three channels at the time, with no endless talking heads to help us understand like they do today, so we were left with images of world leaders saying terrifying things without predictive analyses--we knew the worst was yet to come.

The hardest part of this book was capturing those moments of terror where it's happening offstage. I'm talking in a literary sense here, from the viewpoint of the writer. The day's real story was the Kennedy brothers, McNamara, Rusk, Macmillan, Khrushchev, and the headliners. In retrospect, we find, like we always do, that other players lent intelligence to the moving parts. Spies like the real Oleg Penkovsky, who told Kennedy about the Soviet plans and weapons. Were there critical pieces of that which Penkovsky did not know that Kennedy had to know anyway? Enter my fictional hero, Nikolai Semenov, who did know those special things and was willing to reveal them because he had overcome his entire system of beliefs and exchanged those for freedom of expression. And freedom to take a vacation without spies following you to Yellowstone to watch Old Faithful just for the heck of it. Nikolai had the goods Kennedy needed, leaving me with a story to tell. As I've said before, my stories operate in the seams, the interstices where history has left an opening.

Question: Are we going to be seeing more of Nikolai Semenov?

Answer: Definitely. Next, when we take up his story, he's a widower, living in England, 33 years old, with a young daughter, and thinking about—maybe even obsessing about—the men who murdered the wife he loved, his Yulia. The problem is, those men are in Russia, and he's in England. Which rules them out, unless, and until, the British foreign spy service, MI6, taps him on the shoulder and asks him if he's interested....

ACKNOWLEDGMENTS

Thank you for making this book what it is: Corinne DeMaagd, editor: no wonder you're so busy; Gemma Brocato, fact-checking and continuity editor: you're right, whatever it is; Jan Larsson for European fact-checking and local customs; Adriane Ellsworth for hours and hours of production, advertising, Street Team creation, and lead: yes, we'll do that after the pandemic (sorry, daughter); and most of all to Deb Ellsworth, storyline editor; for speaking truth and listening to me talk about the book for hours and months on end: your turn to talk.

As always, thanks to Max, Toby, and Nina for good company, for dozing beside me in my chair as I wrote this book, and for their endless barking at the world outside, as necessary.

The advance readers for this book numbered 85. I posted a signup sheet for those of the 85 who would be okay with me including their names in this book as my way of saying thank you for their help. Thank you to the *God Save the Spy* Street Team for the care they gave and the great fun we had discussing *God Save the Spy*, reading several drafts, also for suggestions on structuring the book, and all the rest of what we covered. They are:

David Quackenbush, Joyce Zeitz, Bernice Ilmrud, Charles Rotenberg, Carolyn Holtz, Ginnie Caricofe, Howard Richman, Sharon Buddette, Nikki Little, Maryjane Schwartz, Rhett Bassard, Mary Schreckenghost, Genevieve Chesky, Teresa Kuhl, Richard Kaufman, Lorintha Moore, Kris King, Helen McDonald, Georganna Turnbull, Jennifer Hickman, James Coad, Bruce Gibson, Bob Morrison, Charles Young, Jill Lopez, Bill Whipple, Jacki Tibbitts, Jane Haver Brown, Suzanne D. Bower, Bj Kammerer, Sharon Gilbank, Robert Penrod, and Ann Grubbs.

Thanks to proofreaders: Suzanne D. Bower, Ann Grubbs, Debra Ellsworth, Bernice Ilmrud, Sharon Buddette, Georganna Turnbull, Jacki Tibbitts, Yvonne Kanocz, Tamra Smith-Wasel, and Lorintha Moore.

Cover design by Nathan Wampler—you're always spot on and ever the best. I can't say enough good things about your art. nathanwamplerdesign@gmail.com

Thanks to the gang at IAC, who helped with cover selection and blurb creation. You know who you are.

As always, a special thank you to Dr. Elva MacAllaster, who saw a glimmer of some facility with words in a young student. To Edward Zahniser for teaching that student to write inner life.

Blessings, all.

ALSO BY JOHN ELLSWORTH

Cold War Series

God Save the Spy (book 1)

THADDEUS MURFEE PREQUEL

A Young Lawyer's Story

THADDEUS MURFEE SERIES

The Defendants

Beyond a Reasonable Death

Attorney at Large

Chase, the Bad Baby

Defending Turquoise

The Mental Case

The Girl Who Wrote The New York Times Bestseller

The Trial Lawyer

The Near Death Experience

Flagstaff Station

The Crime

La Jolla Law

The Post office

The Contract Lawyer (pre-order)

SISTERS IN LAW SERIES

Frat Party: Sisters In Law

Hellfire: Sisters In Law

MICHAEL GRESHAM PREQUEL

Lies She Never Told Me

MICHAEL GRESHAM SERIES

The Lawyer

Secrets Girls Keep

The Law Partners

Carlos the Ant

Sakharov the Bear

Annie's Verdict

Dead Lawyer on Aisle 11

30 Days of Justis

The Fifth Justice

PSYCHOLOGICAL THRILLERS

The Empty Place at the Table

HISTORICAL THRILLERS

The Point Of Light

Lies She Never Told Me

Unspeakable Prayers

HARLEY STURGIS

No Trivial Pursuit

LETTIE PORTMAN

The District Attorney

FREE BOOK FOR EMAIL SIGNUP

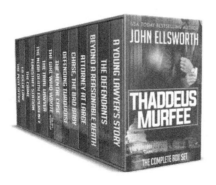

Can't get enough John Ellsworth?

Sign up for our weekly newsletter to stay in touch!

You will have exclusive access to new releases, special deals, and insider news!
Join today!

SUBSCRIBE

FREE BOOK SIGNUP!

ABOUT THE AUTHOR

I used to be a lawyer. Now I'm not. Huge improvement in quality of life.

Presently, I'm writing my 35th novel. I published my first book, *The Defendants*, in January 2014, when I was trying to figure out how to make $500 a month so I could make it on Social Security. Well, I made it.

Reception to my books has been phenomenal; more than 3,000,000 have been downloaded in 60 months. All are Amazon best-sellers. I am an Amazon All-Star every month and a *USA Today* bestseller. How it all happened is anybody's guess. But I think it began the day I turned off the TV.

Thank you for any review you're able to leave on Amazon.

Website and email:

ellsworthbooks.com
johnellsworthbooks@gmail.com

AUTHOR'S REFERENCES

• Haynes, John Earl (2009). *Spies: The Rise and Fall of the KGB in America*. Yale University Press.

• "Milestones: 1961–1968 - The Cuban Missile Crisis, October 1962". *history.state.gov*.

• Scott, Len; Hughes, R. Gerald (2015). *The Cuban Missile Crisis: A Critical Reappraisal*. Taylor & Francis. p. 17.

• Rodriguez (October 1989). *Shadow Warrior: The CIA Hero of 100 Unknown Battles*. John Weisman. Simon & Schuster.

• Alexeyev, Alexandr. "Interview" (PDF)

• Wingrove, Paul (October 22, 2012). "Cuban missile crisis: Nikita Khrushchev's Cuban gamble misfired | Paul Wingrove". *the Guardian*.

• "The Soviet Cuban Missile Crisis: Castro, Mikoyan, Kennedy, Khrushchev, and the Missiles of November". The National Security Archive. October 10, 2012

- Helms, Richard (January 19, 1962). "Memorandum for the Director of Central Intelligence: Meeting with the Attorney General of the United States Concerning Cuba" (PDF). George Washington University, National Security Archive.

- "Department of State Telegram Transmitting Letter From Chairman Khrushchev to President Kennedy". *The Cuban Missile Crisis, October 1962*. John F. Kennedy Presidential Library and Museum. October 26, 1962.

- Dobbs, Michael (2008). *One Minute to Midnight: Kennedy, Khrushchev, and Castro on the Brink of Nuclear War*. New York: Alfred A. Knopf.

- "Aldrich Ames Criminal Complaint" (PDF). Archived from the original (PDF) on 2016-03-04.

- "Aldrich Hazen Ames". FBI.

- Suzal, Savas (1997-03-02). "Disislerinde CIA Köstebegi". *Sabah* (in Turkish). Retrieved 2008-10-13.. Ames made multiple payments for information that included the names of Dev-Genç members Gezmiş knew and the details of their activities.

- Powell, Bill (2002-11-01), *Treason: How a Russian Spy Led an American Journalist to a U.S. Double Agent*, Simon & Schuster.

- Pincus, Walter (September 24, 1994). "CIA: Ames Betrayed 55 Operations; Inspector General's Draft Report Blames Supervisors for Failure to Plug Leak". *The Washington Post*. p. A1.

- Weiner, Tim (November 2, 1994). "Senate Report Faults C.I.A. for Ineptitude in Spy Case". *The New York Times*. p. A1 https://www.nytimes.com/1994/11/02/us/senate-report-faults-cia-for-ineptitude-in-spy-case.html.

- "Assessment," 33–35. Ames's immediate supervisors were aware of his alcohol abuse and his proclivity to sleep at his desk, but his annual performance reviews "consistently rated him a strong performer".

- "The People of the CIA ... Ames Mole Hunt Team – Central Intelligence Agency". Cia.gov. April 30, 2013. Retrieved 2014-01-03.

- Christopher Lehmann-Haupt, "Aldrich Ames: Brilliant or Bumbling?" *New York Times*, February 24, 1997, review of Pete Early,*Confessions of a Spy*.

- "FBI History: Famous Cases – Aldrich Hazen Ames". FBI.gov. Retrieved 2013-08-18.

- Bromwich, Michael R. (April 1997). "A Review of the FBI's Performance in Uncovering the Espionage Activities of Aldrich Hazen Ames". Retrieved 2011-04-26.

- Fischer, Benjamin (2016). "Doubles Troubles: The CIA and Double Agents during the Cold War". *International Journal of Intelligence and CounterIntelligence*. 29 (1): 51–52. doi:10.1080/08850607.2015.1083313.

- Carlisle, Rodney (26 March 2015). *Encyclopedia of Intelligence and Counterintelligence*. Routledge. pp. 273–274.

- David Wise. "Thirty years later, we still don't know who betrayed these Cold War spies" Smithsonian Magazine, November 2015.

- "Spy who came in from the cold thanks to a packet of crisps". 7 July 2015.

- Harding, Luke (11 March 2013). "Gordievsky: Russia has as many spies in Britain now as the USSR ever did". *the Guardian*. Retrieved 16 October 2018.

- Ben Macintyre (2018), *The Spy and the Traitor: The Greatest Espionage Story of the Cold War*

- "This KGB Officer Was a Double Agent for British Intelligence". *Spy Wars with Damian Lewis: The Man Who Saved the World*. Smithsonian Channel. 11 March 2020

- *Time Out* magazine: Oleg Gordievsky: Interview

- videofact.com

- Gordievsky, Oleg; Martin, Christopher (1990). *KGB: The Inside Story*. Hodder & Stoughton.

- Gordievsky, Oleg; Martin, Christopher (1990). *The KGB*. HarperCollins.

- Gordievsky, Oleg; Martin, Christopher (1991). *Instructions from the Centre: Top Secret Files on KGB Foreign Operations, 1975–85*. Hodder & Stoughton.

- Gordievsky, Oleg; Martin, Christopher (1992). *More Instructions from the Centre: Top Secret Files on KGB Foreign Operations, 1975–85*. Frank Cass Publishers.

- Comrade Kryuchkov's Instructions: Top Secret Files on KGB Foreign Operations, 1975-1985 by Christopher Martin and Oleg Gordievsky | Feb 1, 1994

- Gordievsky, Oleg (1995). *Next Stop Execution (autobiography)*. Macmillan.

- The Main Enemy: The Inside Story of the CIA's Final Showdown with the KGB by Milton Bearden, James Risen, et al.

- Schecter, Jerrold L.; Deriabin, Peter S. (1992). *The Spy Who Saved the World: How a Soviet Colonel Changed the Course of the Cold War*. New York: C. Scribner's Sons. p. 284.

- Schecter, Jerrold L.; Deriabin, Peter S. (1992). *The Spy Who Saved the World: How a Soviet Colonel Changed the Course of the Cold War*. Scribner.

- Wynne, Greville (1967). *The Man from Moscow*. London: Hutchinson & Co.

- *Spy Catcher*, p. 212

- Kalugin, Oleg (1994). *The First Directorate: My 32 Years in Intelligence and Espionage Against the West*. St. Martin's Press.

- Sakharov, Vladimir (1980). *High Treason*. Ballantine Books. p. 177.

- Suvorov, Viktor (1986). *Soviet Military Intelligence*. London: Grafton Books. p. 155.

- Tennent H. Bagley, *Spymaster: Startling Cold War Revelations of a Soviet KGB Chief*, Skyhorse Publishing, 2013,

- Aleksandr Fursenko and Timothy Naftali, *Khrushchev's Cold War*, 2006.

- Coleman, David G. (2012). *The Fourteenth Day: JFK and the Aftermath of the Cuban Missile Crisis*. New York: W.W. Norton.

Made in the USA
Monee, IL
26 November 2020